The *Ganzfield* Series

Minder
Adversary
Legacy
Accused
Operative
Soulmate (2013)

Praise for the *Ganzfield* Books

"Fresh and thrilling, *Minder* has breathtaking romance and heart-stopping action. No doubt one of my favorites."
— Jennifer L. Armentrout, author of *Half-Blood* and *Obsidian*

"I completely lost myself in this story—rooting for the characters as they discovered more about their abilities and also following along with the logic and theories. I didn't pause once to question if something wasn't plausible, I simply nodded along, caught up in the world...when I love a book this much I can go on and on... Ms. Kaynak is an amazingly talented writer. I loved the voice of this story, and I fell in love with the characters. If you're looking for something fresh in the YA Paranormal Romance department, do yourself a favor and check out *Minder*. "
— Trisha Wolfe, author of *Destiny's Fire*

"Fantastic. *Minder* is an engaging read with unique characters and a steamy romance that sizzles off the page. The ending had me begging for more."
— Wicked Awesome Books

"Chock-full of romance, action, and supernatural powers, *Minder* is a book you won't be able to put down."
— Book Lungs

A Blkosiner's "Top Ten Authors" Pick
"5/5...*Adversary* did not disappoint...the action starts quickly and doesn't let go...Kate writes with beauty and fluidity. Her characters are real to me, and the way she writes them, I laugh with them, mourn with them, and am joyful with them."
— Blkosiner's Book Blog

A Reading Teen "What to Read This Summer" Pick for 2010: *Minder*
"Absolutely flawless!... 6 out of 6...I loved this book!... one more completely, entirely, absolutely, totally, wholly, amazing book by Kate Kaynak!"
— Reading Teen

A Missy's Reads and Reviews Featured Series: *Ganzfield*
"5 Stars: I thought I was smart by trying to guess throughout the book what was going to happen next...and found myself completely wrong every single time!"
— Missy's Reads and Reviews

"I found *Minder* to be a fantastic read."
— Book Lovers Inc.

"*Minder* is dynamic, original, thoughtful, and entrancing...nothing short of brilliant. Both *Minder* as well as *Adversary* leave you holding your breath while laughing out loud. With its original concepts, dynamic and flawless writing, *Adversary* is a book I am thrilled to have on my shelves."
— Book Crazy

"5 out of 5 Stars: I don't know if it was the author's style of writing, the story line, the characters, or what - but this book had me hooked! I laughed out loud on the subway! People looked at me like I was crazy - but I didn't care. It's been a while since a book made me smile and laugh out loud."
— Good Choice Reading

"The world Kate Kaynak creates is dark and twisted, full of intense young adult issues as well as looming supernatural threats and a mesmerizing and heart-pounding race against time. "
— The Bookish Type

"I LOVED it!! I was totally caught up in the story and couldn't wait to see what would happen next...*Minder* is a terrific read for both teens and adults."
— Sidhe Vicious Reviews

"I give this book an A+."
— Looksie Lovitz: Books and Wits

"*Adversary* had everything I expected and more. If you enjoyed *Minder*, you should definitely check out its sequel. And if you haven't tried *Minder* yet... what are you waiting for?"
— The Wolf's Den

"The story really is addictive...I could barely get enough of it."
— YA Book Queen

"A great start to what I believe will be a really addictive series!"
— I Want To Read That

"*It*. Some books have *it*, some don't. *It* is simply what makes you keep reading, what pulls you forward, what keeps a book niggling in your mind until you simply have to reread it...or pick up the sequel. *Minder* has *it*."
— Elephants on Trapezes

"I can't wait to head back to Ganzfield in the next book!"
— Electrifying Reviews

"I think everyone should give the Ganzfield Series a chance."
— Amethyst Daydreams

"This is a must read. Kaynak brings plenty of action, unique story telling, and lots of romance…be prepared for lots of swooning. "
— Cari's Book Blog

"5/5: Absolutely brilliantly written and extremely captivating. Kate has no problem keeping me hooked onto every word."
— My Bookish Fairy Tale

"Five stars. *Minder* is fast-paced, edgy, highly powerful and thrilling. It will give you that adrenaline rush and make you grit your teeth in anticipation. Read, enjoy and indulge—this is one ride you will not forget."
— Fantasy for Eva

"Holy Heck! You know that feeling you get when you bite into some treat sample that is absolutely scrumptious and leaves you wanting MORE? That's what I was feeling when I finished *Minder*... It pained me to put this book down to do everyday things."
— For the Love of YA

"The plot and premise are unlike anything I've ever seen before. After reading *Minder*, I was left wondering *Damn, wish there were a real Ganzfield around here*...I definitely recommend it!"
— Words on Paper

"I gave this book five coffee cups...Absolutely amazing! I love this book!"
— Elena's Book Café

"I absolutely loved it... *Minder* grips from the very beginning."
— Spellbound By Books

"WOW!... Word to the wise: don't make any plans once you pick up *Minder*; you won't be able to put it down once you start reading!... Absolutely brilliant! The author's knack for storytelling is beyond fascinating. Fans of *Harry Potter* and *Fantastic Four* will enjoy this series."
— The Book Vixen

"I loved this book! I thought it was amazing! Well written and intriguingly suspenseful, with an incredible romance thrown in...a MUST READ!"
— The Wormhole

"A fast moving and compelling read."
— Eating Y.A. Books

"5-stars...I loved this book...The author did it again! *Adversary* had taken hold of me and didn't let go, even after the book was closed. If I was asked, "What Young Adult series would I recommend?", The Ganzfield Novels would be it."
— Escape Between the Pages

"I cannot wait to read the next book in the series."
— Everything To Do With Books

"*Minder* was addicting from page one...5 STARS!"
— Read For Your Future

"A compelling, exciting new series to keep your eye out for!"
— Girl In Between

"I will not only give this book 5 stars, I will be giving it an extra star for 'I could read this again right this minute.'"
— Reading, Writing, Raisin' Boys

"I don't think I've read such an intense opening to a novel...ever. It was nail biting."
— Confessions of a Book Addict

"A fun and intriguing read that pulled me in immediately."
— Candace's Book Blog

"*Minder* is fast paced, unique, and is addicting...I wish for more books like *Minder*."
— Ramblings of a Teenage Bookworm

"Snatches your attention from the first paragraph and doesn't let go."
— Critique this WIP

"Packed to the gills with twist, turns, action, and suspense. There is so much awesomeness... I can not wait to see what *Accused* brings to the table."
— Urban Fantasy Investigations

"Suspenseful, enchanting, and romantic."
— Ellz Readz

"*Minder* is a fun, perfect read for anyone who looks for love, excitement, and a great plot."
— If You Give a Girl a Pen

"Fun, action-packed and well-thought-out; it's a YA novel that's relevant to this day and age. I honestly cannot wait to see what happens next."
— Erika Breathes Books

"*Minder* is an amazing read. It is truly fantastic. I started reading *Minder* and I just couldn't stop...I cannot wait to read the next book in the series."
— Everything To Do With Books

"5/5: Amazing. Kate Kaynak's world is both incredibly original and believable at the same time. The characters are fun, passionate and completely unforgettable... Kate's ability to blend humor, danger and grief all into one amazing book is truly admirable... I love, love, love this series!"
— Books Complete Me

Copyright © 2012 by Kate Kaynak

Sale of the paperback edition of this book without its cover is unauthorized.

Spencer Hill Press

This book is a work of fiction. Names, characters, places, and incidents are products of the author's imagination or are used fictitiously. Any resemblance to actual events, locales, or persons, living or dead, is entirely coincidental.

All rights reserved, including the right to reproduce this book or portions thereof in any form whatsoever.
Contact: Spencer Hill Press, PO Box 247, Contoocook, NH 03229

Please visit our website at spencerhillpress.com

First Edition March 2012.

Kaynak, Kate, 1971—
Accused : a novel / by Kate Kaynak – 1st ed.
p. cm.
Summary:
Maddie and the rest of the team must catch the person selling classified information to terrorists—before they become the targets.

Cover design by K. Kaynak

The quotations and parodies in this work adhere to the fair use principles of Section 107 of the Copyright Act.
One Flew Over the Cuckoo's Nest by Ken Kesey

The author acknowledges the trademarked and/or copyright status and trademark/copyright owners of the following wordmarks mentioned in this fiction:
Alice in Wonderland, Annie, Armed Forces Radio Network, BMW, Cujo, Dr. Dolittle, Dramamine, Escher, Ferrari, Formica, Frisbee, G.I Joe, Godzilla, Gravis, Hall of Justice, iPhone and iPod, James Bond, Jameson, Justice League, Kryptonite, Mambo Number 5, Nissan, Nova, Purina Cat Chow, Spider-man, Superman, The Men Who Stare At Goats, Tilt-a-Whirl, Twilight Zone, Velcro, Volkswagen/VW, Wal-mart, Wonder Woman, X-Men

Thank you, Neil Diamond, for writing "Sweet Caroline," the perfect sing-along song.

ISBN 978-0-9845311-8-9 (paperback)
ISBN 978-0-9845311-9-6 (e-book)

Printed in the United States of America

OPERATIVE

THE FIFTH GANZFIELD NOVEL BY

KATE KAYNAK

SPENCER HILL PRESS

*This book is dedicated to
the members of the US Armed Forces,
including many of my former students.
Thank you for your service.*

*And in memory of
Alice "Badger" Washburn.*

Dear Reader,

I owe you an apology for the cliffhanger ending of *Accused*. What can I say? The characters took over and insisted that things were going to happen that way. Personally, I hate being left dangling for months, waiting for the next book in a series to come out, so I'll tell you right now that this book, *Operative*, will have a properly resolved ending. Please stop with the death threats.

Previously at Ganzfield…

GANZFIELD

Ganzfield is a secret training facility near North Conway, New Hampshire. It normally houses and trains about eighty teenagers, whose special abilities have been enhanced with a synthetic neurotransmitter called dodecamine (pronounced "dough-DECK-a-mean"). Thanks to a new deal with General Dale, a bigwig in U.S. Army Intelligence and an old friend of Williamson's, it's now protected and classified by the U.S. government.

Williamson's office and private suite occupy the top floor of the main building, which also holds the dining hall and the library. Across the way, Blake House holds classrooms, girls' dorm rooms, and the infirmary. Maddie and Trevor have been living in the old church that sits back in the woods. The sparks sleep in a cluster of fireproof cinderblock cottages down by the lake. Other houses and cabins dot the property, as well.

MINDERS

Minders are telepathic; they hear the thoughts and dreams of everyone within range. Some can shield their minds from other telepaths, and a few can project thoughts and images to others. They're also immune to the mind control of charm commands. On the downside, they can't block out incoming thoughts so other people's pain, emotions, and nasty thoughts hit them, too.

Seventeen-year-old Maddie Dunn also can overload people's brains to hurt, injure, or even kill them. Thanks to Heather McFee's healing abilities, she's slowly regaining the ability to talk using a new part of her brain, since Isaiah Lerner fried her original language center. Last summer, Maddie was captured and tortured by Colonel Hunter, a member of military intelligence gone bad, but Trevor helped her work through the trauma. She's been tapped to work with General Dale, who wants to see if a telepath can find the source of mysterious security leaks from several bases and embassies overseas.

Dr. Jon Williamson runs Ganzfield. He can shield and project thoughts, and he's pretty good at using his special gifts in the stock market. Maddie's still learning some of his tricks, but she already has a few million dollars in the bank and was declared an emancipated minor so she could handle the financial paperwork.

Seth Black has the largest range of any minder, but he can't project thoughts to non-telepaths. Telepaths can, of course, just think things at each other and have silent conversations. However, with Seth's strong sensitivity, other minders are much too loud up close, which makes Seth keep his distance.

Ann Williamson, Dr. Williamson's niece, has abilities a lot like Maddie's. Both experience other people's emotions as colorful auras and have "special connections" with their boyfriends that allow them to share abilities. Ann has been working on being able to overload other people's brains the way Maddie can.

Nina Dunn is Maddie's mother, and her telepathic abilities aren't as strong as the others', since she didn't receive dodecamine while her brain was still developing in adolescence. She needs physical touch to read people's thoughts, although the other minders are loud enough that she hears them without contact.

TELEKINETICS

Trevor Laurence is Ganzfield's only telekinetic. He controls two mental hands that can extend about fifteen feet from his body and can even pass through solid matter. They change size and shape to do what he needs them to—including stopping bullets. His ability doesn't shut down when he dreams, so he often grabs or throws things that are in range. Because of the special connection he has with Maddie, they share each other's abilities when they have physical contact.

SPARKS

Sparks control fire, and they sometimes accidentally start fires when they're sleeping or when their emotions get too strong. The two main families—the McFees and the Underwoods—make up about half of the residents of Ganzfield.

CHARMS

Charms can lace their words with mind-control and make anyone within earshot do what they say. Zack Greyson isn't just any old charm—he can shield his thoughts from minders and can also shake off other people's charm commands. He also has a special connection with Ann Williamson; when they work together, they can mentally project silent charm commands.

Nick Coleman, a lawyer in New York City, takes care of financial and legal issues for Williamson and the rest of Ganzfield.

Cecelia Mitchell was a student at the University of New Hampshire, but she came back to Ganzfield when they needed help. She and Maddie can't stand each other.

Belinda Nash is the charm who used to spy for Ganzfield in Washington, D.C. She turned on Williamson, charmed a bunch of people to gather intel on Ganzfield, and then sold it to Isaiah Lerner. When Ganzfield people go after her, she has a nasty habit of charming innocent bystanders into attacking her pursuers—or into killing themselves—to protect her or allow her time to escape.

HEALERS

Matilda and Morris Taylor use their healing abilities to instantly mend cuts, burns, broken bones, internal bleeding, and other physical damage by revving up and controlling pople's natural healing mechanisms. Hannah Washington is their current student, and Heather McFee (the only healer in a family of sparks) studied with them before she went to med school. Healers can also knock people unconscious with a touch, which comes in handy during medical procedures... or when someone gets in their way but they don't want to kill them.

REMOTE VIEWERS (RVs)

Rachel Fontaine gets visions of people, places, or things she knows, no matter where they are in the world, and her ability is back, now that she's had her baby. Little Sienna is about a month old. She was exposed to dodecamine prenatally, and it altered her brain chemistry, allowing her to develop just about all the G-positive abilities. Most of the other RVs were killed in the massacre, but a few of the older ones, like Rick Hanson and Rachel's dad, have been back to Ganzfield recently.

AND AT THE END OF *ACCUSED,* THINGS WENT TO HELL...

Everything went into slow-motion. Trevor gasped and flung an invisible arm wide in front of General Dale as Hunter opened fire. Gunshots cracked the quiet evening. *Shots fired!* The heads of the agents sitting in the driveway turned in unison toward the confrontation in front of the porch. Bullets lodged in mid-air in front of the General. His shocked eyes recognized them for what they were.

Hunter frowned as he registered that Dale hadn't been hit. *How the hell—?* He swung the barrel toward Trevor and me.

Lethal energy flared behind my eyes as I took aim right back at him. Behind me, something seemed to explode in Trevor's soul and I gasped and bent double, losing my grip on his hand as the force of his emotions broke my concentration. The floating bullets fell to the ground as an unseen hand reached into Hunter's chest. The strong muscle tissue of his heart fought against the pressure of Trevor's invisible grasp for a moment before it was squeezed into a lifeless pulp.

The crushing pain flashed to us. Ann cried out. I curled forward as my muscles clenched. Williamson staggered back and fell against the front door. The gun dropped from Hunter's hand and seemed to fall through syrup to the ground. His eyes went wide as he crumpled without a sound.

Dead.

For several eternal seconds, no one seemed to breathe. We stared at the limp heap on the grass as his pain faded.

Something ripped through Trevor and the world tilted around us. *Oh, my God!* His eyes impaled mine and his mouth hung slack. *I... I KILLED him! I just reached into his chest and... and I'm a... a killer!* Dark-yellow guilt stained his mind.

Oh, no. My eyes flashed to General Dale. What would he do to Trevor? Would he try to lock him up? Isolate him? Protectiveness surged through me. *We could run away. We could get away tonight and just—*

That... that was... telekinesis. Actual telekinesis! That young man just saved my life. Dale looked at Trevor as though trying to figure out where to pin the medal. The near-panic that gripped my heart eased. The General wasn't a threat to Trevor.

Trevor took a step back. His eyes never left my face as something seemed to tear between us. Horror. Revulsion. Dismay. Guilt. Pain.

Oh, God. He wasn't just pulling away; he was repulsed. His thoughts were a whitewater river filled with jumbling rapids and sharp rocks. Most twisted by too fast for my understanding. *I could have stopped him without killing him. I know I could have. But I didn't. I killed him. I'm a—a murderer.* Daggers of pain shot through him.

I reached out, but Trevor recoiled from me. My jaw trembled and my throat closed up. *What—?*

Shock flashed through him and his breathing sounded too loud. He shook his head. "I—I can't be around you."

Only my extended hand followed him as he threw himself off the side of the porch and disappeared into the dark, pushing off with his ability. I bit back a sob, feeling everyone's eyes on me as I tried to remember how to breathe.

And now, *Operative...*

Kate Kaynak
New Hampshire, August 2011

CHAPTER 1

Trevor's gone.

Seth's words hit like a splash of ice water. I'd barely slept last night, but I forced my eyes to focus in the pre-dawn dark of the old church.

Gone? I looked over the railing of my loft. Trevor's bed was untouched. I drew in a shuddering breath as yesterday's events found me awake again and pounced back into my consciousness. Government forces had attacked us. Trevor had killed Colonel Hunter. Williamson had cut a deal with his old friend, the General, so now I was off to Europe to use telepathy to ferret out security leaks for the U.S. government. Trevor had been horrified at what he'd become—what I'd turned him into and... *Wait. You mean GONE gone?*

He took the car and left a few minutes ago. He asked me not to wake you, but... screw that.

Hurray for minder solidarity. I scrambled to find something to wear. I'd tossed everything into a big bag last night, forgetting to leave something out for the morning. I'd just have to go AWOL—

or whatever it was called—and find him. My jaw quivered as I remembered the last thing Trevor had said to me.

"I can't be around you."

I squeezed my eyes shut as the pain of that rippled through me yet again and the clothes dropped back into the bag as my hands went slack. Trevor didn't want to be around me and everyone at Ganzfield needed me to go with the General today. They wouldn't be safe if I didn't.

Ah, hell. *I can't go after Trevor. And he doesn't want me to go after him.*

Do you know where—?

Hanscom Air Force Base.

Huh? I shut my eyes tight, trying to make his words make sense. *But that's where we're headed this morning, anyway.*

Apparently he wanted to go alone.

Agony welled up within me.

Geez! Keep your emotions under control or I won't tell you the rest.

I took a deep breath. *The rest?*

He had a long talk with Jon last night—by phone, since he's trying to stay out of everyone's range, I think. He wanted off the meds, but apparently General Dale thinks Trevor's some kind of hero and wants him to be in the Secret Service or something. He insisted that Trevor be part of the contingent from Ganzfield, so they set up this whole thing where Trevor drives himself down and Greg goes down with the rest of you and brings back the car he took.

I sniffed as I pictured *"I can't be around you"* written as an epitaph on a tombstone. *Here lies everything that made my life worth living.*

Don't start. Seth's exasperation hit me. *Geez! Both of you— you're like the drama king and queen. It didn't feel like he hated you, or anything. He's... he's just freaked out, or something.*

Yeah. He'd freaked out because I'd twisted him into becoming a killer... like me.

Whatever. I just wanted to let you know where he'd gone so you wouldn't lose it when he doesn't show up when the military does. Apparently, they're sending regular MPs to fetch you guys. Don't fry their brains, okay?

I hugged my arms tightly around myself and tried not to scream into Seth's head. *How long do I have before they get here?* The now-empty shelves in the annex where Trevor's clothes had been mocked me. Had he come in while I was asleep and packed up? I swallowed hard. *Why didn't he wake me?*

It's oh-six-thirty now. I grimaced at the military lingo. *They'll pick you up at eight.*

I nodded, even though he couldn't see me. *Go away, then. I have time to take a shower.* My life might stink right now, but that doesn't mean I have to.

"You trying to ditch me?" Rachel crunched toward me over the frost-covered grass.

I didn't lift my gaze from my coffee as she joined me on the steps of the main building. *I don't want to go. At least you have a good excuse.*

At the sound of my mental voice, month-old Sienna flung a feeler of yellow energy in my direction. I glanced over and smiled, in spite of myself. *Hey, Sunshine.*

The little tentacle of energy led back into a pack strapped across Rachel's front. It looked like she was being hugged by a fabric-covered turtle.

"Drew filled me in on... on what happened. Ellen said you came by in the middle of the night and told her to say goodbye for you."

Yeah.

"Coward."

I snorted.

"What's so funny?" Drew flung his duffel bag down on the edge of the porch. The noise startled Sienna and the collar of Rachel's jacket started to smoke. She slapped it out as she heaved a long-suffering sigh.

Drew flashed a fire suppression thought at the spot, as well. "So, I got the team all set. They should all be here in the next coupla minutes."

I tried to care. *You got another RV?*

"Yeah. Rick's in, at least for a little while. He got laid off after missing so much work a few months ago." His thoughts flashed back to the full house we'd had when everyone had come back for protection from Isaiah.

Drew frowned as Hannah approached his side, but she avoided looking at him. "Maddie?"

I caught the gist of her thoughts. *You're not coming with us?* Trevor, Rachel, and now Hannah? I was spinning away from everyone—like a Frisbee tossed into the dark.

Drew frowned. "Why not?"

"I—I, well... You know how we saved Sienna's umbilical cord, right?"

Eew. Some people just collect commemorative plates, Hannah.

"Seriously." Hannah raised her eyebrows and waited.

I'm sorry. What I meant was, "How interesting. Please, go on."

Drew snorted.

"Stem cells. Sienna's were affected by the dodecamine in her system, and now she makes her own dodecamine naturally. If we can work with her stem cell line, keep it alive and alter it for other people, we can—"

—no one will need shots anymore. I finished for her.

Rachel's brows shot up and she gave her daughter a wide-eyed look. Sienna flashed a burst of pure affection in response.

"Well, we've been able to keep the cells alive so far, but only by using our abilities several times each day. But last night..." Hannah's excitement haloed pale pink around her. "Last night, after I talked with Drew, I went down to the infirmary for my shift and I got to thinking about how we could improve the nutrient bath we're using. And then..." In Hannah's memory, the small sample felt weak—fading. She'd altered how she used her ability, almost like feeding energy into the cells rather than using the tissue's own resources. The cells seemed to bloom under her touch.

You had a breakthrough.

Hannah nodded, eyes bright. "I called the other healers as soon as I'd verified the results. None of them could replicate the effects, but I was able to do it—twice."

So, you're the only one who can continue the research.

"It should only be for a few weeks. You might not even be gone that long." Hannah bit her lip. "I feel like I'm letting you down."

So we don't have a healer?

"Sure you do. Heather said she'd go with you."

Really? That'll actually be okay. Heather had done very well as a medic yesterday.

"Yeah." Drew smiled. "She was really excited about it at breakfast."

But we'll still need—

A scraping noise startled me. Cecelia dragged a wheeled suitcase across the gravel driveway.

I groaned. *Please tell me you're messing with me.*

Drew gave me a pointed look. "You have a better option?" *Besides, she's so hot!*

Ugh. Think of ANYTHING else, please. I did a quick inventory of the charms. Nearly all of them had died last February in the massacre. We had a few new ones, but they barely knew how to use their abilities. The older charm alums hadn't turned out to be that willing to help, and if I saw Zack right now, there was a good chance I'd fry his brain to hell. That left Cecelia—a pissed-off housecat of a charm.

Oh, super.

"Honey?"

Hey, Mom.

Maddie looks terrible. She's so pale! "I need to talk to you."

I'll give you one better. I pulled off my glove and held out my hand. She gave me a tight smile as she took it in her own. I flashed memories to her, minder-fast—the meeting with the General, the decision to send me and my team, Trevor killing Hunter, the chaos in Williamson's office, and how Trevor had taken off this morning alone.

Her eyes welled up. *Oh, honey. I'm so sorry. You don't have to go. I'm sure we can work something else out.*

I shook my head. *This is actually the best solution. I'm not happy with it, but it'll make everyone here at Ganzfield safer.*

Well, that won't include me.

I met her eyes. *You're heading back to Jersey?*

It's time.

I couldn't argue with that. At least now it was safe for her to go. *You going to stay on the meds?*

She nodded. *I think so. I'm now a VERY insightful therapist. If a little touchy-feely.*

My mom pulled me into a hug that glowed white with love. I turned away to avoid seeing more of the worry in her eyes. Unfortunately, there was more bad news waiting for me.

"We're leaving in, like, two minutes!" Drew scowled at Rick. "You can't back out now!"

Rick shook his head. "Sorry, man. I've been waiting to hear from this company for a month. They emailed me this morning. I start next week, after everyone comes back from Thanksgiving weekend, but that means I only have five days to move out to California, so I gotta leave today." He shook his head as he walked away.

Heather shoved a shoulder into Drew's back and he stumbled forward a step. "Hey! Is this the place for the all-expenses-paid trip to Europe?" She frowned as she took in our expressions. *What's everyone so down about? We totally won yesterday and now we get to go on an amazing adventure!*

Hey, Maddie. Your ride's here. Seth's mental voice was faint; he must still be out by the broken front gate.

An olive-colored vehicle—something that looked like the product of an illicit union between a Humvee and a truck—rumbled through the trees toward us. After quick hugs from my mom and Rachel, I found myself strapped next to Greg on a bench seat in the back.

Take care of yourself, Brat. Seth still kept an eye on the gate, and his thoughts showed things were clear for at least a half-mile down the road.

You too, Narc.

We'd been on the highway for a while before I realized that Williamson hadn't come to say goodbye.

CHAPTER 2

"So, you're the goat-starers."

We'd dropped our bags at the door of what looked suspiciously like a classroom. A woman in grey and tan camouflage glared at us from the doorway. Her lips were drawn even tighter than the perfect black doorknob of hair at the back of her skull. *This has got to be a practical joke. Mind-control? Telepathy? No way they're for real. The Captain's not usually one for joking, though.*

Drew frowned. "Goat-starers?" *She'd be kinda hot if she smiled, but she's too uptight. And what's with the goats?*

Heather chuckled. "You know. From that movie."

"What movie?"

"*The Men Who Stare At Goats.*"

"They made a movie about staring at goats? *At goats*?"

Heather cracked up. "It was much better than it sounds. You'd like it."

Cecelia gave everyone a disdainful look then went back to filing her nails.

The woman's nearly black eyebrows threatened to cross. *The* big, red-haired guy's Drew McFee. The red-headed woman must be the doctor—the other McFee. That leaves the skinny blonde and the short, brown-haired girl. Which one is supposed to be dangerous again?* She dropped her own duffel next to the door as she moved to the front of the room. "Okay, listen up. My name is Sergeant Cavallo and my new orders say I'm gonna babysit you on your little field trip. Leave your bags here and follow me." *Just a bunch of ignorant kids. Probably can't even follow simple orders.*

Kids? She probably wasn't more than five years older than me. I nudged a gentle thought into her head as she turned. *Where's Trevor Laurence?*

She didn't blink. *Trevor Laurence needs to stay separate from the others. He was scheduled to fly out at oh-nine-forty this morning on General Dale's plane.*

I looked at the clock—it was just after ten. I bit my lip as the empty place in my chest grew.

Trevor's not here anymore.

"Get a move on!" Cavallo yelled from the hall. "I've got less than eight hours to get you all processed and on a plane to Ramstein."

She had information on Trevor. I jumped up to follow her, sensing the others falling in behind me, and floated another thought into her mind. *Where's the General's plane headed?*

Sergeant Cavallo frowned and shook her head as though shaking out my inserted thoughts. She didn't know where they were sending Trevor. I swallowed against the lump in my throat. Someone here must know. I'd have to keep checking in the heads of people here.

Chain of command.

I turned back to Sergeant Cavallo and floated in another thought. *Who would know where that plane's heading?*

She squeezed her eyes shut with a wince. *That's weird.*

Hey, Drew. The Sergeant thinks my voice in her head is weird.

Drew grinned. *She doesn't know the half of it! What're you doing in her head?*

Trying to find Trevor.

His face turned serious. *And?*

And he's already on a plane. I'm gonna try to find out where they're sending him.

The sharp slap of December hit us as we headed out past several identical blocky buildings. Each had a large number to the right of the door, while some had signs with further information. *Family Services. Education Center.* We entered a building marked only with the number 22. Over the next two hours, we were photographed, fingerprinted, and had to fill out various forms with the same information over and over. *Name. Date of Birth. Next of Kin.* In my case, there were a few extra forms. *Date of Emancipation. Date of Arrest. Criminal Charges. Verdict.*

Sergeant Cavallo let out an exasperated sigh when she realized that neither Drew nor Cecelia had passports. *Are you frikkin' kidding me?* "You're supposed to fly to Germany tonight and you didn't get passports? Where did you think you were headed—Connecticut?"

Cecelia sighed. "It's not a problem. They'll let us through customs when they see our driver's licenses."

That's the stupidest thing I've ever heard. "That's the stupidest—"

"It's not a problem." Cecelia repeated. This time her voice carried charm-resonance—and a hard edge. "Don't worry about it."

Cavallo's thoughts cleared.

I pulled out my phone and sent a message to Trevor's email. **Please call me.**

When would he get it? When would he land there? I let out a breath. Hell, he didn't even have a computer or a phone; he'd always just shared mine. Gah! I hated this! I hated not knowing where he was! The lack of connection to Trevor made the world feel both numb and raw to me. He was out there somewhere, alone and hurting, and I couldn't get to him. I bit my lip and stared out the window as Cavallo and the other military types finished processing us.

With our new military ID cards still warm from the ID-making machine, we headed to lunch.

"—so please make sure your carry-on is stowed in the overhead bin or beneath the seat in front of you, and that your tray table is locked in the upright position. For those of you in first-class…"

Ha, ha. The captain's voice came through the cargo area where we were strapping ourselves in against bench-like seats along the fuselage. No tray tables, no carry-ons. Hell, there weren't even any windows in the C-130 where we were. I'd only agreed to get into this cargo hold once Cavallo had made a few phone calls and ascertained that the General's plane had also gone to Europe this morning. It was a big continent, but at least this way I was heading in Trevor's general direction.

Once the captain ended his little comedy routine, a guy in uniform came through and did the actual prep, which mainly consisted of, "Don't touch anything, stay strapped in your seat unless you have to use the bathroom, and here are some extra barf bags."

Cecelia adjusted the earbuds of her iPod and closed her eyes as she and Sergeant Cavallo disappeared from view. A pallet of what looked like stacks of truck tires wrapped in thick, grey plastic rolled between us. Shipping containers with long serial numbers were forklifted up the ramp at the rear and slid along tracks in the floor, filling the center space of the huge plane.

Drew sat between Heather and me. He swallowed hard when he saw the large, red "flammable" symbol two containers down. "Looks like I'm not getting any sleep on this flight."

I rubbed the bridge of my nose and wondered if all the mental projecting was the reason my head ached. "I'm gonna twy to stay up wid you." Ugh—I felt drained and my messed-up way of talking made me feel stupid. Trevor wasn't here. The only reason I'd been able to keep going all day was to get closer to the place where he was.

"I can't be around you."

My jaw quivered. He didn't mean forever, right? The memory of Trevor's horror at causing the crushing pain in Hunter's chest—of becoming a killer—made a little sob escape me. He was feeling broken… and I wasn't there to fix it.

Another dozen or so people in camouflage uniforms slid into the remaining seats. The rear hatch closed with a hydraulic whine and a final-sounding metallic clunk. Everything in the huge plane began to vibrate as the engines started up. Voices were lost in the roar, although thoughts still came through.

—checklist complete. Request permission from the tower to—

—please don't let us crash. Dear God, I hate flyin—

—think the short, brown-haired girl's on drugs. She hasn't said a word all—

—cheating on me while I'm gone. Can't trust her to—

—so much POWER! Waves of green delight pulsed through Drew as he felt out with his ability into the engines on the wing behind us. I followed along with him, sensing the rush of energy

as the plane began to taxi. I hadn't met a spark yet who didn't get this joy from fire.

"Yuh fust time fwying, Dwew?"

He opened his eyes and grinned at me like a kid in a toy store.

The engines revved louder and we began to roll down the runway. Actually, without windows in here, we could've been in one of those amusement park rides that tilt and shake in synch with the action on the movie screen in front.

Ooh, screen in front—I focused enough to find the Captain's thoughts and followed along through his eyes. Blinking lights outlined the runway and the plane's headlights—who knew planes had headlights?—lit the tarmac that rolled beneath the nose, faster and faster. We tipped up and lifted off the ground. The lights of Boston spread below us, like thousands of tiny stars had fallen from the charcoal sky. I felt the distant presence of people below me as a thrumming murmur of consciousness, but they weren't overwhelmingly loud from up here.

On Drew's far side, Heather swallowed against her nausea and wished for Dramamine—or another healer who could remove the I'm-gonna-barf feeling from her.

The world I'd known all my life receded to ant-sized spots and disappeared over the horizon. The lights stopped at the water's edge, leaving only a few boats to glitter on the dark waters. We lifted into a cloud, and then even those lights were gone.

I didn't need to be in someone else's head to see darkness. I closed my eyes and pulled my arms against my chest. *I'm coming, Trevor. I'll find you. We can fix this. Please don't hate me.*

The cockpit alarm pulled me into the Captain's thoughts. His eyes widened as a spike of fear lanced his spine. *"Fire in Engine*

Three!" He turned and caught a glimpse of the flames out the window. *"Shut down the fuel pump!"* The explosion jarred him sideways as the wing burst into flames. Inside the echoing cargo hold, a single figure sat strapped to a metal chair, secured to a rolling pallet. A second explosion ripped the fuselage apart and the brightness lit his features just long enough for me to scream his name.

"Trevor!"

I jerked awake with a large hand shaking my shoulder. Drew's freckles stood out against his fish-pale skin. "Geez, Maddie!"

Heather's wide eyes peered at me from over his shoulder. *Holy—that was HER DREAM?*

My heart was a scared rabbit in my chest, moving fast and trying to jump out. I felt the nightmare in the minds of the half-dozen people around me. I groaned and covered my face with my hands.

Heather leaned her head back against the vinyl padding. *I am SO glad I'm a healer.*

Drew shook his head and laughed. "Thanks. It was getting hard to stay awake. Now I won't sleep for a week."

I groaned again. "Ahways happy to be of suhvice."

"You know he's okay, right? That was just a dream. Don't throw up or anything."

"Yeah." But right now I really wished we had an RV with us. I needed to *see* him, to know where he was, to know he was okay. The thought of Trevor, alone and in pain… An ache clenched within me, a sense of being incomplete. Broken.

"'Cuz you look like you might throw up."

I rolled my eyes. "I'm not gonna."

"You and Trevor—you guys shouldn't be apart." His memory

flashed back to a tormented Trevor throwing a book against the church wall. "You need each other."

I sniffed. *I couldn't agree more.* Right now, though, I felt so cut off from him. Even that beautiful dream wedding seemed like something childish. *"Hey, let's pretend we're married!"* Who was I kidding? Right now, I had no real tie to him. He didn't want to be around me. I squeezed my eyes shut and sniffed. I wasn't going to cry. I might curl up and rock in a fetal ball later, but I wasn't going to cry.

Pathetic.

"Hey, Maddie. I've got an idea." He glanced around to make sure no one else could hear him. "I'll help you two fix whatever's going on and you can help me score with German girls."

I cracked up, feeling the pressure in my chest lighten. "What? By tewing you what they're thinking?"

"Exactly. Most guys'll tell you that's one of the biggest mysteries of life. You can give me the inside scoop."

"A-ha! So that's why you vohwunteewed for this."

"Hey, I volunteered for this because it's a cool thing to do and half my friends were going. I set things on fire. It's not like I can use that in an office or a classroom or something. Most of my family become firefighters so they can do something good with their ability. Hell, I'll probably do that, too… someday. But right now, I get to be an undercover-superhero-spyhunter for America, hang out with you guys in Europe, and hit on German girls." He pictured a particularly buxom blonde in a red bikini. His imaginary friend gave him a sultry look, blew him a kiss, and purred, *"Hallo, American stud. You can be calling me Inga."*

"You've got youh nationawities confused. I think you had a Swedish bikini model speaking with a Wussian accent there."

Drew pinked up and gave me a rueful smile. "Hey! Don't mock the fantasy. I'm just looking to make my own 'European Union.'"

I winced. "I think you've just wuined that phwase for me fowevuh."

Drew's watch read 3:18 a.m. as we touched down, but the sun was already up in Germany. What was the time difference—about six hours ahead of the U.S.? I was too tired to really care. Cecelia muttered a few charmed words to speed us through customs and soon, Sergeant Cavallo had us packed into a van. The driver's pale scalp shone through his crew cut and he talked with a loud Texas drawl that grated on my sleep-deprived nerves. "Welcome to Germany! Where y'all from?"

Cecelia felt the same way. "Stop talking now."

The driver shut up.

Cavallo looked hard at Cecelia. *Did she just—?*

It was time to get a few things straight with Sergeant Cavallo. *Yeah, she just used mind control. And I'm talking into your head. It's all real, and we're kinda tired of the whole cranky-babysitter thing.*

Cavallo sputtered.

Cecelia?

God, not again. She hissed through gritted teeth. "Dammit, Maddie! I *hate* having your voice in my head."

I ignored her. *Cavallo just figured out about your charming personality and she's having a fit. Wanna tell her to be cool with everything?*

Whatever. Charm resonance filled her voice. "Calm down. You're okay with being around us. We're just regular people with a few special skills." She leaned up toward the driver. "And you—you're going to remember this as a routine drive. Nothing special."

Drew watched Cecelia with a grin. *That's hot—in a dominatrix kinda way.*

Drew didn't worry about charms when I was around. I gave him a half-smirk. *I thought you were saving yourself for Inga.*

He shrugged. "I'm keeping my options open."

"It's like a hotel suite." Drew surveyed the living room filled with flammable materials.

Cavallo scowled at Drew. "Your powers of observation are amazing! Is that your superpower?"

Drew gave her a long look before flashing a fireball up from his hand. "No."

Cavallo paled and her jaw dropped.

Heather burst out laughing. She'd slept for most of the plane ride and now seemed annoyingly chipper. "Didn't you get a memo or something about Drew's housing requirements?"

I had only one question before I curled up somewhere out of everyone else's range and went to sleep. *Sergeant Cavallo, where is Trevor Laurence?*

"Gah! Stop doing that! Why don't you talk like a normal person?"

I sighed. Speaking aloud was even harder when I was this tired. *Long story. Where's Trevor?*

"I have no idea."

Alarm pinged through me. *He's not here?*

"He might be at Vilstein with General Dale."

Heather frowned. "So why are we *here*?" *And where is here, anyway?*

"You're here because Captain Bell ordered me to bring you here. This is TDY billeting for GS-10s and up, which makes it one of the nicest places on base. Tomorrow, we're all supposed to report to the consulate in Frankfurt and you get to do your thing."

Does Captain Bell know where Trevor is?

"I don't know." *God, she's so intense. What's her fixation with this guy?*

I felt a jolt of lethal energy welling up through the frustration. *ASK. HIM. NOW. And, yeah. In case you're wondering again, I'M the dangerous one.*

Cavallo punched the extension into the phone with shaking fingers.

The voice on the other end of the line came through in her thoughts. "He's in a briefing with Major Stiles. Is it urgent?"

I started to nod, but then had another idea. *Can you call New Hampshire on this line?*

Cavallo hung up the phone. "Yes, but it's expensive and you'd need a credit card."

I dug around in my purse. *Not a problem.*

I had to hit about forty digits before the phone started to ring. "Hello?"

"Way-choh." Her name *would* have to be full of Rs and Ls.

"Maddie? Is that you?"

"Yes."

"What's wrong? Why're you calling at... 4:18 in the morning?"

I winced. "Oh! Sowy." Stupid time difference.

"Actually, I was up with Sienna, so no biggie. And Ann and Zack stopped by less than an hour ago to get the details of the latest Belinda vision out of my head. They just took off for Atlanta; she's holed up in a mansion there. What's wrong?"

"Whe-yuhz... Twevuh?"

"Gimme a sec." I pictured the golden rays of her ability bursting like a sun around her head, although nothing but silence came through the phone.

"He's asleep in a big, empty space. Concrete floor, high ceiling. It's not completely dark. Looks bigger than the sparks' training building here." I heard Sienna cooing in the background. "Let me see... You're..." She drifted off. "Hey, who's the woman with the stick up her butt?"

I humphed. "Baby-sittuh."

Rachel's voice rasped with concentration. "It's like... he's not too far from you. I think, maybe a hundred-fifty, two-hundred miles? North-northeast."

"But Twevuh... He's okay?"

"Looks like he's fine. Hey, does that babysitter of yours actually expect Drew to stay in a hotel room?"

I nodded, knowing she could see me. "Uh-huh." Hey, maybe we should learn sign language or something—or I could just hold up a written sign.

"I'll let you get back to explaining it to her. Bye!"

"Bye."

Drew looked over as I hung up. "The baby okay?"

Yeah. I heard her in the background. I turned to Cavallo and my game-face slid into place. *Here's the deal. It's December. It's cold outside. Drew needs a place to sleep that won't burn down around him. I need a place that's at least a hundred feet from any other person or I'll throw nightmares. We need them now or things will get ugly.*

Cavallo bristled. "Are you *threatening* me?"

I shook my head. *Cecelia? Tell her to find appropriate places for Drew and me to stay and you won't see or hear from me until tomorrow.*

Cecelia smirked. *Good deal.* "You. Get them appropriate places to sleep. Now."

Cavallo picked up the phone. Fifteen minutes later, Drew had a cinderblock barracks room and I found myself alone in a cold trailer in the middle of an empty parking lot. I curled up in a nest of blankets and dreamed of a time when Trevor still wanted to be around me.

CHAPTER 3

"I'm so *bored* of watching you watch other people think."

I was pretty bored with wandering around the Frankfurt consulate, floating thoughts about security into the heads of strangers, but I wasn't about to give Cecelia the satisfaction of agreeing with her. She'd shadowed me all morning, charming people to ignore us whenever they took too much interest in why a bunch of teenagers was hanging out in secure areas. I slumped back from the Formica table; I wasn't really hungry, anyway. The clatter of eating and conversation surrounded us. *Why'd you even come, then?*

"Dr. Williamson needed a charm here. I owe him." *I should've known coming on another mission with Maddie was a mistake. These things never end well. At least I can still finish my classes from here. Good thing I was doing so many of them online this term.*

I'd only been asking about today's trip to the consulate, but her thoughts hit me like a hammer to the gut. In fact, everyone's thoughts around me seemed to jostle around inside my head and knock stuff over. The population density wasn't too bad here, although I'd received a bunch of thoughts in German on the trip over. I could largely ignore the words, since I didn't understand them, although the flashes of emotion and images were the same in any language.

I closed my eyes as a wave of Trevor-longing stole my breath. I bit my lip as I resisted the impulse to call Rachel for an update.

Stalker-by-proxy. Pathetic.

Heather pointed a french fry at Cecelia. "You're about the only charm who thinks so." She paused as she took another bite. "I mean, I know that Ganzfield's been training people for about fifteen years, and the early groups of G-positives were pretty small, but still, Matilda said there are about a hundred charms receiving dodecamine. You're the only one who came back."

I was the only one stupid enough to come back. "Like I said, I owe him."

I frowned. *It wasn't stupid.*

"Stay *out* of my head!" Cecelia reached into her memories and began to think-sing "Mambo Number 5." Off-key.

I groaned. All the positive thoughts I'd been having about Cecelia—her selflessness, how she'd helped Rachel, how well she'd done during the attack—dribbled away into annoyance.

"So, why are *you* here, Maddie?" Heather took another bite and watched me expectantly.

I shrugged. *I'm taking one for the team.*

"Well, thanks for needing a healer along for this. I've never been to a foreign country before."

I looked around the room. Most people were thinking and speaking English. We were eating hamburgers and fries. *I don't think you're in one now.*

Drew chimed in. "Hey, didn't you spend a summer in Vancouver a few years ago?"

Heather rolled her eyes. "Yeah, but Canada doesn't count. Sure, it's another country—but it's not *foreign*."

It'd felt foreign enough here when I'd woken up in a cold trailer this morning. *Alone in a strange land.* I'd returned to the suite to shower and get ready, and then we'd followed Cavallo into another numbered block of a building.

The coffee machine in the reception area had been broken. I considered that reason enough to scrub today's plans and go back to bed, but Cavallo had given me a dirty look when I'd brought it up.

"I got up at five for P.T., so I've been up for more than three hours already."

I didn't know the exact words P.T. stood for, but I got the impression that they involved sweating and sit-ups.

I'd glanced at the receptionist and started to float *where's the nearest coffee?* into her head when Cecelia's charm-voice had cut in. "You. Secretary. Get us all coffee now."

I'd half-formed a protest out of habit before I'd realized I had no problem with mind-control in this situation.

She'd just returned to hand a box of steaming styro cups around when her desk phone rang and she ushered us into a conference room down the hall.

A man in a green uniform stood at the end of the room as we filed in. His dark skin stood out in vivid contrast to the whiteboard behind him as he stared at us over crossed arms. His head was shaved bald, and he kept his face in an intimidating scowl. *So, these kids have superpowers? You'd never know it to look at them. What's the best way to use what they can do? What CAN they actually do?*

My lips twitched. *Right now, we can drink our coffee and you can tell me where Trevor Laurence is.*

His mouth dropped into a perfect O. *DID SHE JUST—?*

Great. Freaking out military people never seemed to get old. Looks like I now had a new hobby.

Drew grinned at me. "You messing with him, Maddie?"

Just a little. I'll play nice once he tells me where Trevor is.

"Mr. Laurence is at Vilstein." The guy had two metal bars on his uniform. *Insignia.* I figured that metal insignia meant "officer"—and metal outranked cloth.

Rock-paper-scissors.

Or maybe fancy uniform outranked camouflage, or something. If we were going to be on military bases, I probably should look some of this stuff up. Cavallo had a bunch of embroidered stripes pointing up at her face on a patch in the center of her chest. She'd saluted when she'd entered the room and the guy had returned the gesture.

"You're all scheduled to go there tomorrow."

Tomorrow.

Part of me lit up in anticipation and started singing that song from *Annie*. Another, cynical part told that first part to shut up, since Trevor didn't want to be around me anymore. The rest of me shushed the first two bits and gulped more coffee.

The guy with the bars zeroed in on me. "Ms. Dunn?"

I nodded.

"You're the expert here. How do you want to do this?"

The scowl slid off my face as I recognized the sincerity in his question. *Respect.* In the few seconds I'd been in his head, I'd confirmed the strength of my ability for him. He's processed that new information and tweaked his plans on the fly.

Well, start with your name and then give us the details of the situation.

He gave a half-smile and nodded. "Looks like General Dale's assessment wasn't an exaggeration. Captain Jacob Bell, Army Intelligence. Here's the situation. Classified databases are being accessed from secure locations here in Europe—mostly embassies and consulates—but we can't find the security breach. We keep sensitive information on closed systems with no internet access... or in SIPR. There's no evidence of hacking—the systems have only been accessed with valid passwords and protocols."

Cecelia frowned in confusion. "What's sipper?'"

"SIPR—or SIPRNet—is the Secret Internet Protocol Router Network. It's like a second internet for the DOD and State Department."

Drew set his cup down. "If there's no evidence of hacking, how do you know you've got a security leak?"

The captain nodded. *Smart question.* "Classified documents and information have been sold to some... disreputable customers." *Terrorists.* "The money trail is cold and the CIA has investigated and cleared the personnel who've had access to the intel." Captain Bell set his fists on the edge of the table and leaned forward. "We keep these files classified for good reasons. We have spies and informants who'll be killed if their covers are blown. We don't want our enemies to know national security protocols— what we do to find and catch those who wish to harm America or its people. If terrorists know how we operate, they'll plan ways to work around our systems. Every compromised document could lead to a planeload of people crashing into a building or a bomb exploding on a crowded street."

I felt a jolt that had nothing to do with the coffee kicking in. This was important.

Real.

I needed to do this right or innocent people could die. I swallowed hard, and then nodded. Getting info without hacking—I could do something like that. It sounded like we might be looking for another telepath... or maybe a charm. *Get me near the people involved. I'll see what they know.*

So, now we got to eat burgers surrounded by people who'd given us no clues about any security breach. At least we'd been able to stop by the passport office here at the consulate and put in applications for Drew and Cecelia.

Charms never need appointments.

Cavallo frowned at us from the doorway and jabbed an emphatic finger at her watch. *Back to work!*

A half-smile formed on Drew's face. *Damn, she's hot when she's being bossy.*

I groaned.

"Anything?"

I shook my head. *Frankfort consulate's clean—at least as far as I can tell.* We were back in the conference room on base and my internal clock was whining that it hated me and wanted to go home.

Captain Bell looked at the pile of papers in his hand. *Travel orders.* "We'll head to Vilstein tonight. The most recent incidents have been in the Berlin Embassy. We'll send your team there tomorrow. Actually, given the size of the embassy facility and the number of personnel, you'll probably need several days there."

Cecelia gave a martyred sigh.

I rolled my eyes. *If you're so bored, you could ask a few questions, you know. You could charm the truth out of people.*

Her next sigh made me cringe. "Whatever."

"Grab your gear, kids. You leave for Vilstein in twenty minutes."

Heather scowled. *Who's he calling a kid? I'm twenty-six!*

I closed my eyes. We were going to where Trevor was. Anticipation and anxiety played tug-of-war in my gut.

No speed limit? I gotta try that! From behind the driver, Drew watched the speedometer slide past 180 and inch toward 200. That was in kilometers, but in miles-per-hour that was like… well, it was really fast. A yellow sports car roared by us on the right and Drew's jaw dropped as something within him whimpered *Ferrari!*

Cavallo leaned against the back corner of the VW bus and tried to sleep. Cecelia had snagged the front seat after the soldier who'd been assigned to drive us had flashed what she'd considered a sexy smile. My lip curled with disgust at the direction of his thoughts. Ick! Did he think she was some kind of a gymnast? I shuddered. Should I warn Cecelia about this guy's perviness? I shrugged. She could put a stop to anything she didn't like.

Distraction time. I flipped channels.

—Enzo with a V12 engine and dual overhead cams—

—looks like without his shirt on. I bet he's ripped and—

—just shut up so I can get some sleep—

—not much good at the consulate. Maybe I can sneak into the base hospital and help injured soldiers. Heather frowned in concentration.

My forehead cleared and I sent her a thought. *Why sneak? I bet General Dale can give you whatever approval you need.*

She jumped, and then grinned at me in the dim light. "Yeah, but it's more fun to sneak."

You may as well go. I don't think we're going to need much healing at the Berlin embassy. Heather really didn't have much to do. I had minds to read; Cecelia charmed away interference or suspicious memories. Even Drew had been sensing for electrical fields that would indicate surveillance equipment. He'd found a bunch, but they were all supposed to be there.

My thoughts turned back to Trevor.

"I can't be around you."

I squeezed my eyes shut as I tried to force the words out of my head. The same arguments ping-ponged back and forth. *He just needs some time alone—but he hates that he became a killer because of me. We have something wonderful together and he'll want me back. We're soulmates, after all—we're meant to be together. He was a good person before I twisted him into a monster like me, and he knows he'll never be able to be like he was if I'm still around.* A lump formed in my throat.

Arrrgh! I hated how... *broken* I felt without him. Could I... could I just apologize to him, tell him how sorry I was that I'd brought all this ugliness into his life? Would that be enough to fix this? I blinked back tears and tried to swallow around the throat-lump.

I'd never wanted Trevor to kill for me, but I'd reveled in his protective side—he'd made me feel so cherished! He'd *saved* me—Hunter had been swinging that gun my way.

But Trevor could've blocked the bullets.

Instead, he'd gone for Hunter's heart and squeezed the life out of it. Blood-red anger bubbled up inside of me.

If only Zack hadn't set Trevor up...

The three-hour drive seemed to take the better part of a year. My sense of European geography was sketchy, but I was pretty sure we'd landed in central Germany and had gone north. Or east. Ugh. I didn't really care.

We pulled up in front of a security gate—and found ourselves staring down the barrel of the huge gun mounted on a massive tank. I breathed more easily when I realized no one was inside.

While one MP checked under the bumpers with a mirror on a stick, another collected our IDs and compared the photos to our faces, and then swiped them through a scanner whose little light glowed green with approval of our existence.

"Report to building 2327," the MP read off the computer screen. He pointed around the tank that still aimed its gun at us like an incredibly intimidating lawn ornament.

You kids stay the hell out of my yard!

"You'll wanna take the second right, go straight about two clicks then make another right onto Access Road Three."

The driver followed the directions and we found ourselves staring up at an enormous half-barrel of corrugated metal—an old airplane hangar—large enough to house a football stadium or two with room to spare. The open door showed as a pale rectangle of light in the dark.

The driver put the van in park. *Should I ask the blonde for her phone number before she gets out?*

My feet hit the packed gravel. I slung my bag over my shoulder and half-ran inside the huge, echoing space with its scattered islands of light.

"Welcome to Vilstei—"

I didn't catch the soldier's name, rank, or anything else. *Where's Trevor Laurence?* If this guy wasn't supposed to know about our abilities, Cecelia could charm him to forget my question.

What's-his-name's eyes opened wide. *Laurence? Building 2335.* "What—?"

My glare made him pale. *Which way?*

His head jerked right. I dropped my bag and took off running into the darkness.

CHAPTER 4

What am I doing?

Memory of Trevor's horrified reaction the last time he'd looked at me hit me in the gut.

"I can't be around you."

My feet stumbled on things that were too dark to see and I slowed to a walk. Lights illuminated more of the giant, half-barrel hangars spaced along the side of the access road. I felt like Alice in Wonderland, too small for the world I now inhabited. The November night was silent except for the scrape of my footsteps on the asphalt.

Should I just go back? No. I *needed* to know he was okay. He'd been so upset—so hurt.

Traumatized.

I pulled a subtle shield up around my mind, the spiderweb camouflage I'd learned from watching Zack. A spark of remembered anger lit me from within at the thought of him.

If only he hadn't set Trevor up that way!

Afterward, Trevor had been so horrified when he'd looked at

me—I rubbed a hand across my face. Trevor might not want to be around me, but what he didn't know...

Gah—a telepathic stalker. Yeah, I'm REALLY mature and healthy.

I felt the touch of his thoughts in the gloom ahead of me—barely perceptible at the end of my range. A few steps closer and I felt the minds of the two MPs just inside the door.

Guards?

Were they there to keep others out—or Trevor in?

I melted off the side of the road. Dead, frost-covered grass muffled my footsteps as I skirted around the side of the building. Trevor's mind became clearer; he occupied the center of the building. I crouched down next to the icy metal wall and drank in his existence.

Anguish whirlpooled through him as he sat on a lonely air mattress in the middle of the huge space. *I miss her so much, but it's better that she's not here. I don't know what I'd do to her.* A vivid image of him crushing my heart inside my chest filled his thoughts and made him shudder. I gasped. *No, it's better if I'm not around her right now. Where is she tonight? Is she okay?*

I fell back and sat down on the frozen ground. Frigid dampness invaded my legs, but I didn't really feel like I was in them right now. I started to shake. Trevor was so upset with me that he thought he might kill me? His thoughts were a confused jumble of intense approach-avoidance.

Love her. Miss her. Think I might kill her.

I took a shuddering breath and wrapped my arms around myself. A single tear left an icy mark down my cheek.

Trevor sighed and dragged himself to his feet. I felt the cold air hit him as the blankets dropped back onto the bed. He deliberately cleared his mind and started making slow, controlled movements. He stepped to the side, and then moved his arms up, repeating the arc with his larger, invisible arms.

Tai-chi? Since when did Trevor do tai-chi?

Bending his legs and lunging to the side, he forced himself to focus on his breathing and on controlling the movements, weaving his steps and making adjustments for a second set of arms. Stretching, bending, turning—always calm and in control. He went through a series of movements that lasted several minutes, and then repeated them, calming with each iteration. I closed my eyes and lost myself in him.

I stayed in his head until he drifted into an unsettled sleep. When his thoughts dropped away, the aching cold in my legs brought me back to the fact that I was sitting on the frozen ground in the dark on a military base somewhere in central Germany. I couldn't feel my feet as I shuffled back to our quarters.

The door to hangar 2327 refused to open when I yanked on the handle, but Drew's mind was in range. *Wanna let me in?*

The code's 5-1-7-1-9-star.

I located the little keypad under what looked like a nightlight in a recessed box next to the door and punched the keys with shaking fingers. *Thanks.*

Inside, the hangar smelled of diesel and disuse. The walls arched and disappeared into the dark above me. A series of trailers formed ranks along the wall to my left, an archipelago of lights in the blackness. Cold pervaded the space and my breath formed a little cloud as I moved toward the trailer where I could feel Drew and Heather watching TV.

Behind me, Cecelia listened to music alone in her own trailer. I couldn't feel Cavallo—she was either asleep or staying somewhere else.

Drew saw me through the trailer window and opened the door as I arrived. *Did she find Trevor?*

I did, but I don't wanna talk about it.

Drew nodded.

A wave of heat enveloped me as I stepped inside.

"Hey, Drew! Don't let all that cold air in!" Heather looked up from the TV. Her eyes widened. *Maddie's shaking. Has she been outside since we arrived? That's more than two hours and it's below freezing out there. It looks like she might have the beginnings of hypothermia.* "Get over here and let me check you out."

She grabbed my hand as soon as I was in range. Heather's eyes scrunched closed as she did her inspection. "Take that coat off and sit. I've gotta do some work on you."

I plopped down on the carpeted floor, feeling mottled patches of pain and numbness in my legs as I did.

"Coat off," Heather repeated.

I shrugged out of it and let it puddle behind me on the floor.

Heather sighed. On each side of my face, her hands seemed fever-hot against my skin. I gasped as pins and needles surged through my system like I'd stuck a fork in an electrical outlet. Every muscle in my body seemed to spasm. My fingers, ears, nose, and legs went from the freezer to the broiler as spring-green energy hummed through me.

"All set." Heather let go of my face and I slumped down, breathing fast.

What the hell?

Heather grinned. "Like it? Morris and I worked out a new technique. We wanted to be able to patch up people quickly in the field. I didn't get much of a chance to try it when the feds invaded Ganzfield, though. We didn't have many injuries."

I feel like I've been touched by the... the sledgehammer of healing.

She cracked up. "Yeah, and it burns up a lot more energy on my end, but that's cool. I need to take off a few pounds, anyway."

I humphed. Now that the intense feeling had faded, I actually felt warm and comfortable. *So you're healing me as part of your diet?*

She tipped her head to the side with a smile. "Mutually beneficial, don't you think?"

Generic soda. All that stuff tastes like—ooh, grape! Drew closed the fridge and flung himself down on the couch. The trailer-sized furniture made him look even larger than usual. "You okay now?"

I shrugged. *I'll live. So, did I miss anything?*

Drew chugged half the can of soda. "We're scheduled to leave for Berlin at oh-seven-hundred tomorrow."

Anything else?

"Well, you're not going to like that your trailer's so close to the rest of them."

I winced.

"Yeah. At least you've got heat and windows. They hauled in a shipping container for me to sleep in." *But no firewood or a way to vent the smoke. I'm gonna freeze tonight.*

I snorted. *Your tax dollars at work.*

"Yeah. Maybe we can drag your trailer to the other side of this place tomorrow."

"Thanks, Dwew."

"Please! Like I want another peek into your dreams. No way—too intense." *Now, if you'd just dream about Inga...*

I let out a bark of a laugh. *Sorry, she's not my type.* The only person on the planet who was my type didn't want me around.

Love her. Miss her. Think I might kill her.

I didn't feel like laughing anymore.

I didn't wake myself or anyone else up screaming during the night. I chalked it up as a success.

Cavallo smacked the metal side of my trailer shortly after 6 a.m. "We leave in forty minutes. Be dressed and ready."

I heard her move off down the line of trailers to repeat the banging and instructions. I decided to wait until the coffee hit before I did anything else. At least my trailer was warm, clean, and stocked with the essentials. I plugged in the coffeemaker and found a few packets of fake sugar in with the filters. No milk, though, so I drank it black and scalded my tongue.

I tore open a mini-box of cereal and ate it dry. The overly-happy cartoon tiger on the box mocked me with his exuberance.

Half an hour later, I was showered, dressed, and standing in the cold hangar. The sparse lighting didn't add to the ambiance, and the barrel-roofed structure looked colorless and dim—like we were standing beneath the most depressing rainbow ever. We all squinted against the too-bright daylight as we climbed into the minivan.

G-positive mole-people.

Our driver this morning seemed almost colorless in her paleness. With her straw-light hair pulled into two French braids that ran along either side of her head, she also looked to be about twelve, like she was playing soldier.

Private Pippi, reporting for duty.

At least Cecelia wouldn't flirt with this one.

I settled in and watched the base roll by in daylight. No leaves littered the meticulous rectangles of lawn. Every sidewalk had been swept clean. We passed a supermarket marked "Commissary."

We should stop for supplies on the way back.

Drew grinned. "Good idea."

Next came a movie theater and a bowling alley, as well as several fast food places. It was like Main Street U.S.A.—acres of a clean, wholesome version of America right here behind the razor wire. Both civilians and people in uniform moved quickly against the cold. Many thought in English—at least I thought most of it was English.

—ask my CO: if I'm going TDY to SHAPE will I need DIPCLEAR?
—drop the kids at school before I go to the PX and—
—podemos ir a Munchen este fin de semana—
—back from Afghanistan. If my next deployment doesn't—
—send it Space-A, will it get there in time for Christmas? Should I—
—Ich brauche diesen Job. Vielleicht sollte ich für ein Visum beantragen und—

It somehow seemed *too* wholesome—like a sanitized version of real America. The whole place was almost like a *Twilight Zone* set-up in which the only thing missing was the creepy, clean-cut kid who could make things happen using only his mind.

Oh, wait. That would be *us*.

We showed our IDs again at the exit checkpoint, and then followed blue "A" signs to the highway. Driving to Berlin took less than an hour. The tide of mental voices rose as we drew closer. Memories of the mental crush of New York and Chicago made me squeeze my eyes shut and brace against the onslaught. The tan, stone embassy looked newly built, and it had been set well away from other structures, which cut the volume of thoughts pressing into mine. Layers of security ringed the active parts of the compound.

Fortress America.

We started in the basement and took it a room at a time. The departments blended into one another. Heather and Drew started a game they called "Office Affairs." We'd enter a room with a dozen or so people at their desks and they'd watch them and figure out which ones were involved romantically. They called on me to render the final verdict.

After standing around disdainful and bored for the first hour, Cecelia began conducting a few quietly charmed interviews, just to speed things up and alleviate the tedium. "Tell me if you've misused classified information, and then forget I asked."

Oh—maybe I should be shielding. If another telepath were here, he or she would've heard me coming. If I'd been spying using my ability, I'd either shield or leave if an enemy telepath came into range. I felt out with my mind anyway, letting the thoughts of several dozen people roll though me. No one pinged back minder-loud.

I didn't expect anyone to be thinking, "—and now I can sell this information to terrorists." It would've been nice if it were that easy, though.

I wanted to whine about the boredom, but I also felt guilty. The other three were here because I had to be here. Could I talk Cavallo into letting the rest of the team do something else? I was pretty sure General Dale wasn't planning on sticking us into a secret prison and torturing us. We left Department B114 and headed to B115. *I'm going to talk to Cavallo and see if you guys can get out of interrogation duty. Why do the rest of you have to suffer?*

"You don't need backup?" Drew frowned.

For the main mission, yeah. But not for this stuff. You've seen how much security they have here; this embassy's like the safest place on the planet. C'mon, I know how bored you all are. In fact, if Cav—

A ghost stepped out of the wall, crossed the hallway, and disappeared into the wall across the way.

My jaw hit my chest and I stumbled to a stop.

What. The HELL. Was THAT?

Heather took a sharp breath. "What's wrong, Maddie? Your autonomic nervous system activity just spiked."

Drew stared at me. "You okay? You look like you've just seen a ghost."

I started to move down the hall. No. *A ghost?* Ghosts weren't real.

And they certainly weren't pale-purple with long, trailing tails.

I yanked open the door, startling the people inside. The wall was too close. I turned and moved down the hall, past the place where I'd seen it disappear, and grabbed the doorknob. This one didn't open.

It's locked.

What the hell is Maddie doing? Did she hear someone's thoughts? Whatever it is, she's really freaked out, and that can't mean anything good. Cecelia eyed the door for a second. "Anyone inside?"

I felt two minds and nodded. *Two people.*

She knocked. "You, in there. Let us in."

An overweight guy in a white oxford opened the door. I pushed past him and scanned the room. I stopped breathing. The head of whatever-it-was poked up through the top of a neglected filing cabinet against the wall. It was still lavender and… translucent. His pale, glowing eyes—it definitely looked like a "he"—remained fixed on the monitor where the other man worked. Thick, dark hair framed the rugged, chiseled face, and a hint of broad, well-muscled shoulders stuck out above the cabinet.

No thoughts—I didn't *feel* anyone there. I just "saw" him. Gah—I was looking at a washed-out, purple… *wraith* of some sort.

Maybe the new embassy was built on an old graveyard.

The ghost's gaze turned toward me. Those creepy, glowing eyes widened as they met mine and my breath froze in my chest until he ducked down into the filing cabinet and disappeared.

What the hell? I started to shake and my hand came up to cover my mouth. It wasn't a telepath. It didn't even feel… human.

But it'd *seen me.*

I closed my eyes and took a deep breath, and then let it out with a groan.

I *really* wasn't looking forward to telling the General that there was a good chance his security leak was a glowing, purple, long-tailed ghost with surprisingly manly features.

CHAPTER 5

"What?" Cavallo stared at me. "What do you mean, a ghost?"

I didn't say it was a ghost. Ugh—my head hurt. *I said it LOOKED like a ghost. I could see through it.* I flashed her yet another image of it.

I can't put that in my report. "What am I supposed to tell Captain Bell?" *Maybe the girl needs a psych eval.*

Tell him we may have a lead. We'd moved through the embassy for hours, looking for the… thing.

Disappeared without a trace… like a frikkin' ghost.

No one else had seen anything. At least Drew had enjoyed watching Sergeant Cavallo as she searched—particularly when he'd followed her up the stairs. Ugh. I stared out the window at the now-dark sky and the lights on the highway.

Ann.

Ann might be able to see it. We both had the same affinity for "seeing" the energy of emotion and when people used their abilities. The ache in my chest sharpened. Too bad Ann now hated me for threatening to fry Zack.

Grr—he'd SO had it coming, though!

Back on the base, I slid out of the van before the driver had it in park and took off toward Trevor. I nearly forgot to shield before I was in his range. His thoughts flashed to me like a beacon in the dark. In the middle of his big, empty hangar, he lay back on an air mattress that hissed with every shift of his weight. The remains of a dog-eared paperback threatened to disintegrate in his hands, and he propped the book at an awkward angle to catch the dim light.

"I been silent so long now it's gonna roar out of me like floodwaters and you think the guy telling this is ranting and raving my God; you think this is too horrible to have really happened, this is too awful to be the truth! But, please. It's still hard for me to have a clear mind thinking on it. But it's the truth even if it didn't happen."

Oh, crap. What did it say about my life when *One Flew over the Cuckoo's Nest* became relevant?

I sank down, leaned against the cold metal wall between us, closed my eyes, and listened to his mental voice. I tuned out the rest of the world, ignored the irrelevant thoughts of the MPs at Trevor's door, and stopped worrying about whether it was better to be hallucinating or be going up against invisible purple ghosts.

I simply breathed in Trevor's thoughts. Yearning tightened in my chest and I drank in his existence. I bit my lip as he replayed his actions that night back at Ganzfield—when he'd killed Colonel Hunter. The rubbery resistance of Hunter's cardiac muscles as he'd crushed them made his gut clench.

I killed him. I'm a killer. I'm dangerous.

I'd done this to him. I crumpled against the metal wall as a wave of self-loathing stole my energy and twisted my face into an aching grimace.

My fault.

Another mind touched mine, and soon light flared red against my eyelids. I opened them to see Drew coming across the frost-covered ground, his eyes on my footprints, a pale ball of fire floating in front of his hand. He stopped moving when his eyes met mine. "Hey, Maddie. Heather sent me to make sure you didn't freeze."

I rubbed my arms. I still had to shield so Trevor wouldn't sense me.

Drew took in the hangar at my back. "Trevor in there?"

I swallowed hard and nodded.

"He okay?"

I bit my lip and sniffed.

"C'mon." He held out the hand that wasn't directing the fireball and pulled me up. I followed him back to the hangar, feeling possibly crazy, but definitely broken.

Metallic pounding dragged me from sleep and Cavallo's bristly thoughts poked at my brain. "You need to report to the General. Now."

Ugh. I downed a cup of black coffee and ran a brush through my hair. Dark-circled eyes stared back at me from the mirror.

I grabbed my coat as I stepped out of my trailer, and then stopped. At the far end of the hangar, General Dale sat in a pool of light cast by a single panel high in the arched ceiling. How did they turn on the lights? We hadn't been able to find any switches. Would we be able to keep them on after he left, at least? I was all for energy conservation, but it was always so dark in here! At the sound of my door slapping closed, the General looked up and waved me over. The walk through the huge, dark hangar seemed surreal. In the center of the huge building, no one was in my range and my world was silent except for the rubbery squelch of my sneakers on the cement floor.

The General's thoughts got louder as I approached him. He pointed at the empty chair across from him and I sank down into it.

"So, Ms. Dunn... you found something?" *What am I supposed to do with a "purple monkey-ghost"?*

Monkey-ghost? My brows pulled together. *He didn't look like a monkey. Oh, the tail-thing. Well, see for yourself.* I flashed him the memory of the whatever-it-was passing through the walls.

The General's gaze fixed on me. "I need to know... is what you saw—is it... *real*?"

If you're asking if I really saw it, then yeah. But I have no clue what it is. I thought I might be looking for another telepath. Whatever this thing is, I couldn't sense any thoughts from it.

"Did anyone else see it?"

I shook my head.

"I understand that you didn't want to come here, and that you've been under a lot of stress lately. The events involving Colonel Hunter—"

My chin came up. *You mean the part where Trevor had to kill him when he opened fire on us, or the part where Hunter kept me in a secret underground cell and tortured me?*

"Like I said, you've been under a lot of stress lately." The General's voice held an edge. *Her mental stability is in question.* "I'd like you to speak with one of the psychiatrists at the base hospital." *If she's become a danger to herself or others, what can we do? She's powerful. We'd need to keep her sedated for the trip back to New Hampshire. Would Jon be able to handle her there, or would she need to remain unconscious permanently?*

Permanently? My whole body glowed sickly-yellow. I had *not* signed up for that. *General, if you think I'm insane, then send me—send all of us—back to Ganzfield. But I'm NOT going to any hospital and I WON'T let you knock me out.*

The General frowned. "You'd disobey an order?" *Dammit, she always knows what I'm thinking!* Trepidation frosted his thoughts steely-grey.

I'm a civilian. I don't take orders. I also don't voluntarily go into buildings filled with people in pain. You wouldn't believe what it's like to feel all that at once. I considered showing him, since I was getting kinda pissed off, but I really didn't want to add fuel to Dale's "sedate her forever" fire. Gah—I needed a working phone. I had to make sure Williamson could check on me and make sure these army guys didn't try something like that. Or Coleman could do it. Was he back from hiding in the Caymans yet?

"Fine. I'll order the psychiatrist to come here."

I'm not hallucinating. Probably. *I see things that other people don't. It's why you needed people from Ganzfield in the first place.* Wait—why was I arguing to keep this job? I leaned forward. *Whatever it is has free access to your secure areas. If it's not the cause of the leak...* Ugh! Screw this. I couldn't concentrate. I knotted my arms across my chest. *Why is Trevor Laurence being held in isolation a few hangars over?*

What has THAT got to do with the security leak? "He requested it."

So he's free to leave whenever he wants?

"I don't think that would be wise."

Wise?

"He's dangerous."

No. I shook my head. *My sweet Trevor would never— Wait, what do you mean?*

"Mr. Laurence requested that he be kept in isolation until he regained control of his ability."

Regained contr— The hangar tilted around me.

"I can't be around you."

He thought he would… hurt me accidentally? It wasn't because he blamed me? Fingernails dug into my palms. *Oh. Oh!* My chair crashed backward as I headed for the door.

"Where are you going?" Frustration colored the General's echoing voice. I felt him reach for a phone as I moved out of range.

The outer door banged against the siding and the cold wind bit into me. My feet slapped the asphalt and icy pain ripped through my nose. I didn't care. The need to see him—to know for sure what I now suspected—propelled me forward like I was tied to the front of a moving truck.

Two MPs stood alert in front of Trevor's door. One shook his head as I approached. "Ma'am? This area's restricted."

Did he just "Ma'am" me?

I stopped in front of them. My breath caught up with me a few seconds later. Restricted, huh? Rules like that hadn't applied to me for a while. I looked at the one on the right and floated a thought. *What's the access code to this building?*

The MP scowled. *4-4-9-0-5-star.*

Maddie? Is that you? Confusion filled Trevor's distant thoughts. I hadn't shielded, so with our special connection, he was able to sense my thoughts, even at this distance.

"Sowwy about this." I flashed the MP an apologetic smile, and then reached into his head and blasted a quick spike of energy into his motor cortexes. Right, then left. His entire body flashed with yellow fear as he fell limp on the ground. "Help!" *I can't move! I'm paralyzed!* The left side of his face hung slack. Oops—I must've overzapped that side. Whatever—he'd recover.

I turned on the other MP.

Lather. Rinse. Repeat.

The whites showed around his terror-filled eyes as he stared up at me from the ground. "Oh, God! What *are* you?"

I made a mental note to call Cecelia for a clean-up of these guys' memories as I stepped between their prone bodies and keyed in the code. Inside, my eyes needed to adjust to the darkness.

Maddie? What's going on? Trevor pulled himself to his feet in the middle of the oversized structure. Seriously? An entire *aircraft hangar* for one guy?

He stood in a pool of light that angled in from above and cast him into silhouette. The sight of him pulled me like a magnet. *I need to know. Did I do this to you? Did I ruin everything? Do you hate me?* I tried to catch my breath as I hurried toward him in the dark.

"What?" His voice echoed. *No! I could never—*

You left. I squeezed my arms around myself as the pain of my accusation flowed through me. This ridiculously huge building went on forever. *You said you couldn't be around me anymore and you left and didn't—*

"You were there!" *You saw what I did to Hunter. I killed him! I didn't have to. I'm a killer. I LOST CONTROL.*

My jaw quivered. *You looked at me and you were so... horrified.* I was close enough now to see the shadows under his eyes and the bits of dark hair that poked out from under his green knit hat.

Maddie, I lost control and I KILLED SOMEONE. And I've hurt you before. I broke your leg!

That was an accident.

I've had other "accidents!" I hurt Reed back when we roomed together. What if I accidentally—oh, God. Even the thought of crushing my heart drained his face and caused purple flashes of pain within him. "I couldn't live with myself if I hurt you like that."

You won't hurt me. I stepped into the circle of light around his pathetic-looking air mattress. My breath formed a little cloud in the light; it was still freezing in here.

"Stop! Don't come any closer. I can't be around you. Not while I still have my ability."

Trevor, that's the STUPIDEST thing I've ever heard you think. Angry-red energy sparked from me.

"You're too important to me to risk hurting you."

So... what? You're going to just stay in isolation?

"Until I'm safe to be around."

You're safe to be around now. I always felt safe when I was with him.

"I just can't take the chance."

You're being ridiculous. I moved toward him.

"Stay back!" *I'm too dangerous!* "Please, Maddie."

I shook my head. *I'll risk it.*

Invisible hands pressed me back.

My eyebrows hit the ceiling and something in my chest roared to life. *Did you just PUSH me?*

"It's not safe!"

I stepped toward him again. Again, he pushed me back. *Knock it off!*

"Please don't! I can't—" The arms formed a barrier between us. I could see them as golden light; Trevor kept his invisible fists clenched. He shook his head. *No. I can't let you.*

Blood-red anger pounded through my head. *Are you frikkin' KIDDING me? I've been freaking out for days, wondering if you blamed me for twisting you into something you didn't want to be, worrying that you were all traumatized because of me! But instead, you've been staying away from me out of some stupid belief that you might HURT me?* I narrowed my eyes, focused in through the energy of his ability, and sent portions of both his overactive motor cortexes into seizure with tiny bursts of energy. The golden limbs melted away, His physical arms also hung slack at his sides as bright surprise filled him.

For an eternal, breathless second, we just stared at each other. *Oh, my God.* What the HELL had I done? Shock and horror washed cold through me. My hands flew up to my face. *Horrible. Unstable. Dangerous. Crazy.* I fell to my knees with a sob.

I'd just... *blasted Trevor.*

My face contorted as agony clutched my soul. Hurting Trevor was so, so wrong. *I'm a terrible person.* Maybe I *was* going over the edge. Maybe I'd become as crazy as Isaiah had been. Maybe there wasn't such a thing as a *good* killer telepath. Right now, Dale's threats of permanent sedation sounded almost tempting.

Trevor's heavy breaths became louder and I realized that he was... *laughing?*

I looked up through the gaps in my fingers. *This is FUNNY to you?*

His yellow surprise had morphed into a geyser of giddy green joy.

My jaw dropped.

"Oh, Maddie..." He stumbled over to me and knelt, staggering a bit as his flopping arms threatened to unbalance him. His beautiful brown eyes met mine and they sparkled with relief. "You *blasted* me."

Two tears broke loose as I shook my head. *I am SO sorry.*

"No! Don't you get it? If I ever lose control around you—you can *stop* me! You... you *disarmed* me. Literally!" *I never thought you'd ever—I couldn't have asked you to.*

I tried to swallow. He was... *okay* with this? I squeezed my eyes shut and rubbed my temples. This had to be the most dysfunctional week of our relationship. General Dale wanted me to see a shrink? Maybe Trevor and I could convince him to turn it into couple's counseling.

I took a deep breath. *So, just so we're clear, you never felt like I corrupted you and turned you into a monster?*

His eyes widened. "What?"

You looked at me after— A whimper formed at the back of my throat. *You told me you couldn't be around me anymore, and then ran into the night!*

"You didn't see the reason why in my head?"

Frustration curled my hands into fists. *If you'd stuck around for more than two seconds, I might've had time! All I got was a look of horror, "I can't be around you," and you were gone!* I shook my head again and rolled my eyes. *But now, after I stalked you telepathically and blasted your brain, NOW you're happy.*

"You *stalked* me?"

Yeah. I've been shielding and listening in for the past couple of nights.

His grin widened. "Really?"

Tai-chi. Cuckoo's Nest. Oh, and I got Rachel to check in on you, too, so we can add stalker-by-proxy to the list.

He chuckled. "It's not stalking if the stalkee is cool with it. By the way, any idea how long this paralysis'll last? I really want to put my arms around you right now."

I could breathe again. My hands came up to cup his face and a sense of rightness returned to the world. He leaned forward. I closed my eyes as our lips touched, feather soft, and then I moaned and pulled him closer as the kiss caught fire. We tipped and my butt landed on the cold cement as we tumbled together. I didn't care.

Our breath mingled in a little cloud between us. *So you still love me?*

"Maddie, I will *always* love you." *Don't ever doubt it.* Silver-white energy flowed over us. I closed my eyes and drank it in, and then kissed him until we were both dizzy.

Okay. I wobbled awkwardly to my feet, feeling a giddy smile pull at my cheeks. I braced Trevor to help him stand. I felt like I might lift off the ground at any moment.

Trevor still loved me!

He looked down at his slack arms. *So, my ability's gone?*

Nope, actually, it's still here. I borrowed his telekinesis and lifted his right hand into a floppy wave.

"Huh?" He looked at his hand. He could feel it moving. *That's so weird.*

I zapped your motor cortex, not your basal ganglion. Your ability's still working, but you have no way to control it. I grinned. *But, since I still have MY motor cortexes and we share abilities, I can do this. Ha! You are now my puppet!*

He raised his eyebrows with a smile. "Oh, yeah? Prove it."

I used his ability to pull his arms around my waist.

He sighed. "Finally."

I leaned my cheek against his chest. He pressed his lips against the top of my head and we held each other in the dark, like a slow dance without music, until the rhythm of our breathing matched each other's.

So, you wanted to go off dodecamine?

He nodded. "Yeah. I was going to stay away from other people until it left my system. They wouldn't give me the antagonist—I asked."

I pinked up, remembering what'd happened the *last* time

we'd been darted with the dodecamine blocker. *That's probably for the best.*

"Yeah, if I'm going to lose my inhibitions, I want you there with me."

I grinned and swatted him on the shoulder.

"Hey! You're hitting an unarmed man!"

I groaned. *Will you stop with the puns? Maybe I'd hit more than the motor cortex with that blast.*

"Let's see... armchair, arms race, Armageddon... I think I'm out."

Good.

"Hey, Maddie, what would you call me if I was in a swimming pool right now?"

Huh?

"Bob."

I grinned as I shook my head. *That's sick. You're pretty chipper for a guy who's at the mercy of a killer telepath.*

"I still can't believe you blasted me."

Well, I promise not to use my ability against you like that again... crush my heart and hope to die.

He paled. *How can she still love me after what I did?* "Seriously, though. Does it bother you that... that I'm dangerous? That I could lose control of my ability and basically kill you?"

I twisted up to give him a look. *You're asking ME that?*

Something uncoiled within him and he gave a little humph of a laugh. "Good point."

Trevor Laurence, you may be strong and powerful and dangerous, but you're not dangerous to ME.

He buried his face in my hair. "Thank God."

I nuzzled in closer, absorbing a warm dose of Trevor-ness. *I've missed you.*

"I've missed you, too."

Hey, if you ever feel like you can't be around me again, call me or something, all right?

"Okay. I would've, but I don't know your phone number—do you realize I've never called you before? And I don't know any of the Ganzfield ones. We've always had them programmed into your phone. I didn't think about it before I left. I tried to get information to look them up, but Ganzfield's numbers are unlisted. Hey, does your cell even work in Europe?"

I shook my head. *Nope.* I'd shut it off after finding that it wouldn't work in Germany. *Ooh—let's go get new ones.*

"Today?"

Right now.

"Are we even allowed to leave?"

Trevor, I just ran out of a briefing with General Dale and disabled two MPs to get in here. Getting permission to go shopping isn't the issue. It may be more on the scale of preventing the General from ordering me shot full of sedatives for the rest of my life.

Trevor's embrace stiffened around me.

Hey, you're getting control of your arms back!

"He *threatened* you?"

Indirectly. He's a little concerned that I may be going insane.

"What?" He pulled back to study my face. "Why would he think…"

I saw—ah, hell. I just showed him the memory.

His eyebrows crinkled together. "A purple ghost?"

More lavender than purple.

"That's freaky."

Yup.

"So you think that might be how the intel's being leaked?"

I shrugged. *Maybe. Whatever it is, I'm the only one who saw it.*

"Like the emotion colors. I wonder if there's a chance that Ann could see it. Maybe she could come check it out, too."

I hissed in a grimacing breath. *Ann... kinda hates me right now.*

"What? What happened?"

Yeah. After... after you left that night, Williamson had us in his office and I... I may've threatened to fry Zack's brain for setting you up like that, and we sorta ended up— I trailed off into the memory of rapid-fire angry thoughts and brain-blasts.

Trevor winced. "Minder cat-fight?"

More or less.

Invisible hands began to stroke my back. The watery weakness dissipated into smooth strength as he re-established his control. I melted into him and closed my eyes. The zipper of his jacket pressed into my cheek so I shifted until I lay against his heart.

Safe. Together. Right. Whole.

A metallic bang echoed through the cavernous room and a rectangle of daylight appeared against the black wall. Silhouettes flashed across it as we turned.

Ugh.

There's nothing like seeing myself in a riflescope crosshairs in a sniper's thoughts to ruin a good mood.

CHAPTER 6

"Mr. Laurence, I thought you said you needed to stay in isolation." General Dale scowled at Trevor. We'd been escorted back to the other hangar where the General still held court in his pool of light.

Trevor's fingers tightened around mine. "I think… I'm safe to be around as long as I'm with Maddie."

I smiled at the little thrill that shivered through me.

At the other end of the hangar, an opening door clanged against the side of something metal. "Hey, what's going on?" Drew's groggy voice echoed in the taut silence. "Trev! You're back!" He waved.

His shout brought Heather and Cecelia out, as well. The three of them took in the circle of soldiers around us. *That can't be good.* Drew stopped smiling, tilted his head in our direction, and they all started moving through the dark toward us.

As they came closer, I felt Drew reach out with his ability and suppress the weapons the soldiers pointed in our direction.

Heather looked from us to the soldiers. *What's going on?*

OPERATIVE

Cecelia sighed. *What's Maddie done NOW?*

General Dale glared at me. "You *assaulted* two soldiers. Give me one reason I shouldn't have you locked up."

I felt Cecelia roll her eyes at my back. *What's the use in charming the people we're working with here not to have a problem with our abilities if Maddie's just going to go out and mess with everyone else on the whole damn base?*

I met the General's gaze with my game face. *First, I never touched them. Second, they're fine. Third, you still need my help with your security problem.*

"You're becoming more trouble than you're worth."

"She's a pain." Cecelia's snarky tone came from behind me. Her next words carried charm resonance, though. "But you aren't going to punish her for this."

I twisted around to catch her eye as she came into the pool of light by the General. *If you fix this, I'll owe you one.*

"Whatever. You already owe me."

The General made a hand gesture and the sound of running boots filled the hangar. Within seconds, we were surrounded by more stone-faced guys with guns. Drew's focus sharpened—which meant that now we were surrounded by a bunch of soldiers who didn't know their weapons were no longer functional.

Neither did Cecelia. "Put down your weapons."

Guns clattered onto the cement floor.

The General paled. "You can't—"

"Everyone stand down!" She gave him a twisted half-smile and took a step toward him as she pointed at his chest. "Look, we're here to do a job and we're going to do it. But you need to Back. The Hell. Off." She cast a glower in my direction. "Any more messes for me to clean up?"

Well, those two over there... I gestured to the two MPs. *They need* a little extra to, um, forget that I paralyzed them.

Cecelia rolled her eyes again. "Geez, Maddie!"

I shrugged a half-apology to her. "They got between me and Twevuh." It'd seemed like the most direct solution at the time, but I was now starting to realize my actions might've been... well... a bit extreme. I leaned closer to him.

Trevor's arm came up around my waist. *"A bit" extreme?*

I pinked up and met his gaze out of the corner of my eye. *I had to come more than three thousand miles to track you down! I wasn't going to let two guys stand in my way when I was only a hundred feet away from you and had finally figured out you didn't hate me!*

"Whatever." She zeroed in on them. "You two. Forget anything weird that happened around *her.*" Her pointing finger now accused me. "And everyone... just accept the weird stuff that happens around us as normal. You're fine with it, but you aren't going to talk about it with anyone." She gave me another glower. "Anything else?"

I sighed. *Just that we need to go off-base today.*

Cecelia smiled at the General. *I'm up for that.* "You're ordering us off the base for the day, right?"

"Absolutely." He nodded, and then frowned. *Was that the plan?*

Heather's jaw dropped. *Is she allowed to do that?*

Drew leered at Cecelia. *So mean, but so hot.*

"You." She singled out one of the soldiers. "Do you have a car here?"

His eyes went wide. "Yes, Ma'am."

"What kind?"

"An '89 Nova."

Cecelia grimaced and turned to the next soldier. "What about you?"

"I—I've got a pickup truck."

She sighed. "Does anyone here have a decent car? Answer me!" Charm resonance echoed in her words.

One soldier raised a hesitant hand. "Uh, mine's okay."

"What is it?"

"Four-year-old Nissan."

She huffed. "I guess that'll do." She focused on the soldier, who paled. "You want to give me the keys now. You're happy to let me borrow your car."

He beamed as he fished the keys from his pocket and handed them over to her. "Lot 16. Just down the road from here."

I grabbed my purse from my trailer as we headed out.

"Let me drive." Drew held out his hand for the keys.

Cecelia shook her head and her voice resonated. "I'm driving. Get in the other side."

"Okay." Drew went around to the passenger door, only realizing as he slid into the seat that he'd been charmed. *Hey, no fair!*

I gave Cecelia a warning look, but let it slide since she'd just saved me from whatever the civilian equivalent of a court martial was. I'd already had enough experience with "military justice" to last several lifetimes. I ended up in the middle of the back seat between Heather and Trevor.

Trevor pulled my hand into his as the car started to move. He fiddled with my wedding ring as anxious little thoughts nibbled at him. *Is it really safe for me to be around everyone in here? What if I lose control?*

I leaned against his shoulder. *Not gonna happen.*

It'd be safer for everyone if I was off the meds. But... would you be,

I mean, would you still—?

What? You think I only love you for your ability? I raised an eyebrow at him. *Don't you know me better than that?*

Trevor pinked up and smiled into my eyes, making my heart flutter in my chest. Now that the ache of missing him was gone, my soul seemed to overflow my body. I settled my head against his shoulder and chafed my thumb across his knuckles. I couldn't seem to get enough of touching him.

We showed our IDs to the guard at the gate. In another minute, we sped up the on-ramp. Cecelia's thoughts flashed a happy green as she pushed the accelerator down.

Next to her, Drew watched her drive with the look of a dog watching a steak come off the grill.

Cecelia cast a quick glare at him. "Forget it, fire-boy. I got us the car, so I'm driving."

Heather turned from the window. "So, where're we headed?"

"I dunno." I shrugged. "Buhlin, I guess."

"Cool."

I turned back to Trevor. *Hey, maybe we should get our own car. That way, we won't have to beg, borrow, or charm one whenever we want to go somewhere.*

The feds unfroze your accounts?

I shrugged. *I dunno—maybe, since I'm now their super-secret special spy-hunter. I'll have to call Coleman and find out.* We really needed to make getting cell phones our first stop today. Everything else would be easier once we had a reliable means of communication.

Speaking of special spy-hunter skills, when did you start seeing ghosts?

I sighed. *I... It didn't feel like a ghost. Not that I know what that's like, but...*

But?

It was... weird. I mean, I don't even really believe in ghosts, you know?

Trevor's lips quirked. *Yeah, something invisible that can go through walls. We've never seen evidence of anything like THAT.* He slid an unseen finger up my spine.

I gasped and squirmed upright in my seat. *That's what I mean! It was... well, like your ability, but an entire body!*

But you didn't hear any thoughts from it?

I shook my head.

So, if it was someone with a G-positive ability, they had to be out of your range.

I shrugged. *Not hard to do; it's a tiny range.* My eyes widened. *Wait, so you think...*

Trevor's jaw tightened. *I think I'm going with you back to that embassy.*

My fingers hugged his and tears pricked behind my eyes. *Thanks. You're the only one who didn't at least consider that I might just be losing it.*

He chuckled. *Well, I know you better than they do.*

So you don't think I'm crazy?

No, I don't think you're crazy. He smiled. *Why? Are you having other symptoms?*

Well, now that you mention it—I keep hearing voices in my head. All the time. And I believe I'm hearing other people's thoughts.

He humphed. *That DOES sound crazy.*

We drove into Berlin and the mental noise increased as the traffic picked up. I closed my eyes for a moment and braced myself against the press of minds that surrounded me. Should I shield from Trevor? I didn't want to overwhelm him by sharing the undertow of mental voices.

Don't bother. His fingers tightened around mine. *I'm telepathic when we're sharing abilities and I'm not letting go of you.*

Good. I rested my head on his shoulder with a sigh.

A huge lightboard spanned the highway with a single word. STAU.

Cecilia groaned. *Great—a traffic jam.*

My brows rose. *Hey! You know German?*

"Stay out of my head, Maddie!"

Whatever. I flashed back to my early days at Ganzfield, when I'd taken a language class with the charms. *I was just thinking that it could come in handy. Does that mean you can charm in German, too?*

She sighed. "Yeah, of course I can."

"Can what?" Drew asked.

She shot him a "shut-up" look.

Cecelia speaks German.

Drew flashed a huge smile at her. "Cool. So you've been here before?"

She shook her head. *This is my first time really going anywhere. My dad used to go on trips to—* She glanced at me in the rearview mirror and forced her thoughts back to the road.

I shrugged. Hey, having a German-speaker was a bonus. We really should've made sure we had the language thing covered when we'd picked out the team. I knew some Spanish and French; did the others know any foreign languages? *Trevor, do you—*

Japanese.

My brows rose. *Seriously?* How had I not known that?

"Watashi wa nihongo o sukoshi hanasu. Anata wa utsukushii."

My lips quirked. *You just said something really sweet, didn't you?*

He blushed and grinned. *I think I said that I speak a little*

Japanese... and that you are beautiful. It's been a few years since I've used it. There's not much call for it in the woods of New Hampshire.

How'd you end up studying Japanese?

I grew up in a college town. My old school offered Japanese, Mandarin, and Arabic in addition to French and Spanish.

Can you say, "Watch out! Here comes Godzilla!"

He snorted and his lips quirked. *Of course. That's the first thing they teach in any Japanese class.*

I snickered as I heard him actually figure it out in his head. *Ki o tsukero! Koko de wa Gojirada!*

The autobahn became a city highway as we inched—or centimetered, or something, since we were in Europe—along with the traffic. Cecelia rode the brake as she kept her eyes on the bumper ahead of us. Anxiety tickled through her mind, but she kept her face a mask of disdainful calm. *I don't know where we're going—or what I'm even doing here.* The traffic picked up to the left and she switched lanes to catch the increased flow.

I felt a stab of concern for her—fear and loneliness tinted her thoughts. I'd never sensed that kind of vulnerability in her. I frowned—I didn't like that at all; it was easier when she was just a cold bitch. *You're finding us a place we can buy cell phones. What kind do you want?*

"What?" Cecelia nearly left her lane as she turned to look at me.

I gasped and pointed through the windshield. "Dwive!"

She returned her eyes to the road. *I can't afford a cell phone, at least until Williamson's first paycheck clears in a couple of weeks. Until then, I guess I'm basically here to chauffeur them around and clean up Maddie's messes.*

Ah, *there's* the Cecelia I knew and loathed. *Hey, the phone's on me. I owe you, remember?*

Really? Cecelia's thoughts deteriorated into a mix of annoyance, temptation, and stubborn pride.

"So, where are we?" Heather asked.

Drew spotted a sign. "Bis-mark-strayb." *Funny-looking 'B.'*

Cecelia rolled her eyes. *Strasse. It's a double-s. Bismarkstrasse.*

Drew didn't hear the unspoken correction. "And we're headed to 'Ernest-rooter-plates.'"

Ernst-Reuter-Platz. Cecelia mentally pronounced the middle word so it rhymed with "loiter." Annoyance swept the discomfort of vulnerability from her thoughts. *Gah, fire-boy's pronunciation sucks!*

We hit a traffic circle surrounding a grey, paved park. The large, rectangular fountain was now drained for the winter, giving the circle an abandoned feel. On the far side, Cecelia caught sight of a sign that read "GRAVIS." Vague recognition sparked within her. *That might've been the name of the tech store in that dialogue we read in German class a couple of years ago.* She swung us around the circle, veered off onto a side street, and then tucked the car into a parking spot located in the center of the road.

The store interior was sleek, clean, and pale—which also described the clerk who came forward to assist us. "Kann ich Ihnen helfen?"

Cecelia's thoughts whirred in translation. "Wo kann man…" *Oh—what's the word for cell phone?* She bit her lip and looked up at the ceiling as though it might be written there. "Um… handys kaufen?"

The clerk tilted his head. "Are you Americans?" His accent clipped each sound.

She nodded and mint-green relief flavored her mind. *He speaks English. Good—I don't have to keep coming up with the right words.* We followed him into the store.

Trevor and I stayed in the back of the group. *Cecelia, what does "doppelte belestung" mean?*

She startled. "Huh?"

The clerk just thought something like "doppelte belestung." I was proud of being able to keep the sounds in order in my head.

Her eyes narrowed at the back of the clerk's head. *He thinks he's going to overcharge us? Guess he's never dealt with a charm before.*

My lips twitched as I stood back and watched her work. Twenty minutes later, we'd gotten five of the latest generation iPhones—at Klaus-the-clerk's employee discount price. I pulled out my credit card as he ran through the activations.

Klaus waved us out of the store like departing friends.

Heather surveyed Ernst-Reuter-Platz like she was looking for a place to plant the flag. "Now that we're here, let's check out Berlin!"

Trevor caught my eye. "You doing okay?"

I nodded. There weren't that many people outside today, so there weren't thousands of minds pressing against mine out here in the open, away from large buildings. The sky was pearly white and it felt like it might snow soon, but we were used to the cold.

"So," Drew looked across the open plaza, "where to?"

I'm thinking we should find a café, get some coffee and something to eat, figure out how these phones work, and then go from there.

Cecelia tipped her head toward a sign on the left. "Tiergarten's that way, so there should be lots of touristy places around it where we can get coffee or something."

Drew's brow crinkled. "Tiergarten?"

"Like Rock Creek Park in D.C.—but not."

"Never been to D.C., so I have no clue what you're talking about."

Cecelia rolled her eyes. "Trust me, fire-boy."

Drew glanced back at me and I gave him a tiny nod. *You can.* No charm commands had laced her words. Actually, Cecelia had been really good about not using her ability on our group.

We piled back in the car and took off toward the forest in the middle of Berlin. After a few turns, we spotted a café and parked on the next side street.

Inside, we ordered coffee and a bunch of pastries, and then huddled over our new gadgets, adjusting ring tones and entering each other's new numbers. I pulled out my old cell phone and copied the existing contact info from it. Good thing I'd shut it off when I'd figured out it didn't work here; the wimpy little battery still held one bar of charge. I then passed it around so that everyone else could get the Ganzfield numbers, too.

Drew frowned at his. "So, we can call the States on these?" *Is Rachel okay? The baby?*

I nodded. *Yeah.*

"But it costs a bundle, right?"

I shook my head. *Don't worry about the cost.* I looked at the time. *But I think it's about 4 a.m. in New Hampshire right now.* Or was it already 4 p.m.? Which way did those six hours go again? Ugh. I grabbed my coffee as soon as the server set it down, took a long sip, and then closed my eyes and blissed as the liquid awesomeness that was European coffee splashed into my soul.

Trevor settled back with a grin to watch the show.

"'Don't worry about the cost?'" Cecelia's eyes narrowed. *I knew it! Williamson's given her some kind of stipend. She's probably getting a much bigger salary than the rest of us are making as "subcontractors." I knew... I KNEW he played favorites with the minders.*

What? My eyes flew open. Way to kill my coffee buzz. *Cecelia, I put the phones on my OWN credit card—it's not Ganzfield money.* Well, technically, at least. Ooh, that reminded me—I needed to call Coleman about making sure my account was unfrozen before the Visa bill came.

"Why would you...?"

I shrugged. *We need them.*

"So—you're rich?"

What was I supposed to say to that? I ignored her and sent a quick text to Coleman with my new contact info. *Call me when you get this.*

Heather rose to my defense. "What does it matter to you, anyway? You can go into a store and ask for anything—and they'll let you just walk out with it."

Drew's eyes widened as he considered the possibilities.

Cecelia frowned at her coffee and crossed her arms. *That's over the line. Why do they think that, just because I'm a charm, I'm also a thief? I'll use my ability to get a good deal, but I won't hurt anyone just to get nice stuff.*

A flash of memory surged through her. "Daddy!" Ten-year-old Cecelia had shrieked with joy as a pickup truck pulled up in front of her apartment building. A huge cardboard box tied with a pink ribbon squatted in the truck bed. She'd flown down the stairs and into the arms of the man with pale-blond hair and a half-smile like he knew a private joke.

"It's the one you wanted, Princess. Happy birthday. The man at the store had set it aside for another little girl, but I convinced him to give it to you."

"Thank you! Thank you, Daddy!" *It's mine.*

"Only the best for a Mitchell."

The memory dissolved into another in which her father had taken her to a jewelry store. He'd pointed out a diamond necklace to the clerk. "You want to give that one to me as a gift."

The clerk had handed it to Cecelia's father with shaking

hands. "My boss already thinks I might be stealing from him. If anything else goes missing, he's going to fire me—and probably have me arrested."

Cecelia's father had given the man a hard look. "You won't tell anyone that you gave this to me."

The clerk had paled as he nodded. "Of course not."

Once they were back in the pickup truck, her father had clasped the necklace around Cecelia's neck. She'd touched it with tentative fingers, as though it might burn her. "Won't that man get in trouble, Daddy?"

"That doesn't concern us, Princess. We're special, and special people get what they want." He gave her a hard appraisal. "But, just in case you get any ideas, you won't talk about this to anyone."

Cecelia hadn't known why her father's words made her mouth feel full of glue, but the sensation had returned every time she'd thought about telling her older brother, Jared, or any of her friends. As for her mother, even if she'd sobered up long enough to listen…

She startled back to the Berlin café and went wide-eyed when she caught me watching her. Tendrils of pink flashed across her mind and she flushed. *Oh, no. What did she see?* "Stay the *hell* out of my head, Maddie."

I returned my eyes to my cool new phone, which we'd paid for, even though the clerk had been a jerk who'd been planning to cheat us. Telepathy made it harder to despise people for their sharp edges—I now saw how those edges had been cut into them.

We paid the bill with my credit card, putting a few hundred extra euros on the tab and getting the café owner to give us some cash. I suppressed a smile when Cecelia noted the exact amounts, making sure they balanced.

We wandered down the street under the overcast noonday sky. Trevor kept guiding Drew back onto the sidewalk with an unseen hand on his shoulder. He'd grabbed an app that displayed our location and avidly followed the map on the tiny screen, even when it led him into oncoming traffic.

Cecelia fumed behind us for a few paces before cutting around Trevor and me. "Will you two give the snugly-cutesy stuff a rest? Do you have to hold hands *all* the time?"

Have to? I chafed the back of Trevor's hand with my thumb. *Nope. Don't have to.*

She threw a glare over her shoulder. "I mean, c'mon! We get it already. You're *in love*." She sneered the last two words.

Trevor frowned for a moment before his eyebrows shot up. "You don't know?"

I shrugged. *Guess she missed the memo.* Everyone else on the team knew about our "special connection." So did all the other minders—and the healers, for that matter.

Drew looked up from the phone screen, grinning as he figured it out.

Cecelia turned, planted her feet, and scowled. "What don't I know?"

Trevor smiled. "Try to charm me right now. Ask me to do… anything."

Cecelia's eyes cut to me.

I shrugged. *Give it your best shot.*

She turned back to Trevor, shaking her head. *Are they trying to set me up?* "No way. You'll just grab my throat or something like last time."

"I said I was sorry for that. I know you weren't trying to do something, well..."

"Charm-like?" Drew supplied.

Cecelia narrowed her eyes at him.

"What?" Drew held up defensive hands. "Like you don't know what I mean!"

"Seriously." Heather nodded. "You can try charming Trevor. You'll see."

I gave her a little nod. *Go for it.*

Cecelia bit her lip. "Let go of Maddie's hand." Charm resonance filled her words.

Trevor grinned. "What? This hand?" He looked down and clasped mine tighter.

Cecelia's eyes bugged out. "You... You're not..." *That's impossible!*

Not impossible, Trevor projected into her head. *Just kinda rare.*

Her jaw dropped. "You're a minder?"

"I am when I'm with Maddie."

She turned to me. "And you?"

I shrugged. *Yeah, we share each other's abilities. I'd pick something up telekinetically right now, but we're in the middle of a public street.*

Cecelia opened and closed her mouth twice, but nothing came out. *Does everyone else know this? Why didn't someone tell me? How is that possible?* Finally, she shook her head. "You guys are freaks."

I snorted.

"So, we've got the day. What do we want to do?" Heather asked as we started walking again. "I mean, there're museums, or the old Checkpoint Charlie, or... well, what else is in Berlin? I don't even know."

Trevor shrugged. "Maybe we could get a guidebook."

The good student I used to be felt a pang of guilt for not being excited to see the pieces of art and history that Berlin had on display. We really *should* experience some of that stuff while we're here. I sighed—I just didn't feel like being exposed to culture today. We were free for only a few hours—it wasn't time for a school field trip. We should do something that made us *feel* free. I looked into the heads of the people around me.

Cecelia wondered if she could ditch the rest of us. Heather was up for anything, as long as it was fun. Drew's mind flashed with envy as Cecelia pulled out the keys.

I'm just happy to be with you, Trevor chafed his thumb across the back of my hand. *So it's your call. What do YOU want to do?*

I raised my eyebrows. "Maybe we should test-dwive Fuhwawees on the Autobahn."

Drew had to think out the fire that flashed up on his sleeve. "Yes!" He grabbed his phone and searched for a Ferrari dealership, and then herded us back to the car. "It's south of here, on Grover-something street."

Cecelia shuddered. *Grover-something?*

Trevor's brows crinkled as he folded himself into the back seat next to me. *I thought you weren't into cars.*

I'm not, but did you see how excited everyone else is?

Trevor glowed back at me.

One of the phones rang as Cecelia started the car and we all shifted elbows into one another as we each grabbed for the one we carried.

Mine! I felt like I'd won something.

"Heh-whoa?" *You've weached Elmuh Fudd. Pwease weave a message.*

Trevor snorted.

"Maddie? Nick Coleman here. I got your text."

My brows shot up. Coleman must be an early riser. "Tanks fow... cawing me back. I wanted... to know if my accounts have been unfwozen."

Everyone else in the car stopped talking.

"Let me take a look." A keyboard clacked in the background.

And we need copies of my emancipation documents sent here. I wiggled my wedding ring at Trevor and watched his eyes light up. After all those days of not having an official claim on him and resorting to proxy-stalking, I wanted a legal tie.

Invisible arms gave me a joyful squeeze.

"Yes, you have access again. It looks like the judge rescinded the order a couple days ago. I just got back from the Caymans last night, so I haven't finished going through all my messages."

I tried to picture Coleman's face with a tan, but it just looked fake and orange in my head. Trevor grinned at the image.

"We-uh wit the gwoup in... G-g-g-many now. Can I get a copy of my eman... cipation owduh sent he-yuh?"

"Just a sec." More keyboard clicks. "Looks like Jon emailed me an APO address for you already. I'll send it out today."

"Tank you."

One last thing. If we don't check in with him after a couple of days, can he call and see that we haven't been... My breath caught in my chest as I flashed back to the basement cell where Hunter had—

Trevor tightened his grip around me and his voice went cold as he took the phone from my hand. "Nick? Trevor Laurence here. We need to—if you don't hear from us after a few days, could you check to make sure we haven't been detained or something? General Dale's already threatened Maddie. He might put her under permanent sedation if he thinks she's become too dangerous."

Heather's shock splashed across me, and Drew had to think out a hot spot in the upholstery.

Coleman's silence lasted several seconds. Was he wondering if he should use his coded way of talking? It's not like the government didn't know about all of us now. Hell, technically, we were part of military intelligence or something; I'd never gotten the details of where we fit in, exactly. "If I don't hear from one of you every forty-eight hours, I'll call. If I can't reach you... well, I'll find you."

Trevor handed my phone back to me in the now-silent car.

I exhaled. *So—Ferraris!*

Heather met my eyes. "General Dale threatened you?"

Not out loud. I swallowed hard. Drew and Heather stared at me with a mix of alarm and concern. Trevor pulled me closer against his chest. Cecelia's eyes stayed on the road, but she listened. I sighed. *Look, this is why we needed to bring an entire team along. The more of us there are—the more abilities we have—the safer we are from people trying to...* I shook my head.

"Is this about the... thing you saw?" Drew played with the phrase "purple monkey-ghost" in his mind.

Yeah. I gave a mirthless snort. *But Dale's not sure which is worse—a purple ghost-monkey-spy or a crazy teenage-lethal-telepath.*

Heather cracked up. "*Those* are the options?"

"I think—" Trevor weighed his words, "from what Maddie showed me, I think it might be another G-positive ability. One we've never seen before."

Drew's eyes widened. "Like an out-of-body thing?"

Astral projection. Cecelia hurried to take the turn as the light changed colors.

What? I caught her eye in the rearview mirror. *Do you know something about this?*

How many damn times do I have to tell Maddie to stay the hell out of my he— "I know that a controlled out-of-body experience is sometimes called 'astral projection.' We aren't the first people to have these abilities, you know. There's, like, a whole history of stuff like this. We're just better at it with the meds."

Drew's eyebrows rose. "That's so cool!"

Heather frowned. "But would they be that strong without dodecamine?"

I shrugged. *Maybe.* My ability had partially manifested before I'd had the drug. *Gah—I wonder what this "astral" guy could do on dodecamine.*

Trevor swallowed hard.

We turned in at the sign with the rearing black horse logo. Drew's eyes danced across the displayed vehicles and he was out the door before Cecelia had shut off the engine.

"Oh, man." He groaned as he stopped in front of something sleek and red. "That's what sex would look like if it was made of metal."

A sly smile spread across Cecelia's face as the salesman approached. She was actually enjoying herself. I didn't catch much of the German, but I think she passed herself off as a Kennedy granddaughter. *Ich bin ein rich girl.* I snorted. With her charming ability, she could claim to be Martian royalty and people would believe it. Who knew? Maybe all those stories of alien abductions were simply the result of charms messing with people.

The salesman reappeared with the keys to the car that'd seduced Drew. The thrill of joy lit him up and his fingers held a slight tremble as he took the keys. Heather looked back at Trevor and me as she climbed into the tiny backseat. *It's going to be WAY too crowded—even though it looks like Cecelia convinced the sales guy not to come.*

Trevor waved her off. "We'll meet you guys back here, okay?" He wrapped an arm around my waist. *You weren't really into that driving thing, were you? Right now I want you in my arms so much it hurts.*

As the Ferrari peeled out of the lot, Trevor led me back to our borrowed car, which stayed locked for less than a second. He pulled me in with him and kissed me breathless. *I've wanted to do that all day.*

I grinned against his lips. *I know.*

More kissing ensued. We were both mussed and breathing hard.

So, tonight...

His brow furrowed. *Sleeping arrangements?*

Yeah.

I... I've got to be out of range of everyone, okay?

How far out of range? Separate building far?

He frowned. *We've been taking too many risks. The way we've been keeping watch while the other one sleeps...*

The sad brown realization made my heart crumble. *You're not going to let me sleep in your arms anymore, are you?*

He shook his head. *Not while I'm on the meds. If you're asleep, you can't stop me if I lose control.*

I closed my eyes as the pain increased. We were never able to both sleep in contact with the other, but it was something I craved. Now, Trevor was taking away the last little crumbs of it from me.

Don't I get a vote?

He shook his head like a macho jerk. *My arms. My rules. No discussion. And did you just call me a macho jerk?*

I crossed my arms and glared. *I didn't say a word.*

"I'm keeping you safe—whether you like it or not. Maddie, you— If you didn't think you could completely control your ability to blast people, would you want to be around me?"

I bit my lip. Dammit, he was right. I sniffed and tucked my head against his chest, aching with a sense of loss.

A shudder passed through him. *How do you stand it?*

What?

He swallowed hard. *Knowing that you've killed someone.*

I have you. That, and the fact that I knew the people I'd killed had been doing terrible things. The world was a better place without them.

Justice.

Trevor sighed and his arms tightened around me. "That settles it. I'm going off the meds—permanently."

My head jerked up. *You're serious?*

"It's—it's just not worth it. It's cool to be able to do things telekinetically, but…" *I have to give up too much for it. And—and I don't want to hurt anyone again.* Horror churned his gut. *Or kill again. Ever.*

Conflicting emotions rippled through me. *I can't ask you to—I don't want you to have to give up your ability for me. But if we could spend the rest of our lives waking up in each other's arms…*

He tipped my face up with a finger under my chin. *You aren't asking—I'm telling you my decision. My arms. My rules.*

It doesn't have to be forever. How could I be responsible for taking this from him? It was like he was… having parts of himself amputated. For me. *You could change your mind and go back on the meds if you wanted to.*

He nodded. "Yeah, but I feel like I'm making the right choice here." He sighed. "So, it's been five weeks since my last shot. I'm due for a booster in a few days. I'll just… skip it. And I should be safe to be around full-time a week or two after that. I still might have occasional flashes of ability, but they'll probably be weak and unfocused, I think—it'll be like when I was a kid."

Bittersweet happiness filled me. *My emancipation papers should be here by then. Maybe we should talk to the base chaplain about making this thing we have legal.*

Trevor met my eyes. "Does that mean you're okay with this?"

Are YOU okay with it?

He grinned. "Think about it. We could have a honeymoon in a little house on a Greek island. In a normal-sized room—with actual furniture. Going to sleep together. Waking up together. Doing *other things* together." He waggled his eyebrows suggestively.

I swallowed hard as a silver-white wave of emotion spilled out of me. Tears pricked at my eyes. *Yeah.*

Trevor stroked my hair. "So I can follow you around on this spy-hunter thing for a while, and then we could go back to the States and let Ann take a turn at it while we go to college."

You've got this all worked out, haven't you?

"You're not the only one who can make plans." He kissed the tip of my nose.

You should do it more often. You're really good at it.

"So you're in?"

Absolutely. I pulled him into a kiss.

A sharp knock on the glass pulled us apart. "Ick. You two've completely steamed up the windows." Cecelia scowled as she unlocked the doors.

Trevor and I both pinked up, but smiled without repentance.

Heather smirked as we slid over to make room for her in the back. *Whoa—I can taste the hormones from here.*

I ignored that. *So, how was the test drive?*

"Oh, man! It was the BEST!" Drew couldn't contain his exuberance. "I have GOT to get one of those someday!"

I turned to Trevor. *We should buy a car.*

"What? Today? You were serious about that?"

Why not? Then Cecelia won't have to charm-borrow one whenever we want to go someplace.

Okay. Trevor leaned forward. "Hey, Drew. We need your opinion. If you were gonna buy a car here in Europe that could fit all of us, what would you buy?"

"TWO Ferraris."

I'm in love. That thing with the Ferrari was lust, but this is the real thing. This one and I have a future together.

I huffed a laugh as Drew continued to stare at the silver BMW.

—535i sedan with rear wheel drive and a 6-cylinder engine and black leather interi—

"—and you have no problem taking an international money order that will arrive sometime in the next week." Cecelia turned away from the obsequiously nodding salesman to appraise me with narrowed eyes.

I finished sending the text to Coleman and met her gaze. *What? You know I'm good for it! I've already sent for the money!*

She frowned and rolled her eyes.

Oh, and get him to put Trevor's name on the title, too.

His hand tightened on my waist. *What?*

I pointed to the ring on my left hand. *Car's half yours. Get used to it.*

His lips quirked.

Rusty-pink annoyance spread through Cecelia. *Williamson's not paying me enough to put up with all of Maddie's crap.*

Trevor frowned at the back of her head.

I sighed. *Well, once we're done here, I think Trevor and I are heading back—and taking all of my "crap" with me. Now that we have a car, we can all come back to Berlin again whenever we want. Cecelia, if you wanna take off with the car you borrowed this morning, we'll see you back... whenever.* I signed another document of unintelligible German in the place the obsequious guy pointed to.

Cecelia actually seemed a little hurt by that. Relieved, but hurt.

I shook my head. *There's just no pleasing some people.*

Drew and Heather both felt torn, looking from Cecelia and back to Trevor and me.

Trevor grinned. "Seriously, Maddie and I haven't been alone with each other all week. Go. Have fun. Do... whatever people do in Berlin on a Saturday night."

Oh, but don't drink too much.

Heather frowned. "Yeah. That would be bad."

Drew turned. "How bad?"

"Remember Uncle Seamus's house?"

"Uncle Seamus had a house?"

"Not after he got ahold of a bottle of Jameson. Fffwwt!" Her hands imitated an expanding fireball.

Drew winced.

"Yeah. G-positives tend to lose control of their abilities when they drink."

"What? Do you go around randomly healing people?"

Heather's blush drowned her freckles. "Well, just that one time in college." *The guy still wore the cast for the next six weeks, but at least his arm stopped hurting.*

I laughed.

Cecelia rattled the keys in her hand and tapped her foot.

Drew gave another longing look at the new BMW as he turned to join the others.

Trevor held up the keys. "You can take it out tomorrow."

Drew lit up. "Sweet!"

Hey, if you get back and can't find us, check the base jail—or whatever they call it in the military.

Brig? thought Trevor.

Ah, my mother would be so proud.

Drew cracked up.

"This is all wrong." Trevor frowned at my trailer. "How can you sleep at night?"

I lucked out the past two nights and didn't throw any nightmares. I shuddered. *Shared a doozy on the plane, though.*

He bent down and examined the undercarriage, and then pulled the chocks out from around the wheels.

I went around to the back to disconnect the water and electric lines. We'd stopped at the PX—which was sort of like the base's smaller version of Wal-mart—and grabbed extensions for both on the way in. A quick stop at the commissary had supplied us with food-makings. We'd also gone back to the other hangar and thrown Trevor's stuff in the trunk of the BMW, which was now parked just inside the large hangar door.

The trailer began a heavy roll forward. Trevor pulled it around and away from the others, disappearing into the dark.

"Say when." His voice echoed.

I stood in the now-empty spot and waited until his thoughts became a faint whisper. *That should do it.*

We ran the extension lines and turned the water and power back on. As soon as we were inside, he pulled me to him. I slid my hands up his neck and into his hair. Rapid breaths hissed through our noses as we kissed and pulled each other out of our coats. We tumbled to the bed and everything faded away as the silver glow drew us together.

Are we going to lose this, too? I bit my lip and sniffed. Trevor's shoulder pillowed my head as his finger drew lazy circles against my arm. We listened to tepid air whistle through the vent in the trailer wall.

Soulmating? I bet we still can, even after I'm off the meds. I think it's a minder thing.

Shared dreams?

Trevor shrugged. *I'm not sure. I think that's probably from you, too. But at the very least, if you throw me a nightmare, I'll be right here to wake you up.*

I snuggled closer to him until we connected from chest to leg in a beautiful line. *There IS that.*

So, tomorrow, let's go see if we can find your ghost.

Purple monkey-ghost, I corrected. *But tomorrow's Sunday.*

He snorted. *Ghosts take off for the weekend?*

Good point.

CHAPTER 7

We played house in the little trailer for the next few hours—putting away groceries, making dinner, and curling up together in bed to read a book. It was the picture of tranquil domesticity right up until the soldiers arrived and surrounded the trailer.

A rifle butt banged on the trailer door, but Trevor and I had already gotten up and shrugged back into our coats by then. "Captain Bell wants to see you."

Trevor pulled wide invisible arms around us as we opened the door. *Gah!* We shielded our eyes against the searchlight's glare. Geez! Did every officer on this base travel with his own lighting crew?

Captain Bell stood by the other trailers. He clasped his hands behind his back and stared at us as we approached. I took in the armed escort and the dramatic lighting shining off his bald head, and the whole situation suddenly seemed ridiculous.

Captain Bell? You rang?

Trevor coughed back a laugh.

Bell's eyes shifted from me to Trevor. "Who's this?"

Trevor Laurence. My husband. It still felt surreal to call him that.

Laurence? That's the one Dale had in isolation. "Husband?"

I held up my hand, wiggling it to catch some of the fancy lighting with the gold ring on my finger.

He raised his eyebrows as he pulled in that new piece of information. *Okayyy.* He nodded and got back to business. "I'm here because I need some answers. Cavallo's report said you encountered a—well, an anomaly."

We're calling it a purple monkey-ghost-spy.

Bell paused as he turned slightly purple himself.

Trevor's lips twitched. "I thought we were calling it a purple monkey-spy-*ghost*."

I grinned. *Or we could go with Cecelia's term—astral projection guy? Astral projector?*

"How about just 'astral'?"

Ooh, I like it.

Bell frowned at us. "This isn't a joke. Lives are at stake. National security. And your team reported this… astral, or whatever you call it, and then decided to take off without leave."

We had leave. Dale ordered us to take the day off.

"What?" Skepticism tinted his thoughts amber.

My lips twisted. *Well… after Cecelia spoke with him.*

Bell's eyes widened and his voice came out as a hiss. "Ms. Mitchell used *mind-control* on the General?"

Trevor took a step closer. "General Dale *threatened* Maddie."

Bell stared at me for an eternal second. "I think you'd better tell me the whole story."

There was something about this guy that I trusted—probably the bit where he didn't plan to sedate me for being dangerously insane. I tilted my head in the direction of my isolated trailer. *C'mon in and have a seat. This could take a while.*

"So, you think you can track this thing down?"

Captain Bell seemed to assimilate the fantastic with remarkable ease. While Cavallo and the General had been reluctant to accept the idea of a disembodied spy, Bell weighed the evidence. He sat across from us at the built-in table and listened, although his knee jiggled a bit when I projected the images directly into his head.

"We're making a bunch of assumptions here." Trevor's hand closed over mine on the table. "We're assuming this thing is the manifestation of an ability, sort of like ours. We're assuming that it—" He looked at me. *He?*

I nodded. *Definitely a he.*

"—he's behind the security leaks. And we're also going with the idea that he has a range similar to what most of us have with our talents."

Something twisted in my gut with that last one. If this guy had a range like Rachel's, he could be literally anywhere on Earth. In that case, tracking him down might take a while. My brow creased. Rachel. *Trevor, I wonder if Rachel could—*

Wouldn't she need something to... well... track?

I bit my lip and nodded. *Yeah, a verbal description won't work. She needs a sense of a thing—and I can't even really sense it.* I had nothing but a vaporous image to project to her, and it was a pretty good bet that if she couldn't see it, she couldn't RV it.

"Hello?"

Oops—we'd just trailed off into telepathy and left Captain Bell out of the conversation. *Sorry.*

"So, you track it, and then what?"

Trevor frowned. "Look, if his ability has a range, then he'll probably need to be near the embassy to use it. If we find the guy, we can—I don't know—detain him or something in a place away from sensitive intel." *We're NOT going to kill him.*

I nodded. *Williamson might have some ideas about how to do that. You know, hold, not harm.* The man had his own soundproofed dungeon, after all.

Such a great role model.

But how hard could it be to detain this astral-person, really? The guy could see things at a distance, kind of like a remote viewer, but like he was actually there. It wasn't like he had any offensive skills—not unless he could possess people or something.

"Possess people?" Trevor's voice went up. So did his eyebrows.

I shrugged. "Pwobabwee not."

Bell frowned. "So, you'll need some place to hold a prisoner—at least if your assumptions hold up."

"Wait. Don't we need a warrant or something?" Trevor shook his head. "We can't just go grabbing people off the street and imprisoning them in secret government facilities."

I hugged one of my arms around my waist and nodded. *Trust me. It's not good.*

Trevor's hand tightened on mine and something jumped in his jaw.

Bell frowned. "Excuse me?"

My jaw quivered. *You're not the first military guy who's tried to get us to do stuff like this. Although, so far, I haven't had a problem with you. The last guy had a thing for trying to "break us."*

"I see. I'll get authorization for the extraction and detention of— You going to be able to tell for certain if you've got the right guy?"

I tapped the side of my head. *That's not a problem.*

He nodded. "All right, then." He stood quickly and it felt like we should get up, too. He turned back at the door. "One more question, though. You two didn't steal the Beemer that's parked out there, did you?"

Trevor's panic flared through me as the world came into focus. "No!"

I twisted around, trying to find him in the Escheresque dreamscape. Gunshots cracked around me, making me jump.

"Trevor!"

He bent over a still figure in a spreading pool of blood. My own pale face stared up lifelessly from the floor and a keening cry began in the back of Trevor's throat. Then the living walls began to splinter and crack, turning into masses of people writhing in pain. Their bodies flew and crashed as grief stole his soul.

I put two fingers into my mouth and tried to whistle. I'd never been able to do it in reality, but I figured it was worth a shot with dream-magic. The sound cut through the air.

Trevor's pain-filled eyes found me. His sobbing breaths were the only sound as he looked down at the dream-corpse and back at me. I stepped over the macabre debris and moved closer—it was a little safer to do so now that his subconscious had stopped throwing people.

He met me halfway and gripped me in a fierce embrace.

I pulled back to wipe the tears and lines of pain from his face. "Hey, it's just a dream."

He drew a shuddering breath and buried his face in my hair. I stroked his back and let him absorb my not-deadness. Everything twisted into focus around us—broken bodies littering the broken world.

I squeezed my own eyes shut, trying yet again to control the dream. I really sucked at it. If I could just borrow Trevor's skill and at least get rid of all the dead people…

I felt a breeze swirl around us and opened one eye to see if the mangled corpses were gone. A world of infinite beige surrounded us. Everything seemed soft and warm, as though the entire place was made of fleece material. We sank down against the side of a pillow-like lump the size of a car.

I gave Trevor a squeeze. "Hey! I did something! It's not Aruba, but it's… different." I pulled him down to lean against a comfortable lump.

He wiped his face with both hands and looked around. "You made… everything… light brown."

I shrugged. "Better than that nightmare."

He gripped my hand and nodded without enthusiasm.

I grinned. "Cut me some slack! I'm not used to being the emotionally healthy one in this relationship. I don't know where to put my neuroses. And how about a little excitement here? I actually got something to change using lucid dreaming!"

His eyes lit up as his soul recovered. "Hey, that's true." He wiggled his shoulders against the lump. "And whatever this place is—it's kinda comfortable."

I rolled and propped myself up on his chest. "Feel free to redecorate, if you'd like."

He placed his hand against the soft surface, and waves rippled from his hand and turned everything green. Then he lifted his chin and huffed like he was blowing out a candle, and the sky fluttered into a brilliant blue.

I leaned in and kissed him. "Showoff," I whispered against his lips.

His laugh quaked against me.

"You guys shoulda seen it!"

Drew's hair stuck up in a major case of bedhead as he threatened to slosh coffee with each emphatic gesture. "We're in this club and it's like, wicked fancy, and Cecelia has this guy convinced that she's... what was it?"

Heather grinned. "The Duchess of Lennox."

"Yeah." Drew nodded. "So this guy thinks she's this Scottish duchess and he's all, 'my friend has to meet you,' and he brings up this actual Scottish guy who's like, 'I'm descended from the Duke of Funny Socks...'"

Funny socks?

"Argyle," Heather translated.

"... like he's totally going to bust her. But she's like, 'We met on my uncle's yacht, remember?' and suddenly we're his best buds and he's taking us back to the V.I.P. room."

Nice. I took a swig of my own coffee.

"So when'd you get in?" Trevor reached for another bagel. We'd brought breakfast stuff over to Heather's trailer when her lights had gone on. In the perpetual gloom of the huge hangar, we always had the lights on in our own private tin-cans.

Heather squeezed her eyes shut. "Just after 3 a.m."

Captain Bell came by last night.

Heather gave a scoff. "Must've gone well. No one sedated you."

I snorted. *But the day's still young. We're going to have another look for that astral today.*

"Astral?" She frowned in confusion.

"Purple monkey-spy-ghost," Trevor clarified.

"Oh." Heather frowned. "We all going?"

I shook my head. *No point. None of you can see it.*

"But Trevor—" *Oh, yeah. Special connection.* "Well, then, if you don't need me, I'm sneaking into the base hospital today."

I grinned. *Have fun performing miracles.*

Her eyes sparkled. "I always do."

"Hey, Drew." Trevor tossed him the keys. "If you don't wanna come along, you can borrow the car while we're in the embassy. We might be in there a while."

"Sweet!" *It's like a James Bond car. Hmm... was it the Justice League, or the Hall of Justice, or the Justice Hall? Whatever, we're kinda like them, except Wonder Woman and Superman keep having PDAs.*

I snorted. *Please! Like I'd actually fight crime in an American flag bathing suit.*

Heather did a spit-take at the mental image. "Where the hell did that come from?" *Seriously? And she's considering doing that in December?*

Trevor's lips twitched as I rolled my eyes. *Sorry. Drew's thinking in superhero analogies again.*

Heather frowned. "You know, there's never been one with healing powers."

Trevor tipped his head. "I think... well, no one who could heal other people. Some of the X-Men could recover fast if they were injured, right?"

Wolverine?

"Jesus?" Drew offered.

Definitely not one of the X-Men. I sighed.

Heather coughed back a reluctant laugh. "Don't let Hannah hear you say that, Drew."

Yeah, that little piece of blasphemy might send her away from Ganzfield permanently.

"Or, at the very least, she might refuse to re-grow your eyebrows the next time you take a fireball to the face."

Drew winced. "Yeah, I really can't rock the no-eyebrow look."

I pursed my lips as I sent the image into everyone's heads.

Drew shook his head with a grin, and then touched his brows, just for reassurance. "So, you have access over at the embassy on weekends?"

Actually, we don't have access without a military escort. I sighed. *I guess we need to take Cavallo along to get us in.*

Trevor set down his cup. "Or Cecelia."

The Bitch Wonder.

"Bring either one." Drew ran a hand through his hair. "They're both hot." *I should probably take a shower before we go.* He looked down at his flannel-covered legs. *And definitely put on some actual pants.*

I snorted. *You got a thing for women who can order you around?*

He grinned at the thought of both of them wearing skimpy leather outfits as they tied him up.

I winced. "Ick."

Drew kicked up the speed and passed a Volkswagen.

"Take it easy!" Cavallo's anxiety speckled her mustard-yellow.

"Hey, this is just a Sunday drive." Drew tossed her a sideways grin. "You should see what I can do when we're in a hurry."

He passed another car and shifted back to the right lane.

Cavallo fumed as she stared at his hands gripping the wheel. *Guy thinks he's all that, just because he's cute and has superpowers.*

In the back seat, my eyebrows rose as I met Trevor's eyes. *Did she just...*

He grinned. *I think they've forgotten we're here.*

We could fix that. *Hey Drew, she thinks you're cute.*

Drew's eyes darted sideways again and a flush crept up the back of his neck.

Trevor frowned at me. *Why'd you tell him that?*

When we were coming over here, Drew and I made a deal. He'd help me fix things with you and I'd give him the inside track on the workings of the female mind.

Isn't that... unfair? Unethical or something?

You think I should tell her that Drew thinks she's hot? That'd even things up.

Trevor sighed. *You're matchmaking AGAIN?*

You've got to admit, I've got a pretty good track record.

He snorted.

But they're not star-crossed lovers or anything, I don't think.

Why don't you let them figure it out for themselves?

My lips quirked. *People take FOREVER to figure this stuff out without telepathy!*

Maybe that's part of the fun for them.

I felt the start of a pout pull at my face. *You think we got together too fast? That we... missed something by just figuring out that we belonged together the way we did?*

He cupped my chin in his hand. *Maddie, what do you think?* He projected a silver wave of pure adoration into me.

I forgot to breathe. *I... think you're the most amazing person in the entire world.*

He pinked up.

... and that I was really smart to figure that out as quickly as I did.

His burst of laughter startled the two in the front seats.

"What's so funny?" Cavallo's thoughts had turned uncomfortably intimate for her and she jumped at the chance for a distraction.

Trevor kept his smiling eyes on mine. "Just that my wife's a genius."

Wife. I'd never imagined that word would apply to *me*. Something in my chest fluttered as this new facet of "being married" caught me by surprise.

Drew cleared his throat. "Hey, how 'bout some music?" He fiddled with the radio. We winced as pounding techno music erupted from the speakers. Drew fumbled to turn down the volume.

"Drew, you drive. I've got it." Trevor leaned forward to get a look at the controls. He frowned at Cavallo, and then raised an eyebrow at me. *Wait, should I do anything in front of her?*

Cecelia's already had a talk with Sergeant Cavallo here.

Oh, okay.

Cavallo gasped as the stations began to change without being touched. *What the—?*

I grinned at her. "My... *husband* is tewekinetic."

On the next station, someone tortured a violin against the backdrop of discordant flutes. Another flip and a gravelly German voice adamantly insisted on something unintelligible. Next flip and my eyes widened at the accentless American speaker.

"—med Forces Radio Network. This next song goes out, by request, to Cara from Vince."

A familiar combination of bass and horns filled the car. "Yes!" Trevor flashed bright with joy, and then flushed with embarrassment.

Drew snickered. "Is that... Neil Diamond?"

Sweet Caroline. Cavallo smirked.

I squeezed Trevor's hand. *Don't be embarrassed—they BOTH know the words.* I could hear them singing along in their heads.

The song hit the refrain. "Sweet Caroline..."

Drew went "bah-bah-bah" along with the horns.

Cavallo laughed out loud then hesitantly joined in to echo, "So good! So good! So good!" to the end of the next line.

Drew grinned at her and added the next "bah-bah-bah!" with greater enthusiasm.

A few more bars in, and they were both cracking up and singing along with dramatic gestures. "... touching me... touching Drew!"

They were both grinning when the song ended.

Drew took a deep breath. *No guts, no glory. Hey, Maddie, if you're in my head right now, go pay attention to Trevor or something.* "So, your first name's not Sergeant, right? 'Cuz that'd be weird."

Cavallo scowled. "Actually it is. You making fun of my name?"

Oh, crap. Drew paled.

Cavallo cracked up. "It's Elena."

Drew exhaled in relief.

I looked at Trevor. *See? They're into each other!*

He snorted. *Yeah, and they're doing fine without you.*

This place has more security than a prison. Trevor rolled his eyes as they confiscated our cell phones at the outer checkpoint.

I raised my eyebrows. *But the food's better in the embassies.*

Trevor paled. *Oh, God. I'm so sorry. I can't believe I—*

I squeezed his hand. *S'okay.*

Cavallo showed her ID and some papers to one of the guards. He pulled up some records on the computer and issued us all clip-on badges.

We started down where we'd seen the thing before and worked our way around the building. It was surprisingly busy for a Sunday morning; I'd been expecting most of the offices to be empty. I didn't stop to read the thoughts of the people this time, but simply scanned each room for the something glowing and purple.

After two hours, I began to doubt my own sanity. Did I *really* see something that weird?

Hey, you're tired. Trevor chafed my fingers. *Let's get some lunch.*

This is a waste of time. Cavallo scowled at the backs of our heads.

The lackluster burgers and fries didn't improve our outlook. I scowled at my plate; the food had been better at the consulate cafeteria. This re-warmed stuff was making me look like a liar.

Actually, no. Prison food had still been worse.

Trevor picked up his soda and took a long drag at the straw. *Maybe you scared it off.*

I frowned. *It did seem like he noticed that I could see him.*

He grinned. *So we can hang the "Mission Accomplished" banner and go home?*

I shook my head. *That'd just jinx it.*

Cavallo looked at the motion. "You two—" She pitched her voice lower. "You two haven't said a word the whole time we've been in here. What's going on?"

"Sorry." Trevor flashed an apologetic smile. "Well, we haven't seen the thing today. We were just discussing whether it noticed Maddie looking at it the last time, and whether that might've scared it off."

"You two really talk to each other like that all the time? The in-the-head thing?"

We both nodded.

"And you don't drive each other crazy?"

I gave an unladylike snort. *"You saw me when he wasn't around and you thought I might be on drugs or something. How am I when he IS around?"*

"Less crazy." *Is that why he's here now? Was she seeing things because he wasn't here?* She looked hard at me. "I… heard you on the phone that one time. Have you always talked like that?"

I shook my head. *Less than a year. I'm actually getting much better, though. Heather thinks I have a good chance of talking pretty normally again, one of these days.*

"What happened?"

I forced myself to say the words aloud. "Got paht of my bwain fwied by a—a bad guy." I swallowed hard, remembering the feel of the hardwood floor against my cheek as Isaiah stalked toward me with every intention of killing me.

Cavallo paled.

Trevor surrounded me in an invisible embrace.

I took a deep breath. "Can we tawk about something else?"

She nodded. "Sure. Like?"

I grinned. "Wike… ah you intewested in Dwew?"

Trevor rolled his eyes. "Maddie!"

She pinked up inside and out. "He's just a kid." *A kid who's built like a Norse god.* "And I'm not looking to start anything serious right now."

I looked down at my fingernails with pretended indifference. "Oh, okay."

Cavallo started imagining Drew shirtless.

I winced.

Trevor snorted and shook his head. *You brought it on yourself.*

After lunch, we continued from where we'd left off on the "first" floor, which was really the second floor. The actual first floor was called the "ground" floor.

Trevor sighed. *I think you were right. Ghosts really do take the weekends off.*

I started playing with a double-entendre involving "day of rest" and "rest in peace," but didn't come up with anything worth sharing.

We headed toward the staircase. I'd felt Cavallo's spike of anxiety when we'd taken the elevator to the basement on our first trip. We didn't need to aggravate her claustrophobia.

A purple ghost dropped through the ceiling and stumbled to its knees as it landed at the other end of the hall. I choked back a gasp and tightened my hand on Trevor's. *Do you—*

He froze with wide eyes. *I see it.*

A sudden thought made me even colder. *What if I'm just projecting "crazy" to you?*

Close your eyes for a second. If it's in your head, maybe it'll disappear or something.

I had to force myself.

Trevor tightened his grip on my hand. *Nope—it's still there.*

My eyes flew open and back to the ghost-thing. Cavallo took a few more steps before she noticed we'd both stopped. The purple specter at the end of the hall pressed its hands against the floor with careful precision. It seemed to test its weight—could a ghost have weight?—before rising. It still hadn't seen us.

Quick—say something office-y. We needed to have some reason for standing in the hall—something so that the astral-thing wouldn't recognize that we'd spotted him again.

Trevor blanked for a second, and then came up with, "Wait, I think I left my key card back in the office."

Cavallo's eyebrows came together like dark wings. "Your key card? What the hell are you talking about?"

I felt a completely inappropriate smile trickling up my face, and my heart raced. *It's there!* The ghost-thing took a few steps down the hall, passing the gilt-framed mirror hanging over a small table at the hallway junction. My veins iced—it didn't cast a reflection.

Purple monkey-VAMPIRE-ghost-spy.

Cavallo's eyes widened and she swung her head around. *Where?*

Gah! Don't look! Say something office-like about where Trevor might've left a key card!

"Uh, did you leave it on your desk?" Her eyes were full-wide and her mind flashed yellow with fear that flicked goosebumps down her arms. *Oh, God! Is there really something right behind me? Is it coming closer?*

The astral examined the sign on one of the doors. He looked different from my memory. I mean, he was still glowing, pale purple, and trailed a tail—*no, a tether*—from one side, like it had been tied inside his navel. *You see the tail-thing?*

Trevor swallowed, his eyes darting over Cavallo's shoulder. *Yeah.*

Whadaya bet his body's in that direction?

The astral glanced in our direction, and then looked harder—at me. *Crap!* My eyes widened and I started to shake. I couldn't look away.

The astral's hard eyes narrowed into snakelike slits as he ran right at me.

CHAPTER 8

Trevor's invisible arms wrapped around me and pulled me back against him. As the astral reached out, he took his eyes off me to stare at his hand, as though willing it to—

He hit Trevor's arms and crashed back. His body disappeared through the floor, leaving the bottoms of his feet and the single, *taloned* hand sticking out. After an eternal second, the feet dropped through and the talons retracted back into normal-looking fingers as the hand slipped away, as well.

The hall echoed with our rapid breathing. I stared at the place where the hand had disappeared. *Claws! It had claws! And it went THROUGH the floor.*

Maddie, lift your feet.

Trevor shifted an invisible hand under me. He adjusted as he placed his feet on either side of mine.

Cavallo gaped as we hovered several inches off the floor in front of her.

Um, maybe we shouldn't leave her unprotected.

Trevor didn't register my words. He held me close as he watched the floor, waiting for the horror-movie moment when the claws would reach up through a solid frikkin' floor and try to grab us.

I slid an invisible hand into the floor under Cavallo's feet, but I didn't have the strength to lift her.

Trevor's shallow exhalations rushed by my ear. *It was solid. I felt it. It was as solid as I am. And it tried to HURT YOU.* His arms tightened around me.

I nodded. *This time he seemed... different. Thinner. Not as tall. I didn't see claws last time.* I shuddered at a flashback of the frikkin' talons reaching for me. I'd remembered his hair as short, but this guy's was shoulder length. *Oh, crap—duh. There's more than one of them.*

I guess if you've seen one purple-monkey-ghost-spy, you haven't seen them all.

We waited outside for Drew. Trevor and I stood back-to-back, looking around us and clutching each other's fingers white. Damp, grey clouds threatened rain. Hey, would the rain sheet off of an astral the same way it did off of Trevor's ability? Maybe even Cavallo could see him coming then.

How long's it been? My heart seemed about to burst.

I only called him eight minutes ago. Trevor's shoulders clenched against the back of my head.

They're punking me. Cavallo crossed her arms as her foot quick-tapped on the concrete. *They didn't see anything, but they think it'd be funny to get me all freaked out about some invisible monster with claws roving the halls.*

The Beemer turned the corner. Trevor flung open the doors before it came to a stop and we launched ourselves into the back. Trevor thunked the back of Drew's seat. "We need to go. Like, right now."

Cavallo's door flew closed as Drew pulled away from the curb. "Hey!" She dragged her seatbelt across herself in protest.

Trevor watched behind us until we'd returned to the autobahn. Then he closed his eyes and rested his forehead against mine.

I leaned into him. *The thing... had frikkin' claws.*

That thing tried to KILL YOU.

I sighed. *Thanks for not letting it.*

"So the invisible monster went after Maddie." Drew kept his eyes on the road. *Thing's lucky Trevor let it live.*

I snorted. My appreciation of the absurdity of the situation increased the farther we got from the embassy, but I still clung against Trevor's side. *If I go to General Dale and report that the invisible purple monkey-ghost with claws tried to kill me, I'm one step closer to a lifetime of sedation. We need to talk to someone who doesn't think I'm losing it.*

"Captain Bell?" Trevor asked.

I shook my head and looked at Trevor. *I've got a better idea. Would you?*

He nodded, pulled out his phone, and hit the number for the main building at Ganzfield. "Jon? Trevor Laurence here."

Trevor put him on speakerphone. Williamson's voice sounded tired. "Is everything all right? Are you back with the others?"

Cavallo frowned. "Who's he calling?"

Drew flashed a glance at her. "The expert."

Trevor humphed. "Maddie tracked me down and… insisted I was overreacting. Just like you said she would."

"She's with you now?"

I made my voice work. "Yes."

"Good." A chuckle twinkled behind the word.

"There's a problem here." Trevor bit his lip. "We found the, um…" *How would Coleman put it?* "We found the individual we came to find, but it looks like… he has an unusual talent."

Dead silence.

"Jon?"

"Sorry. I'm not sure I'm following you."

Tell him there are at least two people. Ask him if he's heard of astral projection.

"Actually, there are at least two of them. Have you heard of astral projection?"

"A new ability?" Williamson's voice no longer sounded tired.

"Yeah."

"Interesting. We haven't seen a new talent since… well, since you."

"But Jon, they… the one we saw today tried to attack Maddie."

Williamson's voice grew cold. "Explain."

"I'm not sure I can. I don't know if this connection's secure."

More silence. "Where are you now?"

"Driving back to Vilstein."

"Is Aaron Dale there?"

Trevor frowned. "I think so. But Jon, he didn't believe Maddie when she told him about the first sighting. He wanted her to get a psychiatric evaluation and… and he considered… sedating her. Permanently."

A seething hiss of frustration came through the phone. "I'll talk to Dale right now. Go directly to his office when you get back.

He can provide a secure connection so you can tell me exactly what happened."

"Yeah, okay."

"And Trevor? Don't worry about it anymore. I'll make sure Aaron knows not to even *think* of doing anything like that to Maddie."

I closed my eyes with a smile as I leaned against Trevor's shoulder. Some wonderfully intimidating people had my back.

After another quick phone call, we met up with Heather and Cecelia in front of building #1. Cavallo shepherded all of us through the layers of military bureaucracy that guarded the inner sanctum of General Dale. A few art reproductions and a surprising number of shelved books saved his office from martial sterility. Dale remained seated behind his desk as Captain Bell straightened behind him. Trevor and I took the chairs in front of the desk, while the other three flopped down on the couch by the wall. Cavallo remained standing, although she took a wide-footed stance once the General returned her salute and "at-eased" her. He then turned his computer monitor to face us.

I gave a startled smile as Williamson looked back at us. "This connection is secure." His voice lagged a fraction of a second behind the video feed. I saw his Ganzfield office behind him. "You can brief both of us now."

I restrained the urge to wave at him. General Dale's thoughts contained enough chagrin that I didn't need to worry about the permanent-sedation threat anymore.

Trevor recounted the encounter with the astral in detail. When General Dale scoffed, I flashed an intense image into his head—with a special focus on the talons. He paled.

I huffed. *That's more like it.*

Dale frowned. "So how do we neutralize it?"

Something ripped within Trevor. He wanted to kill it for trying to hurt me—but he didn't want to ever kill again. Even the thought made his gut heave.

"I tink we need to find him. Dah physical person." I gave General Dale a fake-sweet smile. *You might get a chance to use those sedatives after all.*

"So how the *hell* are we supposed to do this?" Cecelia flung herself onto the bench on one side of the table in Heather's trailer.

I shrugged as Trevor and I slid into the seat across from her. *It may be a moot point. We might've scared them off today.*

"You can charm in German, right?" Heather gave Cecelia a frown. "Practice some basic phrases, like telling it to stop. What's the German word for stop, anyway?"

"Stoppen." Her voice was a growl.

Drew looked up from rummaging through the fridge and snorted. "You're making that up, right?"

Cecelia huffed. "No. We used to have a saying about it in class. 'If you don't know the word in German, say the English word with a German accent. You'll be right about half the time.'" *Stoppen! Nicht bewegen!*

Make sure you look up, "Don't claw me."

"Nicht..." Cecelia looked up at the ceiling for a moment. "Nicht kralle mich!"

I rubbed my hands over my arms. *It's kinda freaky that you already know how to say that.*

Drew grabbed a soda and gave the fridge door a shove. "I wonder if they'd show up on infrared, or something?"

Trevor tensed next to me. "That's why the astral went after you. They've figured out you can see them."

I nodded. *Yeah, 'cuz I basically have built-in night-vision goggles for G-positive abilities.*

"But they didn't see me use my ability. The guy just crashed into me."

I frowned. *He... he seemed to look at his own hand, you know? When he made those claws come out? I wonder if the two of them can see each other.*

Trevor's jaw dropped. "Wait—how are you seeing them at all? If their minds are out of range?"

My brows rose. *Good question. I only sense RVs and everything when I can also hear their thoughts.* I squeezed my eyes shut. *None of this makes any sense!*

Realization splashed cold through Trevor. *Oh... Oh! I can't go off the meds now!*

Suddenly we were the only people in the world. *What do you mean?*

I could feel it—when it hit me. I can touch it. I can stop it from hurting you—but only with my ability. I can't protect you without it.

I swallowed hard and watched his eyes—and his thoughts. I brushed his hair back from his face with borrowed, invisible fingers as he worked through the ramifications. Finally, he gave me a sad smile and nodded. *It'll be okay.*

I wrapped one of his hands in both of mine and nodded back.

His brows shot up. *Hey... actually, I might be able to... to grab it or something. Then we could, I don't know, follow the tether back to the source.*

You think you could hold it?

He shrugged. *One way to find out.*

"—and that's when I decided never to pose nude ever again."

I swiveled toward Heather. "*What* did you just say?"

Heather and Drew cracked up, and even Cecelia smiled. "We were just taking bets on when you and Trevor might get out of each other's heads and let the rest of us in on the conversation."

I snorted. "Okay, how's this? Twevuh may be able to gwab an astwal. We then twace it back to the source and hit the guy with a twank."

Heather held in her smug grin. *Maddie's really getting better at talking. She's almost back to normal now.*

I flashed a grin at her. *Thanks again for that, by the way.*

"Or maybe we could get some of the antagonist darts," Trevor added.

I frowned. "That's kinda wisky. We don't even know if he's a G-positive. And what if one of us gets dahted?"

Drew blew air out his cheeks. "Kryptonite."

Heather jumped up and grabbed a medical bag. "Speaking of meds, you're due for a booster, Maddie."

I sighed and rolled up my sleeve.

Cecelia's lip curled. "Every week? Still?"

I rolled my eyes and focused on my pronunciation. For some reason, I really wanted to say this properly. "Excuse me for not wanting to wisk seizuhs and bwain damage—more bwain damage, that is—just to stick to the six-week schedule the west of you use. You'uh seriously giving me gwief about this?"

She gave a huff. "No 'gwief.' Just leave some for the rest of us."

Something ached within Trevor as we left Heather's trailer. I swallowed hard. *How can I help?*

He sighed. *It's just... I thought I just had to hold it together for another week or two. Now... now it's—* He ran a hand through his hair.

I'm sorry. It's because of me. I squeezed my eyes shut. *Gah—it's ALWAYS because of me!*

He pulled me to a stop and faced me in the middle of the cold, dark hangar. *Maddie, everything changed when you came to Ganzfield. You have a powerful ability, but it's more than that. You see when something's wrong and you work to fix it. Most people don't do that—they wait for someone else to change things. You're one of the people who make the world a better place. You're an amazing person, and... and I'm ALWAYS going to do whatever I can to keep you safe.*

My eyes filled with tears, making everything streaked in the dim light. *I wish you didn't have to do that.* I choked up.

He chuckled. *I never thought I'd be this busy, though. We really do have a way of making mortal enemies.*

I leaned against his chest. *It's a gift.*

I ducked into my trailer to use the bathroom and came out to find Trevor making a series of slow, controlled steps and motions in the shadowy area behind it.

So when did you start doing tai-chi?

His concentration faltered. "A little over two years ago." *After the first time I hurt someone.* He resumed by moving one arm in a slow arc, and then followed it with a similar motion of his invisible limb. "It helped me with my control. When I first started dodecamine, my ability was really erratic. Sometimes I was clumsy—just knocking over stuff I wanted to pick up. Other times, I'd just *think* about doing something and I'd start doing it without meaning to." He stepped, shifted his weight, and turned.

I did exercises like this to help me… stop being a klutz with no impulse-control.

I slid down with my back against the trailer and hugged my knees. *Well, it's sexy as hell to watch.*

He grinned. "You're easily entertained."

I gasped. *Oh, but if you're going to try to catch one of these astrals, maybe you should learn some karate or wrestling moves, or something.*

He faltered again as he considered it. "That's actually a really good idea."

Can I watch you practice that, too? I grinned. *Maybe you could learn it someplace with heat, so you could do it with your shirt off.*

He widened his eyes at me in the dim light. *How* am *I supposed to concentrate if you keep thinking things like THAT at me?* He held out a hand. "C'mere."

I pushed up to stand. *You want me to—?*

He nodded. "You can do this, too. You're a part-time telekinetic." He wrapped an arm around my waist and pulled me back against him.

I prefer "telekinetic by marriage."

A huff of laughter pressed his chest against my back. "Now, clear your head and focus on your breathing and the motion."

His fingers laced with mine and he guided my arm out in a rounded movement. "Like this."

I relaxed into his thoughts, letting him guide us through a series of motions. I borrowed his ability and drew invisible arcs with my own extra set of limbs. In the dark room, with nothing distracting us, the subtle differences in how we manifested our shared abilities shone more brightly. My own invisible limbs were only half as long as Trevor's, and while his always looked gold in my dodecamine-enhanced sight, mine were more like a pale silver. There was some cool sun-and-moon symbolism there.

And now, we were going after guys named after stars. We moved together through the cold and dark in a silent dance.

How… cosmic.

CHAPTER 9

"Whoa!" The thick-necked sergeant watched the weighted bag arc across the gym.

Trevor pinked up. "Did I do it wrong?"

"Damn, kid! How'd you do that?" The sound of West Virginia colored the Marine's words. "I never expected a skinny guy like you to have it in'm."

I leaned back against the bleachers when I realized Cecelia's charm commands were holding. We'd had to get up at oh-my-God-it's-early to get over to the gym to meet Trevor's new martial arts trainer, but it already looked like it was going to be worth it.

Cecelia had gone back to get some more sleep.

Sergeant Jones rubbed his chin with his hand. "I see why General Dale called me in."

Trevor glanced over his shoulder at me. *Am I still in your range?*

I nodded. *But don't worry. You're not going to lose control.*

"The Marines use a combat training that combines martial arts like judo with hand-to-hand combat skills based on fist-fighting and wrestling. There's a crap ton of armed combat training that goes into it, too, but we're gonna focus on unarmed combat. What's your reach with those fancy extra arms of yours?"

Trevor swallowed hard. "Uh… about fifteen feet."

"Alrighty, then. We'll work on some throws and upper-body strikes first, and then start you on a few holds and chokes. If we have time, we'll run through some of the counters for restraints and holds. The idea's to use the appropriate amount of force in a given situation—you don't have to go for the kill, except as a last resort."

Trevor nodded and returned his focus to his fighting stance. Within a few minutes he was breathing hard and shaking.

He'd also managed to hold his own against a Marine brown belt. Something warm swelled within my chest as I watched him run through the moves, slowly at first, and then with speed and power. Two hours later, Trevor dripped with sweat—and a growing sense of confidence.

Sergeant Jones clapped him on the shoulder. "Not bad for your first day. See you back here tomorrow, kid."

Cecelia sighed. *This entire day has been a huge waste of time.*

We'd stayed away from the embassy for nearly a week, getting Trevor into fighting shape and reading everything we could find online about astral projection. Most of it was pretty mystical, with people crossing over into the spirit world or hanging around with talking animals—often after taking heavy doses of hallucinogens.

Not exactly the most up-to-date scientific research.

After prowling the corridors for hours, I didn't want to tell Cecelia I agreed with her about the time-waste. Why would the astrals risk coming back here, now that they knew I could see them? We picked up our phones at the security station as we headed out and into a fading afternoon. The December wind tunneled into our bones as we skirted around the drained fountain and winter-pale grass. The press of understandable thoughts diminished as we left the embassy beyond my range and sailed out into a babbling sea of German. The urban background noise flowed around us as we headed for the side street where we'd left the car—someone had music playing; cars hummed on surrounding streets, and a dog barked nearby.

A flash of wordless, bright-yellow terror hit me as soon as we crossed the street. My gasp caused Trevor to freeze and tighten his grip on my hand. *What—?*

A tiny grey missile of a cat skittered out of a narrow alley and headed for us. Drew and Heather both jumped out of its way. The terror-filled little ball took a running leap directly at Trevor, sank tiny claws into his leg, and climbed him like a tree. A huge black dog appeared in pursuit. Cold fear flashed through the group as they scattered on the sidewalk. Trevor pulled me against his cat-free side.

The dog stopped for a moment to reacquire its target. The brown markings along its face looked like war-paint. A low growl came from the back of its throat as it stalked toward the place where I clung to Trevor's hand and tried to focus into its head. Dog anatomy didn't exactly match up with what I'd studied in humans.

We don't need to fry the dog, Maddie. Trevor put an invisible arm between us and Herr Cujo.

I wasn't going to fry him. Much. Instead, I sent the image of a larger, meaner dog into its head. Its hackles rose as it lifted its muzzle and sniffed the air. After an indecisive second, the dog forgot about the image and growled at us again.

Apparently, it wasn't a smart breed.

The kitten perched on Trevor's shoulder, laid its ears flat back, and gave a ridiculously cute little growl in answer.

"No!" Charm resonance permeated Cecelia's voice. *Oh, hell, what're the words for—* " Nein! Nein! Stopp! Das ist nichts für dich! Setz dich!"

The dog dropped its rear to the pavement.

Cecelia sighed. *Good thing it's trained.*

Drew started laughing. "Did you just..." his voice dropped, "charm a *dog*? In German?"

Cecelia crossed her arms and scowled. *Wouldn't have worked with a dog that didn't know the commands. What could I do to stop a wild animal?* The slap of rapid footfalls came as a jowly blond kid panted up to us. His eyes widened when he saw the dog sitting obediently, its eyes still tracking the kitten.

Cecelia glared at him. *Is that his dog?* "Ist das ihr hund?"

The kid nodded and tried to catch his breath.

How 'bout the cat? "Ist die katze ihnen auch?"

The kid looked at the kitten that now perched on Trevor's shoulder. His cheeks flapped as he shook his head. "Nein. Es ist nur eine verirrte." He grabbed the dog's heavy leather collar and tugged. "Komm!" The dog followed, although its muzzle remained pointed at the cat until they turned the corner.

Trevor reached up and disengaged the tiny claws, one paw at a time. The little cat trembled in his hands. He crouched to put it back on the sidewalk. The cat flattened itself to the pavement and flashed with yellow fear as it scanned around with wide eyes. Trevor slowly straightened and took a step back. The kitten launched itself at his leg again and dug claws in to hitch itself back up the front of his jeans. "Ow!"

I snickered. *I think it's your animal magnetism. See? They stick to you and everything.*

He grimaced. "That hurts, cat!" He reached down and disengaged the claws again. The kitten was small enough to fit in his cupped hands. "Little thing's shaking like crazy."

"Kid said it was a stray." Cecelia frowned at the place where the kid and dog had disappeared.

"Cute!" Heather peered closer. *Ooh—I wonder what nasty diseases it's carrying?*

"Oh, no." Cavallo shook her head. "You're not bringing that… animal back to the base."

We ignored her as we gathered around Trevor. He ran two fingers behind its little ears and the cat arched into his touch and started to purr.

Trevor's face softened.

You're putty in its paws. Watching his tender reaction to this little furball was turning my insides to warm mush. *It's been on its own for a while. The little thing's really hungry.* The hollow, purple ache advanced through its scrawny little body as the wash of fear retreated.

Trevor met my eyes. *Maddie, could we… Do you think—?*

I grinned and nodded. *Sure—as long as I don't have to clean the litter box, okay?*

The cat responded to Trevor's change in focus by reaching out with both front paws, sinking claws into his sweater, and clinging to his chest.

Trevor looked down and beamed. His hands dropped away, but the tiny cat hung on. The fabric was thick enough that the claws didn't make it all the way to his skin.

I snorted. *Like Velcro.*

"Velcro. I think we'll have to call her that." He scooped the kitten back into his hands. Little loops of wool stuck out from the front of his chest.

"No! Don't *name* it! You're not keeping it!" Cavallo glared at us. "Now put it back and let's go!"

I frowned. Trevor wanted the cat. I wanted Trevor happy. "Cecelia, could you—?"

"You have no problem with the cat. It's coming back with us."

Cavallo stopped and stared.

Heather gave her a questioning look.

"What?" Cecelia's voice was defensive. "I like cats, okay?" She reached out and scratched the top of the kitten's head.

"Velcro" closed her eyes and purred.

"Back off, you minx. He's mine."

Velcro lifted her head from where she sat on Trevor's chest and stared at me for a moment. She then went back to licking her paw and wiping it over her face while she pretended to ignore me. I propped another pillow up against the headboard and curled up along Trevor's side.

He smiled at me. "So, we're cat owners."

I grinned back. *Owners? Don't kid yourself. You're completely under her power.*

Velcro glowed a contented green as she tucked her feet under her, closed her eyes, and emitted a rumbling purr. She'd eaten her own weight in cat chow from the commissary as soon as we'd brought her back to my trailer. A fat little furry tummy bulged from her skin-and-bones frame, distorting the subtle striping of lighter and darker grey along her sides. Heather had done a medical assessment in the car on the way home and ramped up the kitten's immune system to purge her of the alley-cat diseases she'd picked up. However, the pins-and-needles sensation had freaked her out.

Trevor had grimaced as Heather had healed his scratches afterward. "Next time we take her to the vet, I won't use my actual hands to hold her."

I sent a quick text to my mom, telling her about the cat. It was hard keeping in touch with her from here. I couldn't talk well on the phone, and I couldn't tell her what we were *really* doing without getting her upset. Besides, texts and emails weren't necessarily secure communication.

That's wonderful, honey! Send me a picture when you get a chance.

I took a photo of the sleeping kitten with the phone and sent it to her. My mom loved animals, but she'd always been allergic. Velcro was the first pet I'd had that didn't have scales.

"Maddie?"

I shifted to meet his eyes. *Yeah?*

"Why'd you say yes to bringing the cat home?"

Seriously?

"Yeah."

I shrugged. *You wanted it. I want you to be happy.*

He radiated joy at that.

And, well, I kinda "get" her, too. She was alone and terrified... and then she saw you. Now look at her.

The lump of grey fluff continued her gentle purr in her sleep on Trevor's chest.

My phone beeped with an incoming text. **Cute kitty!**

Trevor looked over my shoulder. "Your mom?"

Rachel. I waved as though we were on camera, and then made a dismissive, "scoot" motion. *Geez, we're on a different continent and there's STILL no privacy. It's nice to be the only telepath around, though.*

Trevor raised his eyebrows. "I don't count?"

I traced my finger along the line of his jaw. *I don't want to hold things back from YOU. But it's a relief not to have my every thought bouncing around the minder-net.* I lay there and watched him watch the fluffball. *So, did you have a cat growing up?*

He shook his head. "No. If I'd ever brought one home, Lilith would've broken out in hives."

I recalled the unsmiling face of Trevor's grandmother. *She was allergic?*

"Nope."

I snorted. *Another thing Velcro and I have in common.*

I woke with a gasp as something bit my nose. It took a moment for my eyes to focus. The kitten sat back and stared at me, her eyes slightly luminous in the dark. Once she saw I was awake, she jumped off the bed and moved to the outer door. Images of Trevor filled her wordless thoughts. I let out a sigh. *You woke me up for that? Urrgh—don't get on my bad side, cat. You're staying in here with me tonight.*

She scratched at the door. The metallic screech made my teeth hurt.

Yeah, I'd rather sleep next to him, too. We're both safer in here, though. I shook my head and rolled my eyes at myself. *I'm telepathically talking to a cat. A cat that doesn't understand words—and that'd speak German if she did.*

Hey, maybe I could use my ability to actually communicate with her on some level. A half-remembered childhood song from *Dr. Dolittle* floated through my head as I projected an image of Trevor to the cat.

She scratched at the door again then flicked her head to the side as she froze with wide eyes and sharp ears.

I froze, too. Did she just see something *move* in here? My thoughts went to transparent specters with talons and I stopped breathing as cold gripped my heart. What if the astrals found out where we were? Would they come in and slash us with those freaky raptor claws while we slept?

The kitten's body trembled as she flattened into a crouch. I leaned forward, straining to make out what had captured her attention. She filled with wire-taut tension—the need to attack the unfamiliar *thing*.

Velcro jumped high and landed on a piece of carpet fluff. She hit it with two quick taps of her paw, and then darted away and hid under the table.

I fell back against my pillows with a sigh.

"You really think it's going to come back here?" Cecelia scowled at me across the basement corridor of the embassy.

"You got a bettuh idea?"

She lifted her chin and crossed her arms.

Too bad—a good idea would be pretty helpful right about now. And we all needed a break from the search—after more than a week without a sighting, it clearly wasn't working. Trevor's taut alertness quivered through my mind. He kept protectively close—and continued watching the floor for grasping claws, which wigged me out. His thoughts slid back to his most recent training session with the Marine Sergeant—he'd been training with him for the past ten days now—and he imagined trying to perform chokeholds on purple ghost guys.

Would that work on an astral? Did they even need to breathe?

"Maybe you should wear a disguise, Maddie." Drew rubbed

his chin. "So this astral thing won't recognize you if it sees you first."

That's kinda brilliant, Drew. He might be right about the recognition factor, and we could all use a break from this never-ending, frustration-and-fear search. Trying on wigs and fake noses would definitely lighten the terrifying tedium.

We checked back out at the security station and retrieved our phones. As we headed across the walkway toward the front gate, Drew tapped tiny keys with large thumbs as he ran a search for costume shops. "Hey, Cecelia. What's the German word for costume?"

She grimaced. "Costume."

He looked up. "You don't know?"

She scowled. "It's 'costume,' but with a 'K' and an umlaut. Kostüm."

"What's an umlaut?"

"The little dots over the 'U.'"

He looked back at the phone and frowned. "I have no clue how to make those on this thing."

My breath caught in my chest. Across the dry grass, something lavender shimmered in the harsh winter light. *He's back.*

Trevor inhaled with a sharp hiss and fell into a fighting stance beside me. He took couple of steps toward his target—and it vanished from his sight. *It can disappear?* He stopped dead and scanned the area with wide eyes.

I moved up behind him and touched his hand. The astral reappeared to him.

Oh. Conflicting impulses tumbled through his thoughts. *I don't want Maddie anywhere near this thing, but I can't see it without her.*

Operative

I looked up at the sky and blew out a breath. *We probably shoulda figured out that part before now. I could project thoughts to you—show you what I'm seeing—but I don't want to risk getting out of range.* If I fell behind and the thing came at Trevor with claws...

The astral was closer now, cutting across the open lawn next to the concrete bowl of the empty fountain.

Trevor shook his head. *I can't risk you like that.*

I borrowed his ability and wrapped silver arms around us. *You're offense. I'm defense. Let's get this thing and go home.*

I flicked a thought to the others as we started moving along the sidewalk so our paths would intersect. *Guys, we've got one RIGHT HERE. Stay with us and try to act casual.* Trevor and I leaned together as we walked, so we looked more like a romantic couple than a couple of spy-catchers with superpowers on the prowl behind a telekinetic force-field.

"Casual?" Cecelia scoffed.

Fine. How about we get you near it and you can charm the thing?

Oh, crap. Anxiety flowered grey around her. *Can I charm something I can't even see?* "What do you want it to do?"

"Just get it to freeze." Trevor spoke through clenched teeth.

A lump squeezed my throat from the inside as we drew closer. Recognition sparked. *It's the one I saw the first time—the good-looking one.*

Huh? Trevor's head jerked toward me as he flared with yellow energy.

I snorted, but kept my eyes on the target. *As opposed to the scary, snake-like one with the talons. Really? You're jealous of a purple monkey-ghost? Can we focus on grabbing him now?*

The astral turned his head in our direction and slowed as he came to where the edge of the grass met the walkway that edged the embassy building. I slid behind Trevor, feeling a spike of fear as I lost sight of the astral and trying to remain inconspicuous. I watched the thing through Trevor's eyes.

Trevor looked down at its transparent feet. *It's making footprints in the grass.*

That was freaky. I glanced over at the Marines standing by the main entrance. We'd need to do this discretely. While Cecelia could charm the people who witnessed anything strange, we were sure to be recorded by security cameras here, and who knew where the feeds from the embassy went—maybe directly back to Washington.

The astral changed trajectory to go around our group. We moved to intercept him and he froze for a moment. His gaze touched on me and his eyes widened in recognition.

The astral turned and broke into a run.

Trevor took off after him, pulling me along by the hand. The astral seemed slow in comparison, as though moving through something more viscous than air.

Cecelia's charm-filled voice rose above the thudding footfalls. "Don't move!"

Everyone else in the group froze in place—all except Trevor and me. The astral kept going, angling through a topiary bush and cutting through the waist-high, metal fence that edged the grass.

It's still going!

Crap! Cecelia's chagrin flashed pink around her. "Go! Move!" *What the hell's the German word for—* "Nicht bewegen!"

The astral jumped off the curb and cut through a parked car. Trevor caught up with it as it crossed onto the sidewalk. His invisible arms grabbed the lavender ones just above the elbows. The astral glanced back with shock on his face, and then veered into the side of the apartment building, passing through the polished stone like it was water.

Trevor's breath hissed through his teeth as he hung on. He pulled the astral back out of the stone wall. The translucent face twisted in a silent scream.

I stared at the figure. Sunlight washed out the details, but I could still make out the tether that led through the building next to us. I jerked my head in that direction as the others caught up with us. *Around the side.*

The astral brightened in the dim alley. It looked like he was yelling at us, but no sound came out. Mental voices rattled German around me as we crossed the street and entered the alley on the other side.

The tether grew brighter as we approached a boxy, red car parked beside a dumpster. The thoughts from inside the vehicle grew louder as we approached—I glanced back at the astral and saw that his silent gibbering synched up with the strange language. "Shto vy? Kak vy eto delaete? Otpustite menya!"

I frowned. *That doesn't sound like German.*

I used my borrowed ability to fumble around inside the car and finally flick up the weird door lock. The keys hung from the ignition.

I opened the door and wrinkled my nose. *Ugh—it smells like a locker room in here. Has he been living in this car?* The front passenger seat held a plastic shopping bag of dirty clothes. Three black suitcases filled the back seat.

What the hell? It sounded like the gibbering mental voice came from *inside* the suitcases. I looked around Trevor's protective stance in front of the astral.

Tears ran down his translucent cheeks. "Pozhaluysta, sdelaite eto bystro." *Zhal, shto ya emyel vozmozhnost, chtoby poproshchatsya.*

His trembling chin came up as he forced himself to meet my gaze.

I saw images in his thoughts and the understanding made me gasp. *He's in this car, and he thinks we're going to kill him.* "Do you spuh—speak… Engwish?" Actually, it was debatable whether or not I could at this point, but whatever.

Dyevushka razgovarivayet so mnoy. Ona dyeistvityelno mozhyet menya vidyet.

Trevor tightened his unseen grip. "We don't want to hurt you, but you're coming with us."

The astral glanced from Trevor's face to mine and his eyes filled with despair.

"What the hell kind of car is this?" Cecelia shook her head as she shifted the transmission into "bell." At least, the symbol looked a bit like a bell.

I shrugged. *I dunno. Russian, maybe?*

Drew caravanned behind us with the rest of the group in the BMW as we drove back to the base. I heard Cavallo's thoughts as she explained the situation to Captain Bell in a cell phone conversation filled with code words. Good thing I could get the translation from Cavallo's head. I gathered that we'd be met by an armed escort at the base's front gate—and maybe this time, someone would be inside the tank with the big gun pointed at the entrance.

Trevor shifted uncomfortably underneath me. We'd strapped in together in the cramped front passenger seat of the boxy car. He kept his invisible grip on the new prisoner, who'd sunk halfway into the suitcase-shaped box. We'd tried to open the suitcases in the back, but they were actually a single unit and seemed to be locked from the inside. It was like a camouflaged coffin—with a living occupant.

Just the kind of thing a vampire would have… if he lived in his car.

The astral stared out at the highway as his thoughts turned grey. His mournful mental monologue jostled my head full of that unknown language.

The drive took a very long time.

Once back on base, two Humvees fell into line with us, adding to our mini-convoy. We followed the leader back to the line of hangars, pulling up in front of the one Trevor had recently vacated. The large doors swung wide to admit the vehicles.

Once inside, banks of lights in the high ceiling made "woomph" sounds as they turned on.

I sighed. So these places *did* have lighting. Why the hell were we living in the dark in the other hangar?

General Dale stood wide-legged in front of something that looked like a huge fish tank—about twelve feet on a side. Thick glass panels lined the floor and ceiling, as well as all four walls, and they shimmered with a metallic iridescence that seemed sandwiched inside the glass. Seams marked a door on one side, and a thick, snaking tube ran from a grid at the top of the box to a humming air pump. A narrow cot occupied a rubber mat in the center, along with something that looked like a combo folding chair and bedpan.

Eew.

I extricated myself from the front seat and steadied Trevor as he stood, since his focus remained on keeping hold of the astral.

"You really have something here?" General Dale stared at the place in front of Trevor.

I smirked. *Actually, he's still in the car.*

"Come on." Trevor gave the guy's invisible arms a pull.

The astral's movements were slow as he came to stand in front of us. His glowing eyes moved from Trevor to me. His lips moved with the words, but the thoughts—and the sharp, aching pain—came from back inside the car. *Eto bylo slishkam dolga. Ya mog by umeret.* "I... am needing... to be... in my... tela."

"Tewa?" I frowned and tried to speak up so I'd be heard inside the suitcase coffin.

He patted both of his hands on his chest.

I'd played enough conversational charades in the past year to understand. "Body?" I patted my own sternum.

He nodded. "Body."

"Open duh bah—box."

He frowned in confusion.

"Open..." I pointed to the fake suitcases and clamshelled my hands in pantomime. "... box."

"I... am needing..." *rooki,* "hands."

I glanced at Trevor. His game face remained trained on the astral as he shifted his grip—one invisible hand at a time—from the astral's arms to his ankles.

Tverdaya rooka. The astral's thought sounded like an incantation as he focused on his right hand, and then used it to pull open the back door of the car. He slid a small panel to the side then entered a series of numbers—*chetyre odeen dyevyat shest odeen nol.*

The lock clacked and the side of the container swung open. Someone behind me clicked off the safety on his rifle as two limp feet flopped out. The rancid smell that billowed out gave me a shuddering flashback of the prison wing of that hospital in South Boston. The tiny vents set into the seams between the fake cases weren't doing much for ventilation.

Leaning in, the astral flowed up into the body. Trevor's unseen grip moved with him until his hands closed around the physical ankles. The guy's arms thunked hard against the sides of the container and legs flailed as a thunderstorm of energy shot through his head.

I gasped as the burst hit me like a tidal wave. I dropped Trevor's hand and slapped up a mental shield to keep it from spreading to him. It felt like thousands of fingernails scraped chalkboards in my brain. I squeezed my eyes shut and bent double.

"He's having a seizure." Trevor tightened his grip on one ankle and used his other arm to restrain the guy from banging his head. He noticed me as soon as the guy had gone limp. "Maddie?" Concern washed through him as his hands lifted me back to stand. I dropped my arms from where they'd been wrapped around my head.

I lowered the mental shield. *I'm okay.* Weirdly, I now felt... lighter, like the secondhand seizure had scrubbed everything clean in my head. I staggered as I took a step.

Of course Trevor caught me. "You sure?"

I nodded. *Just let me hold on to you for a while, all right?*

Relief filled his smile. "You can hold on as long as you want."

I turned my head to meet Dale's eyes and grinned. *General, I think we've captured your spy.*

CHAPTER 10

I'm a little creeped out that the General can get his hands on a giant, electrified fish tank on such short notice.

We stood on one side of the glass, watching the unconscious astral sprawled on the little cot. He looked like the hunky purple ghost's short, fish-pale cousin—young and vulnerable in sleep. His dark hair clung in small curls against his sweat-dotted face.

On the other side of the tank, Drew kept sticking his hand up near the glass, and then pulling it back quickly as though he'd been zapped. Cecelia perched on the nearest folding chair and fiddled with her phone. Heather had drawn several blood samples and was now being escorted to a lab on base somewhere to run some tests.

Trevor grimaced. *The cage has been here all along. They... they had me test it.*

Indignation flared within me. *They EXPERIMENTED on you?*

It's not like they locked me up. But they wanted to know how high to make the voltage to disrupt my ability.

I frowned. *So, who were they planning to keep in the tank?*

He bit his lip and eyed the tank more suspiciously. *Good question.*

After sending a quick "**We're still okay**" text to Coleman—seeing this containment box for G-positives had reminded me he needed another update—I reached out an invisible hand and touched the electrified surface sandwiched in the double-wall of thick glass. I hissed and jerked the hand back. *It felt like... like it dissolved me!*

Trevor winced. *Yeah.*

I examined the extra hand for damage. It seemed intact, although the creepy tingling persisted for a few more seconds. Trevor leaned his cheek against my temple and looked as well. *It's so amazing every time I see our extra hands like this.* His golden one moved behind my silver and he interlaced our fingers.

It must've been tough, learning to use your ability when you couldn't see what you were doing.

Wonder what it was like for them? He looked back at the astral.

I glanced over at the cluster of uniforms at the far end of the hangar. *I'm more concerned with what those army guys plan to do now.*

Well, we know there's at least one more of these astrals out there, Trevor frowned, *so we're not done yet.*

And that's the dangerous one.

Trevor nodded. *Yeah, this guy didn't try to hurt any of us, even when he thought he was about to die.*

The astral moaned and rolled over.

He's dreaming.

Surreal images, vivid with emotion, flowed through his mind. A girl's face—similar to his own—disappeared into the dark. The astral reached for her, but his hands closed on air. *Vasha syestra neekogda nye ostaveet zdyes, yeslee vy nye.* The scene shifted as a hard-eyed man stabbed a needle into his arm and suddenly the astral was floating toward the ceiling, looking back on his own, younger body lying on a medical table. A bank of machines recorded his slow breathing, but the world had gone silent for him, so he only saw the movements of the white-clad medical people as they monitored his now-empty shell. Panic flooded through him and he reached back for his body, but his hands passed through his own flesh, like the world he'd always known was simply an illusion. He held up his hands and saw right through his now-translucent flesh. When he started to scream, no sound came out.

The astral jerked up with a shout.

All around the hangar, heads turned toward the glass tank.

He's awake!

Gdye ya?

Now we'll get some answers.

Is he dangerous?

Geez—he's just a kid.

The astral's muddled confusion settled as he saw me. *Ona yavlyayetsya tot, kto mozhyet videt menya.*

Mind-reading was pretty useless when I didn't speak the language. Ooh—wait a sec. *Cecelia?*

"What?"

Can you charm this guy to THINK in English? But... I don't know... be subtle about it, so you don't tip him off that I can hear his thoughts?

She sighed and got to her feet. The astral turned his gaze to her as she approached the palm-sized, mesh circle set into the glass next to the door. "You in there. You speak English?"

Da. "Yes." His accent coated the word and fear iced his thoughts. *Oni yavlyayutsya amyerikantsy. Shto oni sobirayutsya sdyelat so mnoy?*

"The people here are going to ask you questions." Charm resonance filled her voice. "You will answer every question honestly, completely, and in English. In fact, you'll even *think* in English while you're here."

His eyes widened further. *Are they going to hurt me?* He tried to gasp, but it caught in his chest and left him racking with deep coughs that made his lungs burn.

"Don't try to leave your body and go out through the glass." Trevor's face was a cold mask. "It's electrified."

The astral's eyes widened as he recognized Trevor. *He is the one who stopped me.* "What… are you? How did you… put hands on me?"

I shook my head as I took a step toward the glass. "No. We ask. You ah… ansuh."

Trevor cast me a quick sideways grin. *You're getting better at talking all the time.*

I gave his hand a squeeze. *Thanks.*

The astral's chin trembled as the military people approached the side of the tank. Captain Bell stepped in front of the others and read from a piece of paper. "According to the Geneva Convention, spies or enemy combatants who come secretly for the purpose of waging war are not entitled to the status of 'prisoners of war.' They are considered unlawful combatants and are subject to trial and punishment by military tribunals. You are hereby designated an unlawful combatant." He folded the paper and tucked it into his pocket.

The astral's face had gone grey. It didn't feel like anything after "Geneva Convention" had registered with the guy, but that was enough for him to understand that he was seriously screwed.

My hands clenched into fists. *At least they made it official, which is more than Hunter did when he detained me. But what are they gonna do to this guy? I'm not going to be a part of torturing anyone.* I moved over to the group of uniforms. *General, I need to talk to you.*

"Not now."

I'll be quick. You can just keep that menacing stare on the scared kid in the box.

General Dale cut a sharp glance at me.

This isn't the dangerous one. But I bet he knows something about the other one. My team needs to know more about how his ability works if we're going to capture the other guy for you without being ripped to shreds by invisible claws.

Trevor shuddered beside me.

Besides, I can tell if he's telling you the truth. The General hadn't heard Cecelia's charm commands, and I didn't feel the need to enlighten him.

Trevor frowned. *Why are you trying to protect the guy?*

Because he didn't try to hurt you, even when he thought you might kill him. He's scared and alone. And a few months ago, it was me in the box.

General Dale peered at me through narrowed eyes as he considered the benefits of a telepathic interrogator.

I raised my eyebrows at him. *Jon Williamson trained me. This isn't my first interrogation.*

I turned back to the astral. "You will talk to me, wight?" *Hey, that sounded pretty good!*

Trevor snorted. *I told you you were getting better.*

The astral nodded. "Yes." *What if I tell them something that they use to hurt Katya?*

I made a mental note to ask about "Katya" later—preferably without the military types around. Maybe I could just float a thought when we weren't interrogating him. "Name?"

"Dmitri. Dmitri Sergeyevich Orlov."

"Age?"

"I have sixteen years."

Dale exhaled in a near-whistle. *Just a kid. Or is he lying? The ID we pulled out of the car said his name was Dmitri Argunov, and that he's twenty.*

I cast a glance over my shoulder to him. *He's not lying. Must be a fake ID.*

"Nationowity?"

Dmitri's features creased in confusion. *Huh?*

"What countwy ah you fwum?"

Countwy? Oh, "country." I do not understand her American accent very well. "Russian."

"What..." I couldn't make my mouth shape the word "were."

Trevor stepped in. "What were you doing at the embassy, Dmitri?"

"Getting... information." He paled again. *Oh, God. They are going to kill me for being a spy. And then Goran will make Katya—*

General Dale stepped closer. "What did you do with the information?"

"I am giving it to Goran. I call him when I find new things."

The General held up the cell they'd confiscated from the car. "Your phone was dead."

"My phone... I am not having, how you say—" He pointed two fingers then stuck them into the fist of his other hand. He pinked up when the gesture struck him as pornographic.

"A charger to plug in?" asked the General. The embarrassment hadn't escaped him.

"Plug in, yes. Mine is... breaking."

"Who do you work for? The FSB?"

I frowned. *FSB?*

Dale frowned back. "Modern version of the old KGB."

"Not FSB." Dmitri paled grey again. *They DO think I am spy. They will kill me!* "I give information to Goran." Shudders wracked him as he started to cough again. I paled and bit my lip; his chest felt like each cough shot burning liquid through him. It took nearly a full minute for him to stop.

This guy was seriously ill—like tuberculosis or lung cancer ill. "How many udders?"

Cecelia snorted. *What? Like on a cow?*

I glared at her. *Do you mind? I'm trying to interrogate a Russian spy here!*

You sound like a retard when you talk.

I glared harder. *You're so politically incorrect. That's as insulting as a racial slur.*

If you'd just stay out of my head, you wouldn't be insulted.

Believe me, I wish I could.

"Only Goran is coming with me to Berlin." The image in his head was similar enough to the purple guy with the claws that I was pretty sure they were one and the same, although the real guy looked shorter and scruffier than his astral form. I snorted—it was like they projected cooler-looking avatars of themselves.

How Matrix-y.

"The others... they are still staying in Russia. But Goran—he is not Russian. He is... Serb."

"Tew him," I pointed to Dale, "ev-wee-ding you towd Gowan."

Dmitri listed a series of projects, classified documents, and passwords he'd seen in the embassy. My mind fogged over the specifics—with that accent, I kept waiting for him to start talking about how "ve must get moose and skvuirrel."

Dmitri seemed surprised with the thoroughness of his own memory.

Guess he's never been charmed before.

Heather came back in the middle of the recitation. I met her eyes. *Well?*

She startled at the voice in her head, and then came close and spoke softly. "He's a G-positive. Looks like he's got some sort of enhancing drug in his system, too, although I don't have any specifics yet. It's not dodecamine, though."

We should let Williamson know about him.

"I already called everything in to Matilda and emailed her the lab results. She'll fill him in."

I nodded. *Good.*

"What'd I miss?"

The guy's named Dmitri. He's sixteen, Russian, and — as far as I can tell — was forced into this with no clue about his ability. You saw that he had a grand mal seizure as soon as he returned to his body, right? And he has a nasty cough that feels really serious; you'll need to check it out. Right now, he's telling the General every piece of information he's passed along to the scary guy with the claws.

"He's cooperating?"

Trevor humphed. "Cecelia had a few words with him."

Heather snorted. "I'll bet."

Yeah, he's even THINKING in English now, which is good, since I was clueless when he thought in Russian.

She examined Dmitri through the glass and bit her lip. "Yeah, he's *not* healthy."

I nodded. *We'll get you in to fix him up as soon as the General's done.*

"Think I'll be allowed?"

I gave her a smile. *We'll make it happen.*

"We should get an X-ray of his lungs. I'd love to get a CT scan of his brain, too—and maybe an MRI."

I swallowed hard. *Are the machines here on base in a separate building from the patients?*

She shook her head.

That could be a problem. Could Trevor keep hold of the guy if he couldn't see him? I didn't do hospitals.

Dmitri shook his head as I tuned back into the conversation. "No. I am... like sleeping when I am... outside my body." He started coughing again and his dizziness gave me secondhand vertigo.

"Does being outside your body make you sick?"

"Yes. Longer times make me—I am not knowing the word—" He shook and twisted his hand around in front of his face.

"Dizzy?" Trevor guessed.

Yeah, he's definitely dizzy. I leaned on Trevor more. *He might also mean the seizures.*

"Short time... is no problem. More than eight or ten minutes... and I am sick. And my body... is not fighting sickness so good after long time as aethernaut. I have now four years. Longest time is six years."

Heather frowned. "It suppresses your immune system and causes seizures?"

Dmitri fell to another wave of coughing. Burning pain from his chest and throat ripped into me.

Heather's chin came up. "I need to get in there."

General Dale shook his head. "No. The prisoner needs to remain secure."

Trevor stiffened. *They're not going to give the guy medical help? His pain's hurting Maddie.* "He'll stay secure."

The General stared at each of us in turn, and then muttered to a guy with a crew cut of right-angled perfection and a single bar insignia on his chest. "Lieutenant, take down the grid."

The lieutenant double-timed it to the other end of the hangar. A few seconds later, the power to the glass cage cut off. "All clear!"

I have to get help! Dmitri's body fell slack against the bed as his astral form made a break for it out the far side of the glass box. Trevor reached for him, but having me propped against him slowed him down.

I narrowed my eyes. Dmitri was still conscious, even though his physical body wasn't responding, but he felt… weird. Once out of his body, though, all sensations of dizziness vanished. I could see the world through his now-silent experience, feel his concentration as he kept his feet slightly solid so he wouldn't sink through the floor or drift away…

I focused in on his basal ganglia and sent a small burst of energy into it. The lavender astral form flared brightly and collapsed as the energy seemed to suck itself back into his body.

On the cot, Dmitri's eyes flew open with a gasp. "What… what happened?"

His aching dizziness hit me like I'd been on the Tilt-a-Whirl for the afternoon. "You wye stiw."

I still am having trouble with her accent.

"Lie still." Trevor repeated. "You're sick." He turned to face me and concern lined his face. *He shouldn't know that you can stop him like that. The other one targeted you just for being able to SEE him.*

I nodded, which made the dizziness worse. *You're right.*

Trevor pulled a second arm around me. "Heather, you can go in now." *Maddie, you'll feel better as soon as he does.*

The door gave an audible click and Heather pushed it open. Dmitri watched her with bleary eyes as she laid hands on either side of his head and looked inside. *What the hell? His basal ganglion's in seizure right now!*

I winced. *Sorry! That's from me.*

Heather rolled her eyes and moved on. *Whatever they've been using to enhance him, it's seriously messing with his brain chemistry. His myelin cells feel... brittle or something. That's NOT good. And he's running a fever, but I think that's from an infection rather than something like a hypothalamus imbalance.* She pulsed healing energy through his throat and down into his lungs, healing the painful rawness. Dmitri gasped and stiffened as the pins-and-needles expanded through his system, chasing out the infection. Sweat beaded on his forehead and his breathing became ragged.

She slowed her efforts. *I can't do more right now—his immune system is already weak. What have they done to this kid?*

She glanced over at the General and internally debated for a moment before knocking Dmitri deeply unconscious. *He needs several hours at least to recover from being treated, and being interrogated won't help that.*

What was it about this guy that brought out our protective instincts? Was it because he was a G-positive? Was it because he was a kid who'd been coerced into this stuff? Did we feel guilty for bringing him here and locking him up? He'd been spying in a U.S. Embassy! We should be more pissed about that, but instead, we were trying to keep the military guys from getting too rough with him. Maybe I was influenced by my own time trapped in a government box, but that didn't explain why the others were on-board with the unspoken, save-the-Russian-kid-from-the-scary-army-guys plan.

The dizziness trailed away from me with Dmitri's loss of consciousness. I closed my eyes, took a long breath in through my nose, and then sighed it out. Heather stepped out of the glass box and shut the door with careful deliberation. A few seconds later, a tiny, high-pitched whine let us know that the electric field had returned to pulse between the glass surfaces.

Heather rubbed her hands as she approached the General. "He'll be out for the next few hours, at least. Maybe 'til tomorrow morning. Whatever meds they've been giving him have really screwed up his brain and immune system. What he said about only lasting six years—he probably didn't have that long."

General Dale scowled. "He's dying?"

Heather flashed a quick smile. *Not anymore. Not if I can help it.* "Not if he doesn't get any more of those meds. I'll need to see what I can do when he's stronger—I might be able to repair the damage. That seizure—" She flashed an accusing glance toward me and I felt pink guilt well up, "—that seizure was just a symptom. He's got some very strange neurochemistry. I'll want to do a spinal tap."

Ugh—I do NOT want to feel that secondhand. I took a step toward the hangar door, feeling Trevor move along with me. I glanced back at Heather. Even with Dmitri unconscious, I wasn't going to take any chances. *Don't start until I get out of range.*

CHAPTER 11

The little growl pulled me from sleep. Velcro skittered up onto the bed with the arched back and puffed-up tail of a Halloween decoration. Her tiny muscles quivered as she looked back to the other end of the dark trailer and hissed.

I groaned. *Urgh—not again, cat!*

My breath caught in my chest. A lavender specter waded through the trailer, coming toward me. The floor hit her about mid-thigh and she examined her surroundings with cold efficiency. Her leather clothes, high cheekbones, and brutally short, pale hair made her look… hard.

ANOTHER astral? Oh, crap!

She swung her gaze in my direction and my heart froze. Ghost-girl was between me and the door. I had no way to defend myself. I started to shake.

How did they find us?

She moved closer, and then walked through the end of the bed, which came up to her chest. Velcro laid her little ears back and hissed again. The astral grinned and faked a lunge toward the kitten. Velcro jumped, landed in a run, and skittered to hide under the table. Astral-girl was still soundlessly laughing as she walked through the headboard and out of my trailer.

Oh, God—Trevor's out there!

Through the window, I could see the astral heading toward his still form, silhouetted on the air mattress. I jumped out of bed and crashed open the trailer door. Trevor jolted awake, but the noise hadn't tipped off the glowing purple thing standing over him.

Trevor! There's an astral right next to you!

"Hunh?" His sleep-muddled brain took a couple of seconds to process that. The astral put out a hand toward him. Everything else fell away from the edges of my vision.

"NO!" My bare feet slapped the cold concrete. Oh, God—I couldn't get there in time! *TREVOR! SHIELD!*

He lifted his invisible arms as her hand descended. The hand stopped. She looked up with wide eyes as I half-slammed into Trevor, who was still on his air mattress and trying to stand. I bounced off the same invisible shield and fell backward. The astral turned with viper-speed and reached toward me, talons forming on the fly. I rolled to the side as the claws ripped down.

The air mattress hissed flat beneath us.

"Maddie!" Trevor pulled me up against his chest and covered us both with wide-spread, invisible arms. The astral's glowing eyes darted between us for a moment before she took off running toward the hangar wall.

I grabbed Trevor's hand. *We can't let her get away!*

By the time we'd detoured through the front door, she was no longer in sight. Trevor pulled me back inside. "How far are we going to get barefoot?"

I looked down, finally noticing the icy pain eating into my feet. I began to tremble. *She tried to hurt you!*

Trevor tucked me close to his heart. *Thanks for not letting her.*

Back inside my trailer, he grabbed his phone from the wall charger and called Captain Bell's direct number. The voice on the other end knew that a call at 3:46 a.m. meant something bad. "Report."

"We had an astral in this hangar a few minutes ago."

"He escaped?"

Trevor shook his head, even though Bell couldn't see him. "Different one. Maddie got a good look at her. This makes three, now."

I sank down on the end of the bed. *They know where we are.* Ugh—I might never sleep again. How had they found us? Did they have RVs, too? Where could we get some of those electric fish tanks with the controls on the *inside*?

Velcro stuck a little pink nose out from under the table and sniffed Trevor's toe. I made a tik-tik-tik sound at her and scooped her up as she came out. I frowned at the little furball, even as I stroked a finger down her back.

She'd *sensed* the astral.

It hadn't been a transparent, purple human in her mind, but she'd *felt* the moving cloud of energy that had made her whiskers itch.

I suddenly became a cat person.

Maybe there was a reason cats were so often linked with the supernatural. Dodecamine enhanced our natural abilities, but our ancestors had been able to use their own abilities to a lesser extent for centuries, and may've been feared or persecuted for them.

Spirit walkers. Shamen. Witches.

I looked down at Velcro and realized that Trevor and I had a very useful little... *familiar*. Maybe I *would* be able to sleep again. I sent a little wave of affection into her head and she snuggled closer, closed her eyes, and purred. I began to picture a few similar set-ups for Trevor's protection, but they all ended with accidentally thrown cats flying across the room.

Ree-OW!

Trevor hung up the phone and reached for his clothes, grabbing his wallet off the counter. "Captain Bell's on his way over. We need to meet him at the other hangar."

"Tew me about de udders."

Dmitri's brows pulled together. *What did she say?*

"The others." Trevor gave him a penetrating stare. The only light in the hangar spotlit the cage—Dmitri saw us ghost out of the darkness as we came close to the glass. "How many of you are there?"

Something has happened. Something has upset them enough to come ask me questions in the middle of the night. Actually, what time IS it? How long was I unconscious? He sat up straighter and his thoughts seemed clearer and stronger than they had earlier. "We are..." he looked toward the ceiling as he did a mental count, "...fourteen who can... leave body."

Trevor took that in. "What else can your people do?"

Dmitri frowned. "Some... make people obey. And some can... see things. Far things."

I met Trevor's eyes. *Charms and RVs?*

He nodded back and returned his focus to Dmitri. "Could they find you here?"

Dmitri's eyes widened. *Someone is finding me? To save me—or kill me?* "Who—?"

The sound of the hangar door opening made us all jump. Captain Bell's brisk footsteps echoed through the hangar and his thoughts floated into my understanding with his approach.

—with no sign of a suspicious vehicle or unauthorized person on base. If I've raised the alert level because that girl was just having a nightmare, I'll have—

I gave a wide-eyed sigh. *Really? Did a nightmare slash Trevor's air mattress with its CLAWS?*

Bell at least had the decency to look chagrined.

Trevor turned back to Dmitri. "How many remote viewers do your people have?"

"Remote wiewers?"

I pressed my lips together to prevent asking Dmitri to say "nuclear vessels."

Trevor's lips twitched. "People who can see faraway things."

"Three."

"What's their range?"

Dmitri frowned. *What is range?* "I don't know this word."

"How far away can they see?"

"One can see... not far, but other two can see in... most of Europe and Asia."

I nodded. *Those two could find him here. They might even be watching us right now.*

Trevor cast a nervous glance into the dark space over his shoulder.

"What about dee astwals?"

Dmitri bit his lip. *The what?*

"Astwals." Hell, I'd mangle the "nuclear vessels" phrase myself. No—wait, Dmitri had used a different word for them.

What was it? *Aethernauts.* "Ay… ter… nauts."

His face cleared in understanding.

"How fah can dey go fwum deyuh bodies?"

Dmitri's confusion clouded back in.

"How far can they go from their bodies?" Trevor repeated.

Dmitri nodded. "Most… not far. Maybe… half-kilometer?" A small flush of pride turned his thoughts green. "I go… most far. Nearly two kilometers. Goran and Tania can both go more than one kilometer. Mikhail can go… near that."

Captain Bell considered the distance from the hangars to the base perimeter. *It would have to be one of those three.*

I caught his eye and nodded. *Tania, then. The one I saw was female.* Bell startled.

Trevor frowned. "What do you think they'll do to you if they find you here?"

Dmitri swallowed hard. "I think… they will kill me." *They won't want people to learn about them. But if I am dead, then no one will save Katya.*

Another mention of this "Katya" person. "Why do you wohk widdem?"

Dmitri closed his eyes and sighed. "They have my sister. She is… born same day as me… tvin."

Trevor frowned. "Your twin?"

Dmitri nodded. "Katya—she has same… ability as me. But she say, 'No. I will run away if you make me spy,' so they keep her to make sure I am not running away." His face twisted as frustrated anger flashed through him. "They want… more aethernauts. So they say that, if I am not good at spying, if I do not do what they tell me, they will… they will make her… mother to more aethernauts."

Cold anger filled me and I hitched in a breath. *A G-positive BREEDING program? With unwilling teenagers? Oh, we're going to have to put a stop to THAT.*

Trevor caught my eye and nodded. *You know you can count me in.* He turned back toward the glass. "Dmitri, do you know where she's being held?"

He hesitated, and then nodded. "The... we call them 'mafiya.' They have her. She is at the place where they... teach us to... to leave our bodies."

Captain Bell leaned closer. "You're not part of a government program?"

Dmitri shook his head. "The first ones—aethernauts—they were in the Soviet time. That was government. But now... is mafiya."

Is he lying? Bell's brow creased.

No. He's telling the truth. My chin came up. *And that means we're going to go up against the Russian mob to put a stop to them selling our state secrets to terrorists. And at the same time, we'll rescue at least one kidnapped teenager before she's forced into a frikkin' breeding program.*

And prevent them from killing people like Dmitri with whatever drug they've been giving him, Trevor added.

Bell did a double-take at the sound of Trevor's voice in his head. Oh, had we forgotten to mention the sharing-abilities thing to him?

Oops.

I faced Captain Bell. *Yeah, Trevor can project thoughts, too. Not the issue right now. We need you to give Dmitri immunity in exchange for revealing the location of their training facility. We'll take a team in and...*

Bell was already shaking his head.

Are they talking without words? Dmitri watched us stare at each other.

Ah, hell. I threw a glance over my shoulder at the prisoner. Cecelia wasn't here to charm Dmitri to forget things when I got sloppy. I tipped my head toward the door. *Let's discuss this somewhere else.*

The light from Dale's desk lamp seemed too bright as Bell brought the General up to speed. The adrenalin from the astral attack was bleeding out of my system, leaving me feeling semi-deflated until another flash of paranoia jolted me back to alertness. Gah! How were we ever going to sleep knowing that invisible, clawed assassins knew where to find us?

Dale squared his frame in the chair and scowled at me across his desk. "We're not going to offer immunity to a spy who's been selling our state secrets to terrorists." *Jon told me I could trust her instincts—that she was probably the most valuable individual I'd ever work with. She just seems like a bratty kid, though!*

I crossed my arms and scowled back. *Bratty kid? You know I can hear you, right?*

Dale frowned at me and I realized that my response didn't exactly contradict his perception. A second later, Williamson's supportive words registered and filled me with a warm glow that took the edge off my annoyance.

Trevor squeezed my hand. *And we know you better than Dale does.*

I grinned and pulsed a quick little burst of adoration at him before returning my attention to the two officers on the other side of the desk. *Dmitri was COERCED. They have his sister. He can give us information on their program—including its location. We could take a team in, take OUT the bad guys, and then rescue the sister and anyone else they're keeping prisoner.*

"I'm not going to give amnesty to a dangerous spy." Dale kept shaking his head.

Right now, you've just got one guy—and he's NOT dangerous. There are at least thirteen more like him, and one of them found us here on base tonight—probably because they have remote viewers. We need to get to the source and we need to do it fast.

Trevor swallowed hard. "You've got Russian mobsters shooting up people like Dmitri with a drug that messes up their brains and kills them. Holding him isn't going to stop that."

I nodded in agreement. *We need to pull their program up by the roots. Get the people in charge. Stop them from making the drug. And if we can free the G-positives who are being held or coerced, there won't be any more astrals spying in our embassies. Hell, you might even convince them to switch sides and spy for you!*

General Dale frowned. *She's right—we do need to take this thing out at the roots. But we can't get caught doing it.* "Status of Forces Agreement—I don't have authority to send troops to act outside of NATO countries. And we're supposed to get their governments' permission and cooperation within their borders."

I smiled. *We know some people who can make others VERY cooperative. What time is it in New Hampshire?*

The video conference link filled Dale's computer screen a few seconds later. In the lower left corner, a little green circle designated the connection as "secure."

"Aaron?" Williamson's voice pitched higher with concern.

"Jon. We've got a situation here."

"Are my people all right?"

Dale swung the screen around to face Trevor and me. Williamson had on a dark blue robe. The collar of a pair of pajamas showed at his neck. Geez—the man even looked immaculate in the middle of the night.

I grinned and gave a little wave. "Hi, Jon. We caught one."

Williamson's face lit up. "Your talking's getting better all the time." His eyes widened as the words themselves registered. "You caught one *what*?"

I glanced over at Trevor. *Would you—?*

"Jon, we've got an astral projector here. He's a G-positive and he's been coerced to gather information because the guys in charge are keeping his sister prisoner. They've been giving him an enhancing drug that causes seizures and it's killing him. I think Heather sent the lab results to Matilda."

Williamson's eyebrows rose. "Who? Who's been doing this?"

I jumped in. "Wush-an mafia."

Williamson gave a snort. "Maddie, are you telling me you've made *more* mafia enemies?"

I humphed—I'd forgotten about Barry Petras in New Jersey. *I wonder if he's broken through Zack's charm commands yet.* At least his last dose of dodecamine must've worn off by now, so we just had a regular mafia guy who wanted to kill us, rather than one with superpowers.

Yeah, much more manageable.

Trevor's tone sobered. "From what Dmitri's told us, it looks like the Soviets used to have their own program like Project Star Gate. Jon, they've got charms, RVs, and at least fourteen astral projectors. But the mafia guys are running it now—shooting kids full of this killer drug, holding family members prisoner to coerce them to follow orders, and selling the government secrets they gather to terrorists."

I swallowed hard. "And dey haf a—a *bweeding* pwogwam."

Williamson's face clouded. "A what?"

Trevor translated. "They've got a breeding program. They're forcing G-positive girls, like Dmitri's sister, to have more G-positive kids for them to use."

Williamson's serious gaze met mine. "You want to go in and stop them." It wasn't a question.

I nodded.

Williamson started typing and his gaze shifted away from the camera. "You'll need at least one Russian-speaking charm. I'll need to check my files to see who we've got who speaks Russian. Do you know the location, or will you need an RV?"

"What are you doing, Jon?" Dale swiveled the screen back, cutting off our direct view. Whatever—I could still see it in Dale's head. "I can't authorize an assault on foreign nationals. If they're in Russia, it could cause an international incident. Relations are more strained between our counties than the public really knows. Damn it all—it could be seen as an act of war!"

Williamson sounded amused. "That's only if you send in military personnel, Aaron. I think we could send a few Ganzfield 'students' to see some of the cultural sights of Eastern Europe without a problem. Especially if we send along a 'guide' who speaks the language."

Dale's cloud of concern evaporated as the potential of our team registered. "You think they can do this?"

Williamson laughed out loud. "You were here last month, Aaron. You saw what my people did when Ganzfield was attacked. That was *Maddie's* plan."

General Dale stared at me over the top of the screen. I gave him a shrug, but felt like I was glowing inside.

Trevor squeezed my hand. *You are glowing a little.*

I smiled into his eyes.

We went back and forth on the logistics over the next couple of hours. The eastern sky had paled by the time we stood to leave Dale's office. Bell was on-board, but General Dale wasn't ready to give final authorization yet. Williamson would get in touch with the charms who might know how to speak Russian, and he'd arrange a place at Ganzfield for any G-positives we rescued.

Concern tinged Dale's thoughts storm-cloud grey. *Will this really work? They still seem so young and undisciplined.* "Check the mail slots by the door on your way out. I believe my secretary said you had an envelope." *I hope she doesn't realize we're reading her mail.*

My eyes bugged as outrage flowed up through my center. *What? You're reading my mail?*

Dale's eyes widened.

Trevor snorted. *You might want to cut him some slack. He might be reading your mail, but you're reading his mind. Everyone's violating each other's privacy. Besides,* his eyes widened with anticipation as his unseen hand pulled the envelope from the slot and floated it in front of me in a little envelope dance, *what do you think's in this?*

Coleman's law office was listed as the return address. I felt my soul brighten as the significance registered. *Oh!*

Trevor clasped my hand as he looked at General Dale. "How do we get to the chaplain's office from here?"

Dale pointed. "Out the door. Go left about six blocks. It's past the temporary housing and the enlisted club."

CHAPTER 12

Dreams and morning thoughts drifted to me as we walked across the base in the pre-dawn cold.

—haven't had that much to drink since Oktoberfest and now my head feels like—

—must... have... coffee—

—where's my jacket? I gotta book if I'm gonna make it to PT in time—

—wanna throw the frikkin' alarm out the frikkin' window.

What're Trevor and Maddie doing out here at six in the morning?

Huh? "Drew?" We picked him out as the guy heading against the tide of people in grey uniform jackets.

Aw, crap! Drew briefly considered ducking around the long line of trailers that the base used for temporary enlisted housing. *Don't think about it! Picture—*

He came up blank. Pink embarrassment stained his thoughts and filled in around his freckles. *I just had the most amazing—okay, the only—sexual experience of my life. How am I not supposed to think about it?*

Trevor snorted. "Try to keep a song in your head. Or think about fireball."

I gave him a fake-serious look. *Oh, Drew. I hope you'll let Inga down easy.*

He grinned. *Oh, well. Busted on my first walk-of-shame.* "So what're you doing here?" He fell into step with us on the sidewalk. A burned fabric smell—like an overly-ironed cotton shirt—clung to him.

Trevor pointed a thumb over his shoulder. "Coming from the General's office."

"At oh-six-hundred?"

We had a purple visitor last night. We had to talk to Williamson.

Drew's eyes went wide. "Is everyone okay?"

Trevor nodded. "Yeah."

But we're putting a mission together. Williamson's trying to find someone who can charm in Russian.

"You think I could—" He glanced around and frowned, and then framed the rest of his thought. *Think I could use my ability to, I dunno, disrupt an astral somehow?*

I turned to look at him. *You should try. I think—well, I can see him. Trevor can touch him. Cecelia charmed him.*

Trevor rubbed the back of his neck. "But only when he was..." *in his body.*

And Heather healed him. And knocked him out with a touch.

Drew frowned as he considered that. "Would that keep him from going astral?"

I shrugged. *I think we're going to have to run some tests. If Dmitri knows we're planning to go in and get his sister out, I bet he'll help us figure it out.*

Trevor nodded. "Yeah."

Drew frowned. "So, where're we going?"

"Chaplain's office."

Drew's brow knit. "At the cracka dawn on a Saturday? What for? Are they even gonna be open?"

Lights shone through the windows, and the front door was unlocked. A guy with earnest eyes who looked only a few years older than us ran some papers off on a copy machine. He looked up as we came in, and the light caught the little black crosses on the collar of his uniform. The pristine embroidery on his chest read *Richardson*. "Do you need some help?"

Drew's eyes widened. *Aw, geez! Don't think about last night in front of a priest! That's just—wrong!* He forced his head full of fireball, but a mangled Springsteen song jumped in along with it. *Cuz wow her kiss, oooh, I'm all FIRE.*

Trevor met my eyes. "We need to get a marriage license."

Chaplain Richardson smiled. "Congratulations. Just a sec." He checked the output of the copier and uttered a silent prayer that the toner wouldn't need to be replaced before the early mass. He turned to a desk stacked high with bins filled with official-looking paperwork labeled in designations that looked like what tax forms and locker combinations would name their children. *My first marriage application! I think I remember which forms to give them.* "Let's see what you'll need. Are you both active duty?"

Trevor shook his head. "Both civilians."

Chaplain Richardson set down the first stack of forms. "Are you military dependents?"

"Subcontractors." Another set of forms went back to the desk. "U.S. nationals?"

We nodded. More papers slid back into their numbered slot. So far so good.

"Both over eighteen?"

I held up the envelope in my hand. "Emanci… pated."

The chaplain frowned. *Is she mentally retarded?*

I suddenly didn't like Chaplain Richardson so much.

Trevor's fingers tightened around mine. *Don't let it bother you. We both know you're brilliant.*

"Uh—" Chaplain Richardson seemed to have lost his own mental sharpness. He fumbled with the paperwork. "As long as that's in order, there shouldn't be a problem. Did you want to have the ceremony in one of the base chapels?"

Trevor shook his head. "We've already had the ceremony."

I held up my hand and flashed the ring.

"We just need to do whatever we need to do to make it… legal. Recognized. Official." *Since we couldn't get out to the town hall when we were surrounded by federal agents.*

"Oh." Chaplain Richardson sounded disappointed. "Your officiant didn't take care of that for you?"

Trevor shook his head. "Not that kind of ceremony."

Chaplain Richardson's eyebrows met. *What kind of—? Maybe I don't really want to know.* "Well, then, all you need are these." He handed a thin packet to Trevor. "I'll need copies of your identification and your emancipation paperwork. Please fill this out. I'll ask the questions to make it official, we'll all sign, and you'll be set."

Trevor's eyes widened. "That's all we need to do?"

Chaplain Richardson smiled. "Since you brought your friend along to be your witness."

"Witness?" Drew's voice had gotten higher.

"Best man." Trevor smiled. He picked up a pen and started in on the forms.

Drew grinned. *Yes!* "Much better." *Wow. They're making it real. Rachel's gonna be bummed she missed this.*

I grabbed my phone and sent a quick text. **Rachel? You awake?**

I didn't get a response. I really didn't expect to—it was after midnight back home.

Trevor flipped to the next page. *Maddie? What county were you born in?*

What a weird thing to ask. I peered around his shoulder. *Morris County. Why do they need to know that?*

No clue. I'm just filling in the blanks. They also wanted to know if we're cousins or anything.

Eew.

The screen lit up with an incoming message. **Just got Sienna back to sleep. Everything OK?**

I grinned; she wasn't going to miss it after all. **Turn off your ringer.** I didn't want to wake the baby.

Drew? Can you call Rachel? Let her know she might wanna watch this.

He pulled out his phone. "Rach? Can you see where we are right now?"

Is that one of those fancy camera phones? Chaplain Richardson shuffled his papers off the copier and ran our IDs and docs through it.

Rachel's voice carried through Drew's thoughts. *"Is that guy a priest? Are they—?"*

"Check it out." Drew pointed a thick finger at the words "Marriage License" at the top of the form.

An un-Rachel-like squeal came through all the way from New Hampshire. A second later, Sienna wailed and Rachel groaned.

I rolled my eyes. *So much for not waking the baby.*

Chaplain Richardson read over the information, and then nodded. "Are you ready?"

"Yes." Trevor's hand tightened around mine.

"Yes." I smiled up into his eyes.

"Do you..." He pulled up the papers, "... Trevor Bryan Laurence, take this woman, Madeline Elizabeth Dunn, to be your lawfully wedded wife?"

"I do." Silver white flared around Trevor as his eyes filled with love.

I heard Rachel's *"aww"* through Drew's thoughts. He sniffed in response and his jaw tightened with the effort to remain cool and unmoved.

"Do you, Madeline Elizabeth Dunn, take this man, Trevor Bryan Laurence, to be your lawfully wedded husband?"

I swallowed hard and concentrated. "I do."

"Then, by the power vested in me by God and the United States Army, I pronounce you husband and wife."

I smiled into Trevor's eyes, feeling the sense of rightness in that one moment. We didn't need fancy clothes or a giant cake. We belonged to each other and now, everyone knew it.

Official.

That's it? Drew raised his eyebrows. *That took, like, three seconds.*

Chaplain Richardson bent over the desk to sign the form.

Trevor cupped my face with one hand. *I love you.*

Silver light spread between us and I tried to swallow the lump of emotion that filled my throat. *I love you, too. Looks like he's not gonna say it, so I will. You may now kiss the bride.*

His lips touched mine and I wrapped my arms around his neck as we smile-kissed.

"Geez, Drew! Don't just stand there. Make yourself useful. Take a wedding picture or something!" Ah, there was the Rachel we knew. In the background, the baby gurgled and I heard Rachel's muffled yell. "Harrison! She's torching the bed again!"

Harrison's voice came through as a distant "Oh, crap!"

The phone flashed. After the third burst of light, Trevor put up a hand like Drew was one of the paparazzi and kept kissing me. We finally pulled back as we felt the beginnings of soulmating start to draw us together.

My hand shook as I signed my name on the line marked "Bride." Trevor took the pen from me and put his name on the next line. Drew signed last as the witness. Chaplain Richardson checked over the forms, and then tore along a perforation and handed a half sheet to Trevor.

A sudden burst of desperate sadness wilted Trevor's thoughts brown.

My eyes flashed to his. *What?*

I just wish I'd had this when you were being detained.

I wrapped my arms around his waist and tried to squeeze the memory of his helpless torment from him. *I get that. I felt a little bit of the same thing when you left that night and came here.*

I'm so sorry about that. Chagrin filled him.

I shook my head and pulled his face down to meet mine. *Just tell me we're never going to be apart again and then kiss me some more.*

"Yes, Mrs. Laurence."

Drew flashed another picture.

Back at my trailer, Trevor swooped me into his arms as he opened the door. I drew him in for another kiss as he kicked the door shut behind us. The world went away for a while as we held each other close. My hand slid along his chest and he trapped my fingers, bringing my hand up and kissing the tips one by one. He put his hand under mine and gazed at my ring.

I snuggled against him. *Yup, it's official. You're all mine.* I splayed my hand out, letting the little gold band catch the light.

He pushed my hair back behind my ear. *I was already.*

Yeah, but now I have the papers to prove it.

Trevor's joy sparkled green and a sense of peace warmed him, driving out some of the haunting anxiety that had shadowed him these past months. We now had all the ties and claims to each other that society could provide, and even his sense of honor was satisfied—we weren't breaking any promises or letting anyone down.

Ooh, and you forgot to get the pre-nup first. Ha! Too late! You're now a millionaire, too.

He rolled his eyes and tsked. *Oh, the sacrifices I make…*

We curled up on the bed together and just basked in the monumental sense of rightness. Velcro scratched at the bedroom door and Trevor cracked it open without moving. The little cat jumped up and made little dents in the blanket with each imprint of her little paws. She came up beside Trevor and purred as she rubbed her cheek against his shoulder.

She saw the astral last night, you know.

Trevor's eyes widened. *She WHAT?*

She sensed the energy field when the astral came through the trailer and she woke me up. I scratched between Velcro's ears and she arched into my hand.

We need to talk to Dmitri—figure out how to keep everyone safe from the other astrals.

Hey, at least I've got Velcro the Wonder Cat to watch my back at night. We need to find a way to keep YOU safe.

He frowned. *I think that means we're going to have to get out of bed.*

No! I gripped the comforter like a lifeline. *Anything but that! There's got to be another way!* I'd kinda wanted to start, well… honeymooning.

He chuckled and kissed my temple. "C'mon. Let's go talk to the Russian spy."

I grinned and shook my head. *Just like all newlyweds do. It wouldn't be a traditional honeymoon if we didn't.*

"We want to stop the people who did this to you and get your sister somewhere safe, but we need your help." Trevor's eyes locked with Dmitri's through the glass.

Hope and distrust warred within him. "You are telling me… truth?"

I nodded. "Yes. We want to stop Goh-wan. Stop the spying."

Trevor joined in. "And we're going to rescue the people they're holding prisoner and stop them from giving that drug to anyone. It was killing you."

Dmitri shook his head. "If we leave, mafiya will find us."

I smiled. "Not whe-huh we'd take you."

His eyes widened. "America?"

Trevor nodded.

Dmitri's thoughts turned grey as he deflated. "Why would you help me? I was spying against you."

Because you're like us, and you were forced into doing it.

Dmitri's eyes showed white as he stared at me.

Trevor frowned. *I thought you weren't going to let him know you could do that.*

I gave him a sidelong glance. *We're asking him to trust us with his life—and his sister's life. I figure we can trust him a little, too.*

You really think we can trust him?

Who—the Russian spy we're holding prisoner who can walk through walls? What's not to trust? I grinned. Besides, if he isn't trustworthy on his own, we can always have Cecelia talk to him.

"You are... what is the word... mind-talker?"

Telepath. I nodded. Here's the deal. We want to take some of our people in and free the people the bad guys are holding prisoner, stop them from making that drug, and make sure they can't do it ever again. We need to know where they are—and what they can do. We want to see what we can do to stop the other astrals. Will you help us?

"You want me to..." *Understanding flared through his thoughts. NOW I know why that mind controller told me to think in English! This one has been listening to me!*

I nodded. That's how we know you told us the truth and that you are... worth helping.

Dmitri gave us a weak smile. "I thought I was... more sick."

Oh! You know you're not dying anymore, right?

Dmitri's hands started to shake and his eyes went wide. "What?" *What does she mean? That they are not planning to kill me—or that I am not sick anymore?*

I grinned. Both.

Dmitri half-fell onto the cot behind him. He rubbed his hand across his jaw. "The red-haired woman..."

Fixed the worst of the damage from the drug. Now, want to help us figure out the best way to save your sister?

Dmitri's eyes shimmered as he pressed his lips together and nodded. *I am not going to die here! And they can help Katya...* "What do I do?"

We'll get the others in here and we'll see if we can find ways for them to use their abilities to stop astrals, okay?

Trevor pulled out his phone. "Drew? Can you grab the others and c'mon over to the other hangar? We wanna try that thing we talked about."

Cecelia and Drew arrived within a few minutes.

Drew ran a hand through his hair as he stopped next to Trevor. "Heather's not in her trailer. I think she went back to the hospital or the lab or something. I left a message on her cell."

Cecelia rolled her eyes. "Why am I here?"

I refrained from snarking at her. *New mission. We're going to rescue Dmitri's sister from the Russian mafia.*

She squeezed her eyes shut. "I think I hate you."

I snorted with surprise, because... she actually *didn't* hate me. Her swirling pink emotions held none of that steely-grey. Sure, we had a mutually assured annoyance thing. But, after years of holding her own in a sea of hostile charms, she found doing stuff to help others was... better than what she'd known before. She wanted in on the plan; she just didn't want to show weakness by letting anyone know she cared.

Trevor shrugged. *Who knew?*

I gave him a quick burst of adoration, and then turned back to the glass. *Ready in there, Dmitri?*

He nodded. "I am ready." His "am" sounded like "yem."

Cecelia gave a quick bark of a laugh. "Gee, Maddie, he speaks English better than you do."

I squeezed my eyes shut as I kept myself from zapping her Broca's area. We still needed her to be able to talk.

Trevor's face darkened. "Cecelia—that's enough."

Her eyes narrowed. "Why don't you let your fake-wife speak for herself? Oh, wait, she can't."

Drew frowned. *She isn't as good-looking when she's being such a bitch.* "They got married for real, you know."

"Dreams don't count."

Drew snorted. "Official army priest guys do. Whadaya call 'em? Chaplains."

Cecelia couldn't think of anything to say to that.

I raised my eyebrows at her. *Are we done with that now? Can we actually get to work here?*

She scowled. "You can't order me around."

My lips twisted into a half-smile. *Nope, ordering people around is YOUR job. Wanna tell Dmitri here to cooperate with us and not try to make a break for it?*

Trevor frowned. *I thought you said we could trust him.*

We can, but we can trust him MORE this way. He's worried about his sister and what they'll do to her if they know he's cooperating with us. He might make a snap decision to try something.

Cecelia faced the glass and her voice resonated. "Dmitri. You won't try to escape. You'll cooperate with us and do what we tell you."

Dmitri's eyes widened. *Mind-control.* He gave a shaky nod. *Why did they ask me first? Why not have this one force me to help them?*

I bit my lip. *We wanted you to be able to make your own choice before Cecelia did her thing.*

"Would you have done mind-control if I had said no?"

I winced. *Um… well, maybe.*

Cecelia snorted. "Yeah, of course we would've. You're a captured spy. At least this way, you know you're only doing what you already agreed to do."

Dmitri frowned.

Trevor looked back into the shadows at the uniformed officer guarding the control panel. "We need you to turn off the electricity to the glass now, please."

The officer paled. "I can't do that without authorization." The guy was less than a year out of West Point, a fact I picked up every time he thought something like, *Wow. Less than a year out of West Point and I'm already part of a top-secret military intelligence operation with a captured Russian spy.*

I rolled my eyes. Lieutenant Whatzizname was basically a doorman in a better uniform in this hangar, but I didn't care enough to explain it to him.

Cecelia?

"Turn off the electricity." Charm resonance was all the authorization the Lieutenant needed. The whiny hum died, leaving only the whispering whistle of air from the vent in the box's ceiling.

Trevor put an invisible hand through the glass. "All clear."

"What do you... what do I do?" Dmitri's confusion twisted within him.

I smiled. *Drew, here, needs to see if he can do anything to your astral body. You know, sense it or disrupt it or something. Come on out and we'll see what we can do.*

Dmitri seemed smaller as he looked at Drew. Weird. I'd always pictured Russian guys as being huge, hulking blond guys named Ee-van or something—not pale, brown-haired guys built on my diminutive scale. Geez, Dmitri looked like he could be my brother.

Dmitri lay back on the cot and took several deep breaths. His body slackened as his better-looking spectral self pulled to sit up from within his own torso. I met his glowing eyes and waved.

She really can see me when I am like this.

I can still hear you, too.

His transparent jaw dropped.

And cats can see you, right?

His eyes widened even more. *How did she know about the cats? Only some cats see—other cats do not.*

Good to know. There might be a genetic strain in cats like the G-positive ability. But I wasn't about to let Heather shoot our little Velcro full of dodecamine to find out. The pouncing on lint was bad enough—we really didn't need a kitten that might start setting things on fire. *Tania stopped by last night. Our cat freaked out.*

A shiver passed through his translucent form. *If Tania finds me here, she will kill me. She and Goran do not want anyone to know about us—what we can do.*

If you show us how to deal with astrals, we'll make sure that she doesn't get a chance to hurt you. If you need to say anything, just think it clearly and I'll pick it up.

Dmitri stared at me for a moment as he considered whether I was being sincere. Finally, he gave a silent sigh. *Okay.* Dmitri focused his attention on the soles of his feet, willing them slightly substantial as he set them on the floor.

I watched closely through his thoughts. *You have to make yourself solid?*

He nodded. *Enough to feel the floor. Otherwise, I will fall through or float away.* I shuddered as I flash-remembered the snakelike one, Goran, with just his feet and taloned hand above the hallway floor at the embassy.

How did the others make claws on their hands? I projected a quick image of Goran's talons to him.

Dmitri's prone body on the cot flared bright yellow. His translucent face contorted in horror. *They—they made claws? Were they trying to KILL someone?* His astral self floated down about a foot into the floor. He froze, spread his hands out wide, and braced them before they hit. Once they made contact, he swung one foot, then the other, up into a crouch, and then focused again on making them solid.

Sorry—didn't mean to distract you.

It is... no problem.

What would happen if you went all the way into the floor?

He shook his head. *I can... make a small part of my hands and feet strong enough to climb out. But it—it is not—I am feeling sick when that happens.*

Actually, I could tell it terrified him. *Buried alive.* With the feel of solid earth not only around his entire body... but *within* it. I gave a sympathy shiver.

Dmitri put a tentative hand against the glass. When nothing happened, he stepped through and stood in front of us.

So, how'd you get the intel out of the embassy? It wasn't as though the marines guarding the embassy would ignore file folders and thumb drives floating through the security checkpoints.

Goran had me put papers into mail in non-secure place in embassy. Send to drop-box—a local house with owners who are not home in the daytime. Use different house every time.

Clever. "Okay, Dwew. He's wight he-uh. Can you feew anyfing?" I really loathed the sound of my voice these days. Was it ever going to get back to normal?

Drew frowned as he stepped in. He focused on a space in the air about two feet to Dmitri's right. Dmitri stepped closer so he was standing in front of him.

Drew shook his head. "Nope."

He's right in front of you. I flashed an image of Dmitri into his head.

"Geez!" Drew staggered back and then recovered with a crooked grin. "Ya coulda warned me."

I bit my lip. *Sorry.* Was there any way Drew could sense the energy of an astral form? *Put out your hand.* I glanced at Dmitri. *You, too.*

Dmitri went as though to shake hands with Drew. His small, ghost-violet hand passed through Drew's.

Feel anything then?

Drew frowned. "Yeah, my fingers got cold. Why?"

Dmitri just touched you.

Drew jerked his hand back. A little flame burst out on his sleeve. "Dammit!" The flame died with a thought. "I liked this shirt!"

Dmitri jumped back as well, using two fingers to make the sign of the cross in front of him. *Demon!*

I cracked up. *Hey, ghost-boy! Don't call my friend a demon!*

What—what is he?

One of us. He can start fires, though. I looked at Drew, and then back at Dmitri. *Hey, Drew. Can you give us a little flame? Something for Dmitri to try working with?*

Drew stretched out a hand and, with a little huff, a golf ball of blue-white fire expanded above it.

Dmitri's glowing eyes caught the light as he gaped.

Try to touch it. See what happens.

The glow from the fireball washed the tentative finger nearly invisible. Dmitri jerked back, looked at his own finger, and then focused it solid and tried again. He looked up and shook his head at me. *I feel the fire, but I am not... burning.*

I shook my head. *It was worth a shot, Drew.*

He exhaled and the flame died in his hand.

"Cecew-ya?"

Her exasperated sigh made my free hand ball into a fist. "What?"

"Youh tuhn."

"I already tried to charm him when he was out-of-body, remember? At the embassy? He didn't stop."

"Just twy. Be woud."

What does it matter if I'm louder? "Fine. I'll be… woud." She looked at a spot in his general direction and raised a charm-laden voice. "Dmitri. Get back in your body right now."

Dmitri's ghostly form sprang back through the glass. Inside, his body went rigid and he gasped.

Cecelia startled vivid yellow. *Did I do that?*

I nodded. "He heawd you. Fwoo da gwass." Or at least through the little bank teller mesh circle everyone kept talking through.

Dmitri still trembled with shock. *I could hear her! I am never hearing anything when I am not in my body!*

"So I can charm astrals—as long as their real ears can hear me?"

Yeah.

"And they have to understand whatever language I'm using."

Maybe you should learn a few words in Russian.

"We going to Russia?"

I turned to Dmitri. *Do you know where they're keeping Katya?*

He nodded. "Yes. It is not in Russia. It is in Belarus… near Brest."

Drew snickered. *Brest?*

Dmitri's eye flicked to him. "What is funny?"

Drew's smirk grew. "Um, is it… hilly?"

Dmitri shook his head. "No. It is… mostly flat there."

Trevor's lips twitched as he tried not to laugh.

I rolled my eyes. *Can we concentrate on the whole rescue mission thing now?*

CHAPTER 13

You're sure? I watched Trevor's eyes and thoughts as ambivalence twisted between us. Was this the right thing for Trevor to do?

Trevor nodded. "I need to." He rolled up his sleeve.

"About time. You're a couple of days overdue." Heather gave him the shot, and then pulled the prick-mark in his arm closed with a burst of healing energy. She slipped the used needle into the red sharps container next to the tiny sink in her trailer. Her mind hummed with satisfaction as she recalled sneaking into the hospital room of a soldier with a traumatic head injury. *When he woke up and thought I was an angel—that was pretty cool. Too bad I had to duck out when that nurse called the MPs on me.*

I pulled Trevor's fingers up to touch my lips, keeping my eyes on his. Anxiety churned within him, making my gut clench. *So, you saw an astral's shadow and now you have six more weeks of winter.*

"I can't go off the meds until I know you'll be safe."

Heather frowned. "You're going off dodecamine?"

Trevor nodded.

"Why?"

He looked away. "I—I hurt people. I killed someone."

"What? Someone on the street?"

Trevor frowned. *She's not taking this seriously.* "No. Colonel Hunter."

I squeezed his hand. *She doesn't know what it did to you.* The act of crushing the life out of someone—even someone as twisted as Hunter—had burned into his soul. The scars to his psyche were no longer raw, but they still ached within him and made him doubt himself.

And they made me yearn to make him whole again.

Heather's eyes went wide. "The guy who got the feds to attack Ganzfield?"

Trevor swallowed hard and stared out the window.

"Look." She sat down across from us at the little table. "It's your choice, but I think the world is a better place when good people like you have the ability to stop bad people like him. The fact that it bothers you to take a life means you won't do it lightly. You have a great responsibility when you have an ability like ours."

Trevor gave a sad smile, and then his brows knit. *Hey, wasn't that from Spider-man?*

"Speaking of being responsible," Heather turned to me. "You two all set with birth control?"

Gah. Seriously, didn't she have any discretion at all? I felt my face grow hot as I nodded. I'd already had this discussion with Matilda.

She gestured to the door with a smirk. "Good. Then carry on."

Trevor's steps slowed as we made our way back across the dark toward my trailer. *They know where Maddie is. They know she can see them. They're probably going to target her.*

I slid my hand up his arm. *There's one obvious solution. We take turns watching over each other.*

"I can't risk hurting you."

Trevor. I wrapped my arms around his waist and met his eyes in the dim light that came from the small bulb over my front door. *I know you won't hurt me. I KNOW it. And I'm much safer sleeping in your arms than I would be if I were away from you.*

The mental image of Goran running at us with those wicked talons forced a shudder through him.

Maybe we should see if he or Tania come back tonight. If you could grab any others, it'll improve our odds and make going into their base less dangerous.

Indecision made him ache.

Please. I pulled him toward the trailer. *You need to stay in contact with me to see them. You need to come in.*

He balled his hands into fists and bit his lip as he decided. *Okay.* He followed me through the door.

I kicked off my shoes, slid into bed, and curled against him.

His mind pinged with concern and he held me too gently. *I could hurt her if I lose control when she isn't awake to stop me. God, I could accidentally kill her if I fall asleep! I already broke her leg that time!* His invisible arms spread wide and the bed tipped a bit as he slid one under the mattress, protecting us from below.

I wrapped one of my hands around the back of his neck and met his eyes. *You know that I'm safer right here with you than I would be anywhere else, right?*

His anxiety simmered back with his sigh and he gave a sad laugh. "I guess that's true. Maybe you should rethink some of your life-choices." *Having me here... it's like sleeping with a loaded gun under your pillow. Not a good idea, unless it's necessary.*

Part of me hopes it'll be necessary for a long, long time. I pulled Trevor into a tender kiss and then made a downy little nest in his thoughts. Even though it was still early evening, I fell asleep within minutes.

I suppressed a yawn and pulled my blanket tighter around me as I surveyed the dark hangar from my perch on the frigid metal folding chair. My feet felt numb, even though I still wore my shoes, and my breath misted in the dim light.

About twenty feet in front of me, Trevor rolled onto his back. The new air mattress—a replacement for the slashed one that now was probably in an Area-51-style evidence locker—hissed with the shift in his weight, and the sleeping bag slipped down his shoulder. I waited for a dream to start, but he settled more deeply into sleep.

After glancing around me once again, I put the earphones back in and cranked up the iPod to keep myself awake. It was a little after midnight, but I could've slept all night if Trevor hadn't needed a turn. Between the jet-lag, the perpetual night within the hangar, and the weird hours we'd been keeping, my circadian rhythm was completely whacked.

I turned my head and looked behind me. One benefit of this ridiculously huge building was that, as long as I kept alert, no astral could sneak up and maul me through a wall or something. I pulled the blanket tighter as a shiver passed through me at the thought, though.

At the far end of the hangar the door creaked open and I heard the light tap of echoing footsteps. After a few seconds, a light flickered in Cecelia's trailer as she returned from another day of... doing whatever she did when she wasn't annoying me. Actually, what *had* she been up to? She really wasn't around much, and everyone at that end of the hangar was well out of my mental range over here. After her shadow moved across her window shades for a few minutes, her lights died. The click of her heels resonated through the hangar as she headed back to the outer door. She was dressed like she was going out somewhere.

I leaned back with a sigh. My folding chair gave a loud creak.

Saturday night in Europe as a spyhunter with super-powers and I'm sitting in the dark as my butt slowly freezes to an uncomfortable chair.

Were the others in any danger if Tania or Goran showed up? So far, they'd pretty much ignored the people who didn't react to them. But their trailers were out of my range, now that Trevor and I'd set up our little homestead at the other end of the hangar here. What if the astrals decided the others were a threat to them? What if they used them as hostages or something to force us to release Dmitri? I huffed at the image of someone holding a talon to Cecelia's throat.

Talk about a no-win scenario.

Trevor started to dream and my entire body got warmer when I realized it was *that* kind of dream. I stifled a breathy gasp as I melted. Out of the corner of my eye, I caught the flare of a blue-white fireball. A metallic creak bounced through the hangar as Drew opened the door of the shipping container in which he slept, but I kept my focus on Trevor and his steamy subconscious. I rubbed my hands across my face as he dropped back into deeper sleep.

Okay, spending the night "in" had a few perks. I'd have to ask Trevor when we could try turning some of his dream stuff into reality. I leaned back on my chair with a sigh as I let that line of thought dance through my brain. After we took care of the astrals, we'd be able to go home, right? How strange was it that returning to an abandoned church in the middle of the New Hampshire woods was now a desirable goal?

The night grew colder over the next couple of hours and the already dark hangar seemed to dim further. I felt like we were in an enormous cave, and images of ancient people with poor hygiene drawing on rock walls filled my thoughts. Trevor slept deeply, making me realize how much strain he'd been under—how much recent events had drained him. He needed this rest and suddenly, playing guardian angel as he slept seemed like the most important way for me to spend my time. A tender smile pulled at the corners of my mouth as I watched him. The light from the pale bulb over my trailer door behind him barely touched his features, silhouetting them in midnight blue. I itched to run my fingers along the line of his jaw.

A dim glow broke through the far wall of the hangar on my left and I gasped as though I'd been splashed with ice-water.

Astral!

What was the female one's name? *Tania.* I forced my eyes down, keeping her in my peripheral vision. Her eyes skimmed over my shapeless blanket lump; I was outside the little puddle of light fanning out from the trailer door. Tania looked at my trailer—and then over at Trevor. My hands clenched with the need to protect him.

"Twevuh." She couldn't hear anything, right? Dmitri said that he couldn't hear anything when he wasn't in his body. But he'd been able to hear Cecelia when she'd charmed him. Maybe charm resonance did something differently—came in through another channel of perception, or something. I kept my head still as I glanced back toward the purple ghost-woman. She still hadn't noticed me. My voice got louder. "Twevuh."

Tania continued taking cautious steps, like a gazelle approaching a watering hole, watching for an ambush. When nothing moved, she settled her gaze on Trevor again. She came closer.

"Twevuh!" Why couldn't I mentally reach people when they were sleeping? Stupid limitations— "Twevuh! Wake up!"

Trevor groaned and rolled over.

My entire body tensed as warring impulses smashed into each other in my head. *She's too far away to do anything to him yet—I can't move and give away my position until she's closer—but I have to KEEP HIM SAFE!*

Heartbeats stomped against my ribs as her wraith-like form glided nearer. My jaw trembled as she focused on him. Her eyes narrowed, and her fingers lengthened into claws. She held them at her sides in an oddly elegant way—like a dancer with impractical fingernails. Her glowing eyes brightened as she fixed them on her prey.

No! I pushed off the blanket and dove for Trevor. Tania's head whipped around at the flash of movement. I landed on my knees beside him, slapped my hand onto the exposed skin of his neck, and threw up my silver arms as soon as we came into contact.

Trevor mumbled and I felt the first stirrings of his mind.

"Wake up!"

The claws slashed down toward us. They slid off my invisible arm, pressing in but not causing any pain. They didn't leave a mark.

Something in my soul started to roar. I threw my silver arm out sideways, hitting Tania in the gut. I felt the leather of her outfit as my unseen hand made contact. As she stumbled backward and lost her balance, she flung out her hands to stop her descent as half of her spectral body disappeared into the concrete floor.

A lump of burning anger filled my throat. I widened my invisible hand and grabbed her around the neck—pulling her out of the floor. She dug her claws into my wrist, pushing her feet into the floor and yanking hard. I started to tumble forward, nearly losing my grip on Trevor. God—if I lost the connection, my hold on Tania would dissolve and she'd slice into us with those claws…

I braced my other invisible arm against the floor and lifted her into the air. She came away from the surface like a magnet off the fridge—once she lost contact with the solid surface she weighed nothing. Her feet kicked for a few seconds as she clawed at my unseen fingers. Her eyes went wide, and then her body went limp.

Trevor stirred under my hand. "Wha—?" *Maddie, what are you—?* His bleary vision caught the astral dangling four feet off the ground in front of us and he blinked to make sure he was really awake. "Oh!"

He peeled my fingers off his neck and clutched them tightly as he staggered upright. His gaze bounced from the see-through girl in the air to where I still knelt by the side of his air mattress, breathing hard and shaking.

The sleep-fuzz in his thoughts cleared a bit as he lifted me to my feet and wrapped an arm around my waist. "You okay? Need any help?"

I kept a raptor gaze on Tania, who looked as though she wanted to spit glowing purple hate at me. *I'm fine. Let's follow this one's tether and see where it leads.*

I slid my hand back to his neck as he shoved his feet into boots. Tania tried to struggle as we headed toward the outer door of the hangar. I narrowed my eyes at her and shook my head.

We came into range of Drew's shipping container as we approached the door. I grimaced as I realized that Drew wasn't alone in his metal box. *Drew! We just caught another astral in here!*

Drew's surprise broke through his lust. *Um... kinda busy here. REALLY don't need an audience in my head, you know? Wait—you mean CAUGHT caught?*

Yeah, she tried to slash Trevor and now I'm dangling her by her throat. Get out here!

This I gotta see.

I flashed him a mental image while he made himself decent.

After a few quick words of explanation, Cavallo buttoned up her shirt as she followed him out. *This is ridiculous. I mean, the kid's good-looking and all, but first he sets my barracks room on fire, and now we're out here fooling around in a shipping box like... hobos. There's got to be an easier way to get some.*

I tasted bile in the back of my throat and nearly lost my grip on killer purple-ghost-girl. Trevor reached up an invisible hand and grabbed Tania's arm.

I scowled. *People do NOT mess with my friends like that.*

Trevor's hand tightened around mine. *Maddie. Maybe this isn't the time to deal with—*

But she's just... using him for sex!

Trevor met my eyes in the dim light. *It's okay, Maddie.*

I shook my head. *Like hell it is!*

"Hey, Drew." He pitched his voice lower as he looked over to where Cavallo was calling in our situation on her cell phone. "You know she's just using you for sex, right?"

Drew's grin stretched wide. "You say that like it's a bad thing."

"Stop! Get on the ground! Now!"

Security lights drew pale lines against the curve of the rifle barrels that the four men pointed at us.

Ah, hell. Cavallo had been right—the big red "RESTRICTED AREA" signs *did* apply to us. She and Drew were still on the other side of the chain link, where she was trying to reach Bell or Dale or somebody to give us clearance to cross between the inner and outer fences that surrounded the base.

Trevor pulled invisible arms around us, drawing my shoulder tight against his arm. I sighed. These guards hadn't been in range when we'd arrived. If we hadn't stopped and wasted time trying to call for permission, we probably could've gotten across and vaulted the outer fence before they'd closed in.

Still suspended in my invisible grasp, Tania watched the approaching soldiers.

Looking for her chance to escape.

I tightened my grip. Apparently she didn't need to breathe when she was like this. My fingers digging into her throat probably didn't even hurt.

"Put your hands where we can see them. Step apart."

Okay, that wasn't going to work for us. Panic flashed through me, and I squeezed Trevor's fingers. *I'm going to have to zap them.* I focused within the closest helmeted head.

No! Wait. Let me take her. Trevor unwrapped an unseen arm from us, shifting his other around me.

I gasped and flung one of my own along his exposed side. *They could've shot you!*

His wide-stretched fingers closed around Tania's waist and her spectral body stiffened under our grips. Trevor moved with deliberate slowness as he pulled me down on my knees with him.

He raised his hands over his head, still holding mine. *Let's just do what they say for now. Drew and Cavallo will be here in a minute.*

I sighed. Where was Cecelia when we needed her?

"Face-down! On the ground!"

One of the soldiers shoved us from behind and we toppled forward. Trevor pinwheeled his unseen arm up, trying to keep Tania off the ground. He spread the other wide across my back like a blanket. His face was pale in the searchlights as his eyes found mine. A boot hooked under our hands and ripped us apart. My invisible limbs disintegrated, and the frost-covered grass felt like it sliced into my cheek.

They're not going to shoot me if we're complying! Just hold on to Tania!

Anxiety crinkled across his skin. *Okay.*

I felt the air stir behind me as he withdrew his second arm from my back and used it to steady his grasp on our prisoner. Rough hands patted my sides and turned out my jacket pockets as they searched me. A knee pressed into the small of my back, pinning me in place.

Ice-water fear splashed through me. What were we going to do if they detained us? How long could we keep hold of Tania? What would happen if we tried to drag her astral form beyond her range? Would it kill her? Would she snap back into her body and get away?

"—secure area. It's a felony to come in here without authorization." *Cuff them and take them in.*

I twisted until I could see the side of the soldier's face, and then zapped a bit of his motor cortex into seizure. The handcuffs slipped from his fingers. "What the hell? I can't move my hands!" *Oh, Jesus. Nerve gas! They're terrorists with nerve gas and—*

One of the other soldiers had been talking on a walkie or some kind of comm device. "Yes, sir, that's what he said." His splotchy yellow fear hit me as he watched the soldier pinning me stare at his unmoving hands.

General Dale's voice came through the speaker. "Is she a short, brown-haired girl?"

"Yes, Sir. That's an affirmative, Sir."

General Dale sighed. "Let her up."

Drew and Cavallo ran up in the company of two additional soldiers. Cavallo still had her phone to her ear. "Yes, Sir. They're here."

The soldier who'd been kneeing me in the back rolled back onto his heels. I staggered back up and reached for Trevor's hand. His shoulders shook with concentration as he held on while Tania braced her legs against his invisible forearm and fought. She looked like she was snarling. My own invisible arms swelled around me and I used them to help pull Trevor to his feet.

Cavallo shoved a phone at me. *Bell's gonna yell at her.* "Captain Bell wants to talk to you."

I reached an invisible hand back around Tania's throat and gave a squeeze, and then took the phone.

"What the hell are you doing?"

"We have anudder one."

"That's no reason to enter secure areas without authorization!"

"She's cwose. We need to—"

"You *need* to keep from putting the entire base on alert!"

"So cancel it. We have to fah-whoa the tedder."

"You have to what?"

I sighed and handed the phone to Trevor. "We need to follow the tether. She's—" he looked at the soldiers within earshot. "She's close and she's higher up in their organization than Dmitri. If you give us authorization and let us do this, we'll have her back where you can talk to her very soon."

It took us longer than we thought. Tania had wrapped herself in a metallic camping blanket and burrowed under a layer of camouflage netting in a ditch off the side of the road. After playing "getting warmer" with the strength of her mental voice and the direction of the tether, we finally located her by the steely glow of hate that simmered from her. *Ya buda rvat ih vnutryennosti eez ih tyel i kupatsya v ih krovi!*

Yeah, I didn't understand a word of what she was thinking… and I was pretty sure I didn't want to know. The beam from Cavallo's flashlight caught Tania's pale face as I pulled the layers back with my one free hand. We pushed the lavender ghost version in the general direction of her body and watched as she sucked back into herself.

The secondhand seizure hit me as her body shuddered against the cold ground. Trevor kept a hand on her ankle until Tania lapsed into unconsciousness. As soon as the intensity faded, I half-collapsed against his chest and rubbed my face with a trembling hand.

You okay?

I nodded. *Two down. Twelve to go.*

Trevor threw her limp form over his shoulder, still wrapped in the foil-like thermal blanket. *Let's get her back inside.*

"You can't keep them in there together." Trevor's eyes darted back to the glass cell. "She'll probably kill him as soon as she wakes up."

Tania's still form sprawled across the cot. Dmitri hovered next to the door, silently pleading with his eyes and his thoughts. *Please do not leave me in here with her.*

Dale frowned. *He's a captured spy who can walk through walls—and who now knows we have G-positives working with us to catch his people. We can't just let him run around loose.* "She's unarmed."

I gave an angry sigh. *Have we mentioned the damn CLAWS? Let Dmitri out. I can keep him in his body if there's a problem.*

"You can what?"

Zap his brain and send the area that controls his ability into seizure. He'll stay put.

The General's eyes bugged a little bit. *Good thing she's on our side. She really is dangerous.* He nodded to another guy in uniform. "Bring him out and cuff him."

Dmitri closed his eyes in relief and leaned against the door. The glass insulated his physical form from the current, but he still felt it when the power shut off. After pressing against the door as it unlocked, he secured it behind him with a cautious hesitancy. A soldier approached him with handcuffs and Dmitri held out his hands. Behind him, the power hummed back through the glass as someone turned the controls back on.

"Thank you." He caught my eye as waves of pale-green relief flowed through him.

I flashed him a smile and tucked in against Trevor. Our attention turned back to Tania when she let out a low moan and stirred. *Oh...* "Does Tania speak Engwish?"

Dmitri frowned. "No. Russian and... German. Maybe some Polish, I think. She was working in Warsaw."

Crap. Even if Cecelia *were* here, I didn't think she'd be able to charm Tania to think in a language she didn't know. I turned to General Dale. "We need someone who speaks Wush-an." Dmitri could translate, but the General might feel he had some kind of conflict of interest.

Wush-an? Oh, she means Russian. He nodded. "I've already sent for a translator."

Where the heck was Cecelia anyway? I pulled out my phone and called, but it went directly to voicemail. We didn't even know where to start looking for her. Was she even on base, or had she taken off in a charm-borrowed car for another fun-filled Saturday night in Berlin?

I know how to find her. Trevor pulled his own phone out. "Rachel?"

"Hey, Trevor! What's with the girl in the big fish tank and the guy in handcuffs? Is it some kind of freaky German performance art?"

He chuckled. "Not really. It's the new guestroom at our place here in Germany. We have a… a visitor we'd like to introduce to Cecelia. Any chance you know where she is?"

"Ah." Rachel paused and I heard a sharp crack from a fireplace log. "She's still on the same base you are. In the hospital. Looks like she's talking to a guy—a soldier… and he's crying."

A wave of goosebumps ran up my arms. Heather had been sneaking in to treat injured soldiers in the base hospital. Cecelia had a special interest in using her charming ability to treat posttraumatic stress. Had she been working a few miracles of her own on the side?

Damn—sometimes she didn't make it easy for me to keep disliking her.

"Thanks, Rachel. How's the baby?"

Rachel groaned. "Eating, sleeping, setting things on fire. You know."

"I can imagine."

I tried Cecelia's number again and left a grumble on her voicemail. *Drew? Cecelia's at the hospital and not answering her phone. We're going to need some charming help with Tania here. Can you see if you can find her and bring her here?*

Drew nodded. "You want Heather, too?"

I looked at the pale face that still seemed hard and cold, even in sleep. *Yeah, I think we're going to need as much help as we can get.*

He ducked out as Tania rolled over and opened her eyes. Her shock popped within her as she took in the cage—and the people in uniform on the other side of the glass. Her gaze fell on Dmitri and her eyes narrowed. He gasped and took a step back, bringing his manacled hands up like a shield.

"Vy slaby i pryedatyeli, Dimka." Her words hissed out through the little mesh circle.

Dmitri's jaw trembled, but he didn't drop his eyes. "I am not a traitor. You are a criminal."

Her brow furrowed at his English words. Oh, yeah—he could only think and speak in English while he was here, thanks to Cecelia. Apparently he could still understand Russian, though.

Weird.

She stood up, looking as scruffy and dangerous as a rabid dog. Her eyes shifted to Trevor and me. "Vy oba stradayut, kogda prihodit Goran dlya menya. On sdyelayet vas proshu, chtoby umyeryet." The splatter of her spit stuck to the glass, and then oozed down the interior wall.

Classy.

Dmitri gasped. *She thinks Goran is coming for her. He will hurt them.*

I gave him a sideways glance and a tiny headshake. *If Goran comes here, he'll end up next to her in the glass box.*

The hangar door scraped open behind us. Heather entered on the heels of the translator. "Drew said you needed me here?"

I nodded. "Headuh, meet Tania. Tania wants to kill us all."

Heather took in the look of hate etched in Tania's face. "And then suck the marrow from our bones?"

"Oh, have you two aweady met?"

She snorted. "Hey, your voice keeps getting better." *We did it!*

Tania stepped back and lay down on the narrow cot with her arms folded across her chest like she was preparing for her own funeral. After a couple of deep breaths, she went limp and her spectral body slipped up to stand. She glanced at Trevor and me as she moved toward the far wall.

I tensed. *Is the current really going to hold her?*

Tania pushed at the glass. The silent shriek of panic came from within her still form on the cot and stabbed me through the temples. Where her astral arms had gone through the glass, they'd dissolved. She jerked the stumps back, staring as the transparent flesh grew back up from her elbows and her hands reformed. With another murderous look at the two of us, she stalked back to her body. When her eyes opened, she stared at the ceiling for a moment. Tania kept her face disdainfully neutral, but yellow sparks of fear shot like tiny fireworks from her. She turned on her side and faced away from us, as though we were beneath her contempt.

Trevor ran his fingers through his hair. "Well, that went well. Now all we need is—"

The outside door opened again as Drew returned with Cecelia. Her heels clicked on the concrete as she fought to keep up with Drew's bounding strides.

My lips quirked. *Speak of the devil.*

Cecelia eyed Tania's sulking back. "Does she speak English?"

I shook my head. *Dmitri doesn't think so.*

Cecelia stalked around to the far side of the glass, so she could see Tania's face. "Hey, do you speak English?"

Tania looked at her with loathing, but no understanding. *Yeslee ya na sdyelat yego obratno, ya nikogda nye ooveedyat moee detee snova.* An image filled her thoughts—two sharp-faced little boys, one half a head taller than the other, but both with the same, pale-blond curls. She clutched at it and pulled it deeper within her.

She's got kids? My brow furrowed. She didn't look very old—maybe college-age—although she had a hardness to her that made me think she'd survived terrible things. She definitely didn't have a mommy-vibe.

Dmitri took a shuddering breath. "Yes. Two boys. They are… they will become aethernauts when they are older."

The breeding program?

He nodded.

I looked at Tania's back, seeing it rise and fall with her breathing, and I felt a stab of sympathy. Then I remembered her claws reaching for Trevor and the soft feelings vanished.

Cecelia suddenly registered Dmitri's presence. *What's he doing on the outside?* "Hey, what's he doing running around free?"

Dmitri held up his manacled hands and gave her a lopsided smile. "What is this 'free' you speak of?"

I was starting to like having the guy around.

Cecelia stared at the handcuffs for a moment. *I guess it's covered.* "Whatever. You speak Russian. How do I say, 'Tell us the truth' in Russian?"

Dmitri's mouth opened, but no sound came out. *I know what to say. Why can't I say it?*

"Skazat nam pravdoo." The military translator stepped up behind her. *The blonde girl's fantastic-looking.*

Cecelia took in his broad chest, clean-cut jaw, and sparkling blue eyes. *Oh, I'm gonna LIKE working with HIM.* "Cecelia Mitchell."

"Lieutenant Daniel Moran." He kept her extended hand in his as he smiled into her eyes.

Something inside Cecelia went "sproing." Her lips parted. They just stared at each other for a few seconds. She suddenly remembered to breathe. "So... you speak Russian?"

"Russian, German, and French." *The language of love.*

I bit my lip. *Oh, he did NOT just think that.*

Trevor's lips twitched. *Give him some credit—at least he didn't say it out loud.*

Cecelia flushed. "How did it go again?" *I can barely think—what did I want to say in Russian? I can't remember. Look at the shoulders on this guy!*

He flashed teeth. "Skazat nam pravdoo."

Cecelia tilted her head, yet still managed to seem like she was aligned to face Lieutenant Moran.

"Skazat nam pravdoo." Her charm-voice held a little extra tremor.

Lieutenant Moran smiled wider. "*Awesome* pronunciation. You sure you don't already speak Russian?"

Cecelia flushed and I rolled my eyes. She had to focus to remember what else she was supposed to ask. "Um, how do you say, 'Answer this man's questions?'" *And be quick about it, so I can see if he wants to—* Her thoughts drifted into R-rated territory. She suddenly whirled on me. *Oh, no. Please don't let Maddie have seen that!*

Seen what? I gave her my most innocent face as I tried not to throw up in my mouth.

Cecelia squeezed her eyes shut.

By the way, he thinks you're fantastic-looking.

Trevor sighed. *Again with the match-making?*

Cecelia pinked further and looked at Lieutenant Moran from under lowered lashes.

"Otvechaite na voprosy etogo cheloveka."

What a mouthful. She giggled… and *meant* it. I'd never seen Cecelia so bubbly without a cynical underlying motive. "Can you tell me again?"

"Otvechaite na…"

She repeated his words with charm resonance.

"… voprosy etogo… cheloveka."

"She'll tell you what you want to know now." Cecelia tugged on her lower lip with her teeth. Lieutenant Moran's eyes locked on the motion.

"Awesome." He meant so much more than her charm ability. He gave a slight shake to his head as he tried to remember what he actually was supposed to be doing.

Captain Bell came forward and read the same Geneva Convention speech to Tania, with Lieutenant Moran giving her a rerun of the info in Russian. Her eyes went diamond-hard before she turned to lie on her back and stare at the ceiling.

Captain Bell folded the paper away into the pocket of his jacket. "What is your name?"

"Kak tyebya zovoot?" Lieutenant Moran echoed.

"Tatiana Alexandrovna Mikhalkov." Surprise flashed through Tania. *Pochyemoo ya otvechoo?* Her eyes shifted to Cecelia. *Kontrolya nad razoomom.* She pictured slashing Cecelia's throat with red-tipped talons; I shuddered as the hate in her thoughts bit at me.

Guess she'd figured out the charm-thing.

Trevor cupped my chin in his hand. *Are you okay? Do you want to get out of here before they start interrogating her?*

Let's find out what we need to know about the defenses in their facility first. We'll probably be going in there soon.

Trevor sighed. *Remember back when we tried to AVOID dangerous situations?*

I snorted. *Remember when we used to ask permission just to go into town? Now we're invading entire countries!*

He tightened his arm around my waist. *You know I'd follow you to the ends of the Earth.* He turned to Lieutenant Moran. "Can you please ask her about the place where they train? We'll need to know the layout, information about the people there, the security measures they're using, and where they're keeping Dmitri's sister and anyone else they're keeping hostage."

Lieutenant Moran nodded and tossed the Russian version at the prisoner.

Tania turned away from Moran to sneer at Dmitri. "Goran vasha syestra v bezopasnom dome za pryedyelamee Berleena. Vytashchitye menya otsyuda, ili on nachnyet otryezat paltsy. Ona mozhet yeshchyo porody, dazhye yeslee ona neekogda ne smozhyet zabrat rebenka." The images of mutilation in her mind filled her with vengeful delight.

Dmitri's face drained white, and then flushed angry red. "No!" He took a step toward the glass, and then stopped as he remembered that other people were still around. *If Goran hurts Katya, I will KILL him.*

"She said that Goran has Dmitri's sister in a safe-house near Berlin. If Dmitri doesn't help Tania here escape, he's going to hurt the sister. And there was something about... breeding?"

Lieutenant Moran shook his head. *This is the weirdest assignment I've ever had.*

I snorted. *You don't know the half of it.*

He jumped back with a gasp. "What the hell!"

I rolled my eyes. *Yeah, it's all X-Men and Goat-Starers in here. Ask Tania where the safe-house is.*

"Gdye byezopasno-dom?"

She rattled off an address in a strange mix of Russian and German. Fortunately, one of Bell's military minions got enough of it to plot it on a map. "Due east of Berlin, about eighty miles from here."

I gasped as a thought hit me. *RVs!* Did the Russian RVs see images of their targets the way Rachel and Claire did? They might be able to see Tania in the box right now. Would Goran know we'd captured her? Was that why she expected him to rescue her? What would happen to Dmitri's sister? He hadn't seemed like the type to make empty threats. Crap—it gave the term "deadline" a more literal meaning. We'd have to go immediately. I looked at Drew. *You know where we're going?*

Drew looked at the screen and nodded. "I can getcha there in half an hour." He grabbed his phone to punch in the directions.

That's like, a hundred and sixty miles an hour.

Drew raised his eyebrows. "And your point is…?"

I flashed him a grin, and then looked at Trevor. *The two of us. Drew. Dmitri. And we'll need space in the car for Katya after we get her out.*

His brow crinkled. "You have a plan?"

I smiled. *It's me. I always have a plan.* I gave his hand a squeeze as I turned. *Cecelia!*

"No." She shook her head. "No way. Every time I go somewhere with you, people try to kill us." *And I'd rather stay here with this hot army guy.*

I hadn't planned on taking her with us anyway. *Fine. Just make sure you answer your phone. And call us if Tania gives any new information about the safe-house.* I had the sudden image of a James-Bond-style villain's lair, complete with a shark-filled moat and legions of henchmen. I pictured the lot of us strapped to metal tables as red laser beams inched toward our feet. *Oh, and if we're not back by tomorrow, feed the cat and send in the Marines.*

I tipped my head at Dmitri and, working on cutting back on my Fuddish accent, said, "Let's go get your sistuh."

His eyes widened. "Now?"

I nodded. She might not have much time, but Dmitri didn't need to know that. I figured she'd be a lot easier to convince to come back with us if Dmitri was with us for the rescue. Heck, did Katya even speak English?

"What do you think you're doing?" Dale glared at me. *There's no way in HELL she's taking that spy ANYWHERE!*

I sighed. *Cecelia?*

Her lips twisted in a tiny smirk and her voice held as much sarcasm as charm. "You think Maddie's plan is just… *super*. You're giving her official authorization to go."

He needs to allow Dmitri to go, too.

"And you're giving her permission to take astral-boy along. Let's get rid of the handcuffs, too."

Dmitri needs to be able to speak Russian again.

"He can't?"

Your "think in English" command.

"Dmitri. You can speak Russian and English and… do you speak any other languages?"

Dmitri paled. "Um, German."

"You can speak German again, too. But you still think in English, got it?"

He nodded, eyes wide.

Thanks. By the way, Lieutenant Awesome is working on the best way to ask you out. Try and look surprised when he does.

She rolled her eyes and blew out a long sigh. "Way to ruin the moment."

Whatever. Just keep the pornographic daydreams to a minimum until I'm out of range, okay?

"The *what?*"

Oh, never mind. Those are HIS daydreams.

Cecelia blushed as she looked sidelong at the Lieutenant, who was still occupied translating Bell's questions. "He's... he isn't—?"

I snickered as we turned to leave the building.

"Geez, Maddie! Not funny!"

"Hold up a sec." Heather blocked the route to the door. Dmitri flinched back when she raised her hands toward his face. "I gotta check to see if your neurotransmitters are still outta whack. I couldn't risk overloading your body's repair abilities last time—you were pretty messed up."

Dmitri got lost in her rapid-fire words.

I gave him a nod. *It's okay. She's a doctor.*

His eyes went wide as she pressed her fingers against his temples, and he gave a little "huh!" as the pins-and-needles erupted within his skull.

"There." Heather dusted her hands across each other and smiled. "That should do it. I don't think you'll have any more seizures. Once the last of whatever they gave you leaves your system, I think you'll respond normally to dodecamine."

Dmitri looked confused.

No more being sick.

"But... I am still aethern—astral?"

"Yup." Heather turned back toward the glass enclosure. "She's not as sick as you were."

"She has only been astral for one year." *No aethernaut drugs when in breeding program.*

"Won't take as much to fix her, then."

I frowned and put a hand on her arm. "Wait." *Tania's vicious. Make sure she's knocked out before you do any treatment on her. You probably should wait until we get back, so I can—*

"Maddie, don't worry about it. I can handle it. She'll be out as soon as I get a hand on her. And Cecelia's here for backup—if Tania tries anything, she can just charm her to stop. Go save that kid from the Russian mob, already."

CHAPTER 14

Drew gave a soft whistle. "Either one of the Russian charms had a talk with the right house owners, or being in the mafia pays *really* well."

We'd parked the car out of sight beyond where the tree-lined road curved, and now we stood in the grey puffs of our own breaths within a stand of evergreen trees that loomed shadow-black in the pre-dawn light. The house was manor-large, with dim security lights at intervals around it. Wide steps led to a front door we could've driven through.

Trevor's hand tightened in mine as he held the cell phone up to his ear. He kept his voice low. "Rachel?"

"Yeah, I'm still here." We'd called in and talked to her about this as we'd driven over. Rachel could find us anywhere in the world because she knew us. Once she'd gotten a fix on our position, she could look around and see other things in our vicinity. Having her case the layout from New Hampshire gave a whole new meaning to the concept of *tele*commuting. "Whoa. Nice mansion."

"What're we looking at inside?"

I frowned at one of the windows. *I can't hear anyone's thoughts at this distance.* I'd need to get closer.

"Gimme a minute." The sound of Rachel's breathing came through the receiver before she inhaled with a hiss. "I don't... I don't see any people on the first floor, but they've... they've got some kind of booby trap on the front door—two guns on trip wires. Looks like you're better off going in through the kitchen in the back."

Drew snorted. *Only two guns? Not a problem.*

"And... nope, there's no one upstairs, either. You sure this is the place?"

I snorted. *As if regular people use loaded weapons instead of welcome mats.*

Dmitri's despair flashed within him. *Katya's not here?*

"Lemme just... Oh. Hey, I found someone. In the basement. Two someones, actually. You're looking for a girl about our age, right? Oh. There's... there's some weird door there. It's like a safe, or... or a bank vault or something. Two of them, back to back, like an airlock." The guy's in a chair in the regular basement—there's a staircase down just off the kitchen. The guy... looks like he's sleeping. The girl's behind the safe-door, and she..." Rachel swallowed hard. "She looks scared to death."

I took a shaky breath as I recalled being trapped in my own underground cell. It was all coming back to me, the helplessness of being at the mercy of a sadistic—

Are you okay? Trevor's arm tightened around me. He hung up with Rachel and turned off his ringer—stealth mode—before slipping the phone into his pocket.

I will be as soon as we get her out of there.

We skirted around the edge of the trees until we got to the back of the manor house. A much-less-grand door opened onto a gravel pathway that led to a separate garage building. As we moved closer, a hint of fear touched my thoughts and I soon heard what I now could tell was probably Russian.

Yeslee onee nye vyernootsya ya sobeerayus oomyeryet zdyes.

Trevor reached through the back door and unlocked it from within. The four of us tried to walk without making the wide wooden floorboards creak. Drew threw a small fireball up over his palm to give us more light, and Dmitri had to bite back his gasp.

Over here. I pointed toward the door at the far end, only to feel kind of stupid when it opened into a pantry.

I think this is it. Dmitri put his gloved hand on the knob and worked on keeping his fingers from trembling.

The stairs descended into darkness. Drew went first, although Trevor stayed close behind and put an invisible arm in front of him. *People who booby trap their front doors with shotguns might have other surprises.* I kept a tight hold of his hand as I followed him down. Dmitri pulled the door shut behind us. His intense need to make sure his sister was safe seemed to pull him down the stairs.

The low ceiling closed in over us and the air smelled damp and mildewy. A narrow hallway led into the gloom, and old-fashioned sconces along the wall threw yellowed light in tepid circles at each door. I could hear the frightened thoughts more clearly now, as well as the dream of the sleeping guy. He imagined coming through a wall as the invaders moved toward—

Crap! Not a dream! *Astral!*

My grip on Trevor pulled him to a stop. A violet form slipped out of the wooden panel and swept nasty talons toward Drew's throat.

Drew bumped into the invisible arm spread wide in front of him. *What the—?*

Dmitri tripped into me. *Why are we stopping?*

Invisible welcoming committee. Trevor's got him.

Trevor nearly growled as he grabbed the astral's wrist and yanked him into the hallway. The lavender face went wide with shock as he struggled against the hold. Trevor lifted him with a second hand around his neck and pushed the spectral form down the hall. The tether disappeared into the wall near the end.

Drew pushed open the door and the guy spasmed and slid off his chair as soon as I had line-of-sight and could overload him. The astral form collapsed in Trevor's grip and flowed back into his body.

Dmitri stared at the limp pile of Russian astral on the floor. "Sergei?" *Is he still alive?*

I frowned. *He's alive—just knocked out.* If he'd succeeded in clawing my friend's face, though, I might've considered doing something more permanent.

We joined Drew in frowning at the brushed metal rectangle set into the far wall. It was the size of a small door, a bit shorter than I was, and it had no handle or keypad or any other controls, at least that we could see.

Drew ran his fingers along the edges. "So how do we open it?"

Dmitri shook his head. "Is she…?"

I met his eyes. *There's someone trapped on the other side. I can hear her thoughts.*

"Katya?"

I think so. *I could ask her, but I think my voice in her head might just freak her out more.*

Dmitri nodded. "Wait here." He sat down on the cold stone floor and braced his back against the wall. "I will see." Closing his eyes, he took a couple of deep breaths, and then pulled himself out of his body. The tether followed him as he stepped through the metal plate. I could see through his eyes as he took in the dim, closet-sized room. The door through which he'd stepped had a wheel set into this side, and three dials formed a line next to it. He faced a second identical door.

Airlock.

The room was vault-secure from both sides. It had been designed so the only way in—the only way to open it—was as an astral. And that astral needed to know the combinations.

Dmitri slipped through the second door. His emotions flared pale green with concern. *Katya!*

The tiny, windowless room barely held the mattress on the floor. The bulb in the ceiling socket cast the huddled figure in harsh shadows. Drawn-up knees hid her face and she had her arms wrapped around her head.

Dmitri willed his hand solid and touched hers. Katya jerked back and scanned the empty room with wild eyes as panic flashed through her. *Kto preekosnoolsya ko mnye?* Her blue eyes narrowed into a scowl. *Ya eestreblyu ih shary s lozhkoy!*

Dmitri jumped back and half disappeared through the metal door. *I didn't mean to make her afraid!*

Dmitri, does Katya speak English?

Yes. The thought came from the still body on the floor as the astral moved back into the room and stared at his sister. *They made us all study languages so we could be good at being spies.*

I focused in on the fierce mind locked behind the doors. *Katya?*

The girl's thoughts fled back into fear as an icy wave flooded through her. She jumped up, backing against the wall. *Preezrak!*

I don't know what a preezrak is, but I'm here with your brother, Dmitri, and we're going to get you out.

Amerikanskii preezrak?

Dmitri told me you spoke English. If you can think something in English, I'll be able to hear it.

Katya slid back down to sit on the mattress. *Dmitri? Dmitri… is here?*

He's there with you right now. He's the one who just touched your hand.

She covered her mouth and took a shaky breath. "Dmitri?" She held out her hand as she scanned the tiny cell for confirmation.

Dmitri, she knows it's you now.

Dmitri gave her fingers a squeeze and she gasped. "Dmitri! Vytashchitye myenya otsyuda!" She jumped up and started pounding on the metal door.

The dull thudding barely registered on our side; Katya was pretty much buried alive.

The slumped form of the guard let out a groan and I spared him a glance to zap him back into unconsciousness.

Dmitri moved back into the center of the airlock. *How do we open these?*

I felt rather than saw Trevor's smile. *Give us a couple of minutes.* His invisible fingers scaled down to match the fine mechanisms within the door. The tiny digits ran across the cut disks behind the dials, feeling for the points that would align. Closing his eyes, Trevor focused in with low, steady breaths. The knobs turned, angling until he felt the little skip as the metal parts caught the right spots.

He exhaled with a deep sigh as the third knob turned into place. Invisible hands expanded to turn the wheel and the teeth of the vault door retracted. The door swung open on silent hinges and I met Dmitri's glowing eyes.

How?

Trevor. I'd never appreciated why Williamson had made him do all those different types of lock-picking in his practicals.

Can I learn how to do that?

I grinned as Trevor nodded.

Drew frowned. "Um, not to stress anyone out, but I just felt a power jolt when that door opened. I think we might've triggered an alarm."

The guard's cell phone began the DAH-dah-dah-dah, DAH-dah-dah-dah of a factory pre-set ringtone.

Um… crap. *Dmitri, maybe you'd better get back into your body. We might need to get out of here soon.*

Drew focused into knocked-out guy's pocket and fried the cell phone's circuits, cutting off the ring in a strangled chirp. He felt out for the alarm wires and toasted them, as well.

Trevor stepped into the little closet to face the other door, still keeping hold of my hand. He started to reach into the mechanism, but a sudden flash of insight made him turn and check the numbers on the first door. He dialed them in manually and gave the wheel a turn. The second door popped free and we were hit with a wall of air that smelled of sweat and desperation.

Pale hands gripped the edge of the door and pulled hard. The girl stared at Trevor. "You… you are not the one who talked into my head."

I grinned and leaned around Trevor's shoulder. "Dat would be me."

"Katya!" Dmitri pulled himself up off the floor. The closet-sized room seemed a bad place for the reunion, especially with the alarm thing and all. We stepped back.

"Let's go!" Drew started for the door.

I sent another jolt into the guard's mind. I didn't want to kill him. He was unconscious and not hurting anyone now; it wouldn't be self-defense. We couldn't have him waking up and raising the alarm, but I didn't want to—

Trevor scooped him up and tossed him over his shoulder. I flashed him a relieved smile. *Thanks.*

Three astrals down.

I felt out for other minds as the five of us headed back toward the stairs. Trevor extended an invisible arm around each end of the group.

He's got the whole world… in his… No—focus!

Katya shivered as we moved out into the grey dawn. She didn't have a coat—only a thin, shapeless, white coverall like a painter might wear.

We moved in under the trees. Trevor dragged an invisible arm behind us to mask our footprints on the frost-covered ground. With the bulk of the unconscious astral over his shoulder, he was breathing hard. After a moment of wondering, "What do we do with this guy?" Trevor shoved him into the back seat and pulled me into his lap in the front. Drew threw the car into gear as we strapped in.

I sank back against Trevor and blew out a long breath. He tightened an arm around my waist and rested his forehead against my hair. "Is everyone okay?"

From the center of the back seat, Dmitri gave his sister's shoulder a tentative touch. "Tebe bolno?"

She shook her head as the pale yellow fear faded from her. Dmitri startled as she flung her arms around him and squeezed "Aaaaayi!" Exuberant, mint-green relief jumped across her skin and she started to laugh.

She met my grin. "Spaseebo! Uh, I mean... thank you!"

No problem.

Her eyes widened. "You are... mind-talker?"

Sure am.

"And you... rescue my brother?"

Dmitri snorted. "Actually, they caught me when I was spy at the American embassy."

Katya flashed grey with concern and the conversation in the back seat fell into rapid-fire Russian as Dmitri brought Katya up to speed. Sergei, the knocked-out astral guard, stirred again, and I sent another quick overload into his brain. Drew pulled us onto the autobahn. The road was nearly empty in the early dawn and he let the BMW loose with a silent *oh, yeah!*

I gasped and pinked up as Trevor slid his hand between us. He chuckled into my ear. *Hold that thought for later. I was just going for my phone.*

He hit Captain Bell's number; we needed to report in. After several rings, it flipped to voicemail. He frowned and hit redial.

I went for my own phone and blew out a sigh before dialing Cecelia. When it also went to voicemail, I started to scowl. *She was supposed to stay in touch. If she's gone off with Lieutenant Awesome the interpreter...* I hit Heather's number next.

Why isn't anyone answering their phones?

I met Trevor's eyes and we shared a flash of rust-brown trepidation. The next number Trevor dialed beeped through several extra digits before it started to ring.

Rachel answered with a groan.

"Uh, sorry, Rachel." Trevor flushed with chagrin. "We didn't mean to wake you, but we can't reach Heather or Cecelia and they were supposed to stay in contact. I hate to ask, but would you mind…?"

Rachel groaned into the phone again. "Okay. Gimme…" She cut into a yawn. "Gimme a sec."

Her harsh gasp broke the whispery silence. "Oh, God!"

My "What is it?" clashed with Trevor's "What? What did you see?"

Rachel swallowed hard. "They're hurt. They're… Oh, God. There's blood everywhere!"

CHAPTER 15

The engine noise filled the car, too loud. Tiny hairs stood on my arms. *Tania. Tania got out and—*

Trevor's pain and guilt slammed into mine, hot and aching. *We never should have left them there. They needed us to protect them from her.*

Oh, my God in Heaven. What had she done to them?

"What has happened?" Dmitri's voice came from the distant back seat.

The phone started to slip from Trevor's hand and I grabbed for it as the tiny light of the display sharpened diamond-hard in my vision. "Rachel! Can you still see them?" *Please don't let her overload. Her vision's the only thing showing us what that sick bi—*

Her voice filled with tears. "Yeah."

"The glass cage." Had Tania gotten out only as an astral, or had she freed her physical body, too? Where was she now? Who else would she hurt? "Is anyone inside? Lying on the cot or the floor?"

"What? What's going on?" Drew glanced over at us with a frown of concern.

After a shuddering breath, Rachel's voice returned, sharp with anger. "I see a woman. She's… she's standing by the side of the glass and pointing… pointing into the dark. She's the only thing moving. It looks like she's yelling."

The only thing moving. Did that mean that everyone who'd been there was— Oh, God. Ice stabbed through my gut. If Tania was still inside the glass and standing, she hadn't escaped as an astral. Which meant…

"Rachel. Keep her in sight. Another astral must be there. Keep her in sight or we'll lose both of them." Rachel might have trouble finding someone she'd never met, but she could follow a person in her vision away from the familiar beacon she'd first used to find a location.

Drew cursed and accelerated. His fingers gripped white on the steering wheel.

"Goran." The snakelike image flashed through Trevor's mind as he said the name. In the backseat, both Dmitri and Katya gasped and shot out yellow spikes of fear.

I nodded. *Probably.* We needed to keep Rachel connected to them. If they were capable of doing that kind of damage, we couldn't let them get away. But Heather and Bell and Cavallo and, hell, even Cecelia—they needed help.

Our people.

The image of Goran's claws growing from his hand closed my throat.

Blood everywhere.

Trevor's hand slid against me, pulling my phone from my pocket since I was using his. He hit another number off the speed-dial and stopped breathing as he waited for it to ring.

Dale's voice was nearly a shout. "Ms. Dunn, haven't you created enough distur—"

"General," Trevor cut him off, "There's at least one astral loose on the base right now, and it's hurt people in the secure hangar. They need emergency medical help—doctors, ambulances—right away."

Rachel's gasp sounded in my ear. "She just pushed the door open. The woman... oh, God, she just stepped over one of the people on the floor... she's headed for the door of the hangar... it opened before she got to it. I don't see anyone else moving."

My throat tightened. "Stay with her, Rachel. Trevor just called in the base ambulances." I imagined Tania running through the grey morning light, making for the fences where we'd been pushed to the ground by the MPs. God, was that only last night?

Maybe they'd shoot her. We should be so lucky.

"There's a car out beyond the fence. The soldiers are running toward her... they're pulling guns and yelling..." Rachel hissed and the phone went silent. "The two soldiers—they... they're down. They just... like something sliced their throats. They started spurting blood and fell."

Beneath me, Trevor went rigid and he half-yelled through his clenched jaw. "We need to get them medical attention now, General!"

Dale's voice sounded too calm for the situation. "I can't risk additional lives until we know the area is secure."

Trevor's voice filled with steel. "The thing that hurt all of them just slashed the throats of two MPs out by the fence! It's getting away!"

I gripped the phone with shaking fingers. "Tell me where she is, Rachel."

Ambulances? What's going on? Who's hurt? Drew's confusion

grew into alarm next to us. Behind Trevor, Sergei, the guard, groaned and I had to pull back from blasting the crap out of his brain. I clenched my teeth and just gave him the telepathic version of a kick to the head.

In the background, I heard Sienna start to cry. "Dammit!" Rachel sounded close to tears. "Harrison? Can you—? I can't lose this vision or…" She hissed in another breath. "She just, like, jumped an eight-foot fence. How did—? She's… she's getting into a car. It's silver and… the license plates are… is that Russian? I don't recognize the letters." I could hear the concentration in her voice. "They're moving. Whoa! Two guys in the back seat just started jerking around like they're having seizures or something. They're… the car's turning. It's going toward the highway. Sign with a big blue 'A' says Berlin."

I looked out the windshield as the grey light grew stronger. Toward Berlin? That meant they'd just gotten onto *this* road.

They were heading right toward us.

Dmitri leaned between the front seats. "What is happening?"

I pulled in a shuddering breath. "Goran just sprung Tania and he hurt a bunch of our people in the process. They're heading this way."

Drew's knuckles went white on the steering wheel as cold grey trepidation curled up in him. "Who's hurt?" *Heather? Elena? Cecelia?*

Trevor forced his voice calm. "They're gone, General. We think there were two more astrals on base tonight, as well as Tania. The three of them just got into a car outside the perimeter fence. A fourth person is driving. *Now* can you get medical treatment for the injured people in the hangar?"

General Dale's voice was hard. "We have no defenses against them when they're in astral form."

"They're *gone!* They're on the highway, out of range of the base. We need to take care of our people now. They need help!"

"Fine. I'll send a medical team to the hangar."

Trevor swallowed hard. "Send as many as you can, General. Rachel said there was blood everywhere." A sick sense of helpless dread ached between us.

Drew hissed in a harsh breath and floored the Beemer's gas pedal, weaving to the left to pass another car. Morning traffic was picking up. "We need to get back there." *They have to be okay! Oh, God, what if they're...*

"Right now, Rachel's vision is the only thing we can use to track them. If we had a healer with us..." Oh, no. Heather couldn't heal herself; none of the healers could. Was she one of the people bleeding on the hangar floor? We couldn't ask Rachel to RV them to check—she'd lose the thread to Tania and the others.

Trevor cut off his call with the General and tried to reach Heather again. *Pick up! Please, pick up. Please let her have gone back to the base hospital, or be a deep sleeper, or be...*

The phone went to voicemail.

"Trev?" Drew tried to keep his voice from shaking. "Could you try to... try to reach Elena?"

"Yeah." Trevor bit his lip as he dialed.

Voicemail.

Drew swallowed hard as conflict pulled at his soul. *I feel so... useless! I should be there. But if Goran gets away then no one will stop him. We need to follow the astrals, find their base, and stop them. If I was the one hurt and lying on the floor, I'd want the others to go after the people who did this. And if they're worse than hurt, then it won't matter when we—*

"Let's get them." He spat out the words. *They can't get away with this. They... hurt our people.* "Before they can hurt anyone else." *Elena. Heather. Cecelia. How badly are they injured? Are they—NO! They have to be okay. Please, God, let them be okay.*

I turned back to the phone I still held against my ear. "You still have them, Rachel?"

"Yeah." She sounded drained. "They're coming up on the turnoff for the one-hundred."

The ring road for Berlin—we'd passed it every time we'd come in. They were getting closer to us. Babbling thoughts grew around me, making it hard to think. We passed out of the cityscape and entered a forest, and the voices in my head simmered back. Was this the Tiergarten again? "Rachel, you gotta let us know if they get off the number five road." I turned to Drew. "Take the next exit and get this car turned around. We need to be able to follow them."

"Never mind that." Drew pulled us into a huge traffic circle. "We'll wait for them here."

We moved in slow circles around the pillar topped with a golden eagle statue. I stared at its spread wings, but the movement of the car made me feel like *we* were the circling birds of prey. Waves of German thoughts washed through me from the surrounding traffic.

"They still coming, Rachel?" A wave of dizziness oozed through me; maybe we'd been going in this circle for too long. Maybe it was the images my brain kept throwing up.

Blood everywhere.

"Yeah. Still on the five, going through trees. Coming up on a big traffic circle."

"The car's description again?"

"Silver sedan, Russian plates. Four people inside."

Trevor and I watched the incoming traffic for a silver sedan with Russian plates. My breath caught as lethal energy coursed through me, coalescing behind my eyes. They'd hurt our people. I wanted to kill them.

Is that—? Yeah! There!

"Up ahead, Drew." Trevor's voice seemed strained.

Drew imagined ramming their car, and then making it blow up in an action-movie style explosion.

Trevor shook his head. "Not a good idea. Too many people here. Someone could get hurt."

We fell in two cars behind them and took the turn back toward the place we'd found Katya. Were they going to the safe house? Our car wove through the commuter traffic as we squinted into the oncoming sunlight and tried to keep the car in view without being too obvious. At least driving a BMW in the middle of Berlin made us inconspicuous. The traffic moved through urban sprawl and past low buildings surrounded by now-bare trees.

Wait—was this road really named after *Karl Marx*? That was something we didn't see in America. Dammit—*so* not important right now. Focus!

The city gave way to houses and farmland after about ten minutes. Sergei groaned in the back seat. Rather than zap him unconscious again, I felt into his head and sent both motor cortexes into seizure. Sergei stiffened, and then went limp. His eyes flashed open and he let out a hoarse scream.

Next to him, Dmitri screamed, as well. He pushed away to crowd up against Katya. *What is wrong with Sergei?*

I sent a thought to Dmitri. *He's fine, but he can't move right now. Yes is "da;" no is "nyet," right?*

He nodded, still pinging fear-filled little yellow flashes of *what the hell?*

Ask Sergei if Goran was planning to go back to the house where we found him and Katya.

"Yesl Goran vozvrativshis v dom, gdyc my nashlee vy?"

Sergei's eyes narrowed and his lip curled. *Nyet.* "On ubet vas za eto, Dimka. On ubet vas, zatyem ispolzovat vashu sestru."

Katya gasped and Dmitri's face darkened.

I frowned. I caught enough of the images in Sergei's head to recognize that he'd just threatened the other two. At least he'd thought the answer to the question.

Ask him where they were—

Something slammed onto the hood of the car. Trevor gasped and threw his invisible arms wide. I whipped my head around just in time to see purple talons slice down through the windshield at Drew's face. The talons skittered off Trevor's unseen arm and the astral dug his other set of claws into the metal of the hood to keep himself from sliding off. His pale face held a predatory sneer.

Goran.

Little shreds of fabric hung down from the ceiling above Drew's head.

"What the hell?" He reached up to touch them, but his hand stopped as it hit Trevor's invisible barrier. "Oh, crap! Is that from invisible claws?"

Katya's gasp seemed too loud in the suddenly silent car.

Sergei jumped out of his body and reached forward. I sent a burst of energy into his head and knocked him unconscious before he could do any damage.

Two cars ahead, a second lavender figure emerged through the back window of the silver sedan and leapt for the top of the car ahead of us. He was larger than any of the others I'd seen—built like a linebacker—with his spectral hair spiked in pale points above an angular face. He landed with a metallic thunk onto the roof one car up and the driver beneath him startled and swerved toward the median. A second jump brought him to land with a clunk on the roof of our own vehicle.

I pulled out my own invisible arms and spread them wide over the back seat. "Two astrals on the car! Everyone stay down!" In the front, Trevor pushed Goran from his perch on the hood. His glowing snake-eyes widened as he slid off the side fender.

Drew let out a snort. "Think they know we're following them?" He sped up his pursuit.

Claws sliced down into my invisible arms from the roof, dragging my attention back. I felt a sick tug, like when I'd gotten a filling at the dentist. I'd been numbed up but the pressure had extended out to the non-numb parts. The talons dug into my invisible limbs and tightened, pulling the limbs up against the roof of the car.

Pinned.

I jerked against the invisible restraints. I should just be able to dissolve out of it, but the claws still sinking deeper into me seemed to prevent that. I pulled harder as a rising panic flowered in my gut. My breath rasped through my too-tight throat.

Oh, God. We can grab them—but they can do the same thing to us.

They might not be able to see the limb, but they could feel it—and grab hold.

A third astral landed on the hood of the car. Tania's diamond-cold eyes blazed at Trevor as she swung claws at his head. Trevor reached out a golden hand, blocking her attack.

Lavender talons slashed into his right leg through the passenger door. We both cried out as the pain ripped through him.

Goran's eyes appeared at the side window, grim and lethal. He pulled back his arm for another strike. Trevor brought his other hand around, trying to shield us. Hot blood soaked down the leg of his jeans with every painful pulse of his heart.

Tania went for Drew's throat, slashing forward with a silent shriek.

With a yell, I pushed my invisible arms straight up. The astral on top of the car had been pulling against me, but now he flipped forward, passing though Tania where she'd braced against the windshield.

The contact between the two astrals jolted through me like they'd been dunked in ice water. My breath rushed from my chest in a sputter and I couldn't seem to draw it back in. I pushed them apart and Tania fell against the steering wheel. Drew let out a curse as the car jerked out of the lane. The side of a small truck loomed large in the side window as Drew yanked us back into our lane, and the truck's beeping honk seemed too cute for the nearly lethal situation. Gruff, angry German thoughts flashed into my brain from the driver.

I shifted my angle and gave Tania an awkward push with my still-pinned arms. She glanced back at the oncoming traffic, spotted an oncoming bus, and made another grab for the steering wheel. I threw myself forward to block her reach.

The guy with the claws in my arms planted his feet on the hood, and then dug in like a pit-bull and forced my arms together, binding them in his sharp grip.

My heartbeat hammered in my ears as Tania jumped toward the roof. With a hiss of pain, Trevor swung one arm wide, batting her sideways. I gasped as she tumbled off the car, and then nearly choked when she righted herself and started floating over the highway opposite Drew's window, keeping pace with our car with a single hand digging into the side, even as other vehicles passed through her.

Ah, hell. That was *so* freaky.

Goran's claws dug into Trevor's invisible arm now. Trevor's physical hand clutched at his leg and blood dripped from between his fingers.

A switch flipped within me, turning me cold and lethal. Energy began to build behind my eyes and my vision got sharp and narrow.

Execution.

"Drew." I clenched my teeth against Trevor's pain. "Get us closer to their car. Right next to them."

Line-of-sight.

"You got it." He moved to the left lane and pulled up.

Tania's glowing eyes widened as she saw where we were headed. She floated up and perched like a gargoyle on the roof of the Russian sedan. I could see the driver now; he glanced back at us with wide eyes and tried to speed up, but traffic reined him in.

I bit my lip. *If I blast him, it'll cause an accident.*

You can't. Trevor's face was pale as cold seeped through him. My heart fluttered with worry and my throat closed. He was losing so much blood! Holding tightly to Goran's arm, Trevor prevented him from swiping at us again, but he was getting lightheaded and woozy. I still had the other guy embedded in my own silver arms. The pit-bull grip tightened as he tried to drag me through the windshield. The seatbelt dug a bruising diagonal stripe across me.

Tania's physical head slumped against the front passenger window of the sedan. Her burning hate and fear painted her in splashes of yellow and grey. She launched her astral body off the roof and flew at me with talons splayed wide. I forced my attention to her still form in the car and focused into her mind.

The lethal energy shot from me with a whimpering gasp. Her astral form flared bright, and then evaporated.

I swallowed hard. Her last thought had been a flash of those two little boys.

Drew pulled alongside the car. I pressed close to the glass, angling up to see into the back seat where Goran and pit-bull guy sprawled down below the window line. Trevor moaned as my shifting weight hit his injured leg and I hissed at the shared pain.

Purple claws raked down toward my face. I flinched back, and then sent a killing blast into the head of pit-bull guy. His body jerked up and jolted Tania's seat. Her limp form slumped forward. His transparent face flashed surprise as he dissolved.

Goran reared up and head-butted Trevor. The crack knocked him back against the headrest with a thud. Blood gushed from his now misshapen nose. I cried out as the pain knifed through me, and then my heart died as Trevor's mind faded.

Trevor!

His grip on Goran slipped as his consciousness fell away.

My own invisible arms dissolved with Trevor's. Panic sent crystalline shards through me.

Defenseless.

Goran raked claws down at me, catching me across my upper arm. I cried out as the pain hit a second later, burning through me. He swiped again and talons sank into my right shoulder—tearing flesh—while the other hand dug into the side of the car, keeping him in place.

I couldn't see his body! He was slumped down against the back door of the Russian sedan. I needed line-of-sight or—

I felt out for the tether from his mind. Aiming through the chest of the looming astral, I shot a bolt of energy across to the next vehicle, using the energy of the tether to focus into Goran's head. I felt it connect as the world spun around me and the purple claws reached for my neck—

The spectral figure was sucked back into his body. Goran whipped his head up and his viper-eyes found mine through the car windows. I focused in, trying once again to fry his brain. The edges of my vision went black and everything seemed to be tipping. I felt the wounds in my shoulder pull apart like gaping mouths. Acid pain burned through them with every heartbeat, every shift of my body. My arm hung limp in my lap as blood soaked down my torn jacket. My mental energy connected again to Goran's mind and I gave one last push. He flared within his own skull, and then went dark. A strange buzzing filled my ears and Katya's sobs registered as a distant sound. Trevor's ragged breathing pushed against me.

Got to stop Trevor's bleeding. He's losing so much blood. Oh, God.

I fumbled to unbuckle the seatbelt. My single working hand trembled as I pulled the belt from the loops of my jeans and wrapped it around Trevor's leg above raw meat gashes that pumped more blood with every heartbeat. I pulled the belt tight.

Drew kept pace with the driver. *They both need medical... so much blood... got to stop this guy...* His mental voice came to me like he was talking into a tin can on a string. "Dammit! They're both— You! Russian guy! What's your name? D something? You still able to do the astral thing?"

"Yes." Dmitri leaned forward between the front seats.

"Okay. That car is about to have engine trouble. I need you to ghost up and get over there and steer. Take it off to the side without hitting anyone, and then hit the brakes. All right?"

"I can do that." *I don't think I can do that. Jump over to a moving car? I barely know how to drive.*

"You…" My voice rasped from me. "You don't jump."

"What?" *I thought she might be dead.*

"Just… float. Like Tania did." I sent an image of her hovering alongside the car. I could barely keep my eyes open and everything seemed to twist and float around me.

Dmitri went still in the backseat. Trepidation flowed through him as he pulled out of his body, took a metaphorical deep breath, and pushed off toward the other car. He slid into the front seat around the now-panicking driver.

"He's… there." Each syllable made the pain in my shoulder flare.

Drew focused into the engine of the Russian car. After a few seconds of fire suppression, the car sputtered and died. Dmitri grabbed the wheel and Drew pulled in front of him as they glided to the side of the road.

The back door of our car opened. I hadn't felt Dmitri get back into his body—or even noticed that we'd stopped on the shoulder of the road. He rubbed his knuckles as the memory of invisibly sucker-punching the driver of the Russian car made him grin for a moment. *He said such terrible things about Katya.* He shoved the unconscious man against Tania's still form as he slid behind the wheel.

Drew nodded to him as they caravanned to the next exit. After they turned us around, we headed back through Berlin. I stirred enough to flop my head back and zap Sergei back into unconsciousness once more on the drive back. I felt cold and numb, even with the heater going full blast, and I still didn't think I could move.

We picked up a large military escort at the base gate. Medical personnel came out to meet the car as we pulled up at the emergency bay of the base hospital. The pain of the people within hit me like a scream. The car door opened and hands reached around me.

Everything went black.

CHAPTER 16

The world was dark and spinning—every cell of my body filled with excruciating pain. Some of it was mine, but the rest came from people around me—recent evacs from Afghanistan, soldiers who'd had training accidents, and a couple of women on the maternity ward—and it seemed to be closing in on me.

—*never walk again, or even*—
—*can't keep pushing. I'm being ripped in ha*—
—*still feel it burning, even with the med*—
—*see his face as the bullets ripped into him*—

I lay on my side on a gurney and curled into a fetal ball as every muscle clenched against the telepathic onslaught.

"Sir! Step aside! We need to get them into the emergency bays!"

I heard Drew's voice from somewhere ahead of me. "She can't go in there—look at her! And he needs to stay with her. Bring whatever you need to treat them outside."

"It's only a few degrees above freezing out here!"

Drew's voice lowered. "You need something warmed up?"

I felt the heat of the fireball on my face as a spot on the gurney cover flared. The shock of the medical people surrounding me broke over me like a sunrise. "What the f—!"

Drew exhaled. "Consider this a hazmat situation. These two need immediate medical treatment and they need it away from the other patients. Can you handle that?" *I gotta take care of Trev and Maddie; I gotta find Elena and Heather and Cecelia; that Russian guy's going to wake up any minute and start clawing people. I don't have time to deal with this!*

"Drew." My voice was a croak. "Go…" Another wave of blackness took my vision. *Get Sergei into the fish tank. Find our people. Then come back and get us the hell out of here.*

"You'll be okay?" He sounded skeptical.

Not at all. "Go." I groaned. "Hurry."

He nodded and ran back to the car.

We were wheeled inside and taken to adjoining stations in the emergency area. The local anesthetic they pricked into my arm and shoulder didn't make a dent in the ambient telepathic torture. I kept swallowing my urge to scream.

I have to stay conscious.

I had to stay close to Trevor. When he woke up, he'd be disoriented and might use his ability. Drew's little display outside could be explained away as a parlor trick, but if Trevor started dreaming…

At least the army medical trauma people worked fast.

While one doctor worked on stopping the bleeding in Trevor's leg, another prodded at Trevor's broken nose. The pain jolted him back into consciousness with a gasp. A tray of medical instruments a few feet away clattered to the floor.

I fought through the pain to send him a clear thought. *It's okay! Trevor! It's okay!*

"Maddie!" His eyes flew open and he twisted around until he found me.

"S'okay." My gasp came from behind clenched teeth. At least he wasn't sharing abilities with me from across the room. He wasn't feeling this, too.

The doctor stepped between us. "Hold still, now. You've got a broken nose and probably a concussion. We've stopped the bleeding in your leg, but if you thrash around, you might pop your sutures."

Trevor's invisible hand snaked over and cupped my cheek. *We've got to get you out of this place. Are you injured? What happened?*

The three astrals are dead. Drew's taking the guy from the basement to the fish tank, but we don't know anything about Heather or Cecelia, or whether they—

The medical people looked up as the clatter of boots filled the emergency room. At least a dozen MPs surrounded us, rifles drawn. "These two need to come with us immediately."

One of the doctors stepped forward, shaking her head. "They both need medical treatment. They're in no condit—"

"General Dale's orders. His exact words were, 'I don't care if they're missing a couple of limbs, get them here now.'"

The truck pulled up at the secure hangar next to the BMW and the Russian car. I tugged the blanket on my shoulders tighter as the cold air hit me and the pressure against my now-thawing wounds made me hiss.

Bruising framed both of Trevor's eyes and the swelling around his nose pulled the skin tight and shiny. The doctors had done a patch-job in the two minutes the MPs had allowed them. Trevor took my hand as we staggered into the hangar, and he leaned on invisible limbs to keep his leg from crumpling beneath him.

Lights blazed from this side of the ceiling. Black bags—body bags—formed a row to the side of the fish tank. The coppery smell of blood still hung in the air. I couldn't pull my eyes from the stains on the floor.

Inside the tank, Sergei slumped on the cot with his head buried in his hands. The driver from the Russian car lay on the floor. Talking into a phone near the door, General Dale looked up as we entered.

I met his eyes. *Our people?*

His face became a cold mask. "All dead but one." *Maybe she can find out what happened.*

I swallowed hard. "Who—?" *Who'd survived?*

He tipped his chin toward the dark end of the hangar. The faces of the victims hung in his thoughts. *Oh, no. Oh, God.* I braced against the silent scream that stabbed into my soul. The walk into the dark took an eternity.

"Hey." Drew tossed up a flame from his hand, guiding us in. The light fell across Cecelia's blonde hair. Parts were streaked dark and matted against her head.

Blood.

She hugged her knees and stared into the blackness. As we stepped forward, pain raked through me.

Her throat.

I knelt down in front of her. At this moment, she wasn't the catty person who made my skin crawl. She was one of us, and something terrible had happened to her.

She startled as I put my free hand on her arm.

Cecelia. I sent the thought into her head.

Her mouth opened, square with horror, but no sound came out.

I remembered the night we'd found Rachel in the basement, the silent understanding that had flashed between us that we were on the same side. *Cecelia, I need you to tell me what happened.*

I jolted back as the sensation of invisible knives ripping through her neck slammed into me.

Trevor's hand on my undamaged shoulder tightened. He'd felt it, too.

Tears filled Cecelia's eyes and she started to rock.

Keeping my gaze on hers, I lowered the hospital blanket and pulled the edge of the too-thin gown down off my shoulder. Her eyes flashed to the wounds, and then back to my face. The rocking stopped.

I gave a sad little half-smile. *Now if I only knew what it was like not being able to talk.*

She inhaled with a snort, and then gave a sob. *Heather.* Guilt inked through her—a mustard-dark stain that tainted her soul.

Show me what happened. Just think about it.

The images jumbled together and voices formed a chaotic swirl that didn't synch up.

Flash.

Heather loomed over Cecelia. Blood stained her shirt black in the dim light—

Flash.

Lieutenant Moran leaned in with a smile and said something about "private language lessons." Cecelia felt her own giddy smile light her face as her heart thudded wildly. Then a scream pierced the hangar, breaking the mood between them. One of the uniformed people arched backward as he collapsed. Blood spurted from a tear across his throat—

Flash.

The light from the fish tank formed a halo around Heather's head. Her face was contorted with pain as she put her hands on Cecelia's torn neck—

Flash.

Two more people collapsed as invisible talons raked bloody lines through them. Shrieks echoed through the hangar and someone started firing wildly into the dark. Lieutenant Moran stiffened, and then stared down at the line of four red stains that blossomed around the rips in his chest. He sank to his knees.

Cecelia screamed. "No! Don't die!" She threw all the force of her ability behind the words, but no one within hearing obeyed her.

As she reached for Moran, an unseen hand tightened in her hair and yanked her head back. With a sick, bubbling hiss, her own neck opened up. The slices felt icy and wrong for a heartbeat—then the pain hit and she couldn't breathe. She clutched at her throat, feeling the hot wetness against her fingers as her legs crumpled and she fell against the dark floor. *Throat slit! Oh, God! Panic and shock and cold and...*

...and then Heather had loomed over her, backlit and bleeding, and the surge of pins and needles had started through her. The bleeding had slowed and air had flooded back into her lungs. Cecelia had spasmed as blood bubbled from her mouth with each retching cough. *Are they still in here? Are they going to attack me again? Am I going to die, too?*

When she'd finally drawn a breath, her gaze had fallen on Heather's still form... and her open, staring eyes.

Cecelia bit her lip and looked up. *She... saved me. Heather saved me, but she died. They're all dead. Why did she save me? Why didn't she help herself first? She could've saved herself.*

No. My own eyes threatened to let loose. *It doesn't work that way.* Hannah had explained it to me once; healers couldn't heal themselves.

And that woman got away. And the astral who killed everyone got away. And—

I shook my head. *They didn't get far.*

Cecelia's eyes darted to my shoulder again, and then to Trevor's battered face. She started to shake, and then something seemed to shatter within her and she sobbed.

I swallowed hard as I tightened my grip on her arm.

"…so you have three dead astrals and another in custody." Trevor and I had gone back to the other end of the hangar, leaving Drew standing watch over Cecelia. I'd given General Dale the play-by-play he'd needed from Cecelia's memories. He'd made notes for his reports, and his cool efficiency in the face of so much loss made me hate him a little bit.

Dale raised an eyebrow. "That's enough, for now. I'll have the MPs return you to the base hospital. You need medical treatment. Both of you."

Major understatement—I'd fall over if I weren't leaning against Trevor. "We can't go back to the base hospital. Or to any hospital."

Trevor pressed against me in a similar state of drained-and-weak and was careful not to put pressure on my shoulder. His invisible arms were the only things keeping us from collapsing in a tangle of bandaged limbs.

Trevor started to shake his head, but the movement made pain lance through his face, so he stopped. "We either need to go back to Ganzfield, or someone needs to come here."

Dale's eyebrows shot up. "Would that person be Hannah Washington?"

Trevor frowned. *How does the General know about Hannah?*

Oh. I heard him remember some of the conversation he'd had with Williamson about two hours ago. "Jon said to tell you that Ms. Washington was on the way. She'll be on the ground here in Germany in about eight hours. Apparently, you have someone there at Ganzfield who knows what happened here." *There seems to be a security leak.*

I gave a quick scoff. "She's not a security leak. She's part of our team. Rachel's ability was critical today. She made taking down the astrals who did this possible."

"Why isn't she here, then?"

I sucked in a breath at the thought. If Rachel had been here, she might well be in one of the black bags in the cold line on the floor right now.

Right next to Heather.

My throat closed up as my eyes filled with tears. Anger burned through me as I remembered how full of life she'd—Aargh! I wanted to drag Goran and the other guy back in here and—and kill them again! I wanted him to... to *hurt* for killing her. I—I wanted to spike pain into their heads over and over until they begged to die. They needed to suffer for cutting her life short—for cutting short *all* the lives that she would no longer be able to save. They should feel all the pain that other people would now feel because Heather wouldn't be there to use her ability to heal them. The hot ache in my chest made it hard to breathe; it was like a scream that wouldn't come out. My face crumpled and the tears flooded down.

Trevor pulled me back against him. He met the General's gaze over my head. "We're in no shape to go after the remaining astrals right now—even if we knew where to find them. Dmitri said they have a training center in Belarus, but it's a pretty good bet that they'll clear out of there now that they know they've been discovered. Right now, we have no way to track them. All the ones we've had contact with…"

I bit my lip. *They're all here, including the ones I killed.* That left no one for Rachel to track.

General Dale frowned. "Our position here—this base isn't secure from them. They found us here already, and they know we've been looking into their abilities. We'll need to relocate this operation."

I took a deep breath and tried to pull it together. "Dmitri—" My throat closed up. *Dmitri and Katya might act as beacons for their people, at least if their RVs locate people the same way ours do. But the Russians don't have the range to find them in America.* Dmitri had been clear about that; they didn't have anyone with Rachel's range.

General Dale nodded. "I'll get them moved to a secure location immediately." He shot a glance at Sergei and the other guy in the fish tank. "Those two, as well."

Secure location. I'd been in one of those and the memory turned my anger into a stone in my gut. I shook my head. "No. No way. Dmitri and Katya should come back with us. Back to Ganzfield."

Trevor gave me a look. *Really? Will that put our people at risk?*

I gave him a tiny headshake. *Not from Dmitri and Katya. And if Ann can see astrals, too, then we'll have a second set of eyes to keep watch for them.* We'd be able to get some sleep. *And Seth would hear any strangers thinking in Russian if they came into range. It's probably safer back at Ganzfield than just about anywhere else.*

General Dale's eyes narrowed as he glanced over at the twins. They stood as far as the MPs would allow them from where

Sergei scowled at them from behind the glass. *They need to be in custody. They're too dangerous. We should have them studied. We can't have spies who can walk through walls and brutally kill with invisible weapons running around loose!*

I stared at him, feeling my face twist into a scowl. "Dmitri worked with us to take down Goran and the others. He was coerced into spying on the embassy, and you know it! Katya's never spied on anyone. You are *not* going to throw them into a cell!"

Would a cell hold any of them for long? Dale scowled back at me. "They're dangerous." *Almost as dangerous as she is. She killed those astrals—the ones that ripped apart a hangar full of trained military personnel... and she didn't even have a weapon. She didn't even touch them!*

"Dmitri and Katya—they're coming with us." I started to cross my arms, but that hurt too much so I let them drop. "We'll train them."

Dale shook his head.

"Look. It's simple. You can either try to figure out how to keep astral projectors locked up, or you can give us a chance to turn them into real assets for our side."

"Our side?"

"You know—America. Truth. Justice. Non-mafia-people who don't sell state secrets to terrorists. *We'd* have the spies who could walk through walls."

Dale's nostrils flared as he considered it. Reluctance and suspicion twitched though him. "If I agree to this—and I'm not saying I am—how long would you need?"

I have no frikkin' clue.

Trevor's hand squeezed mine. *But he doesn't know that.*

Operative 227

True. "Well, Dmitri's already got some training. We'll have to see about Katya. Maybe a couple of months. And I'm hoping we can do a little telepathic show-and-tell and get one of our RVs to locate the remaining astrals." Rachel had been able to make a secondhand connection and see Isaiah from my memories. Could we do it third-hand with Dmitri's? How accurate would it be?

"And you'll need some recovery time from your injuries." The General winced inwardly as his gaze fell on Trevor's bruised face.

"Yeah." I guessed Dale didn't know how fast our healers worked. Whatever. We all could use a little break now. The physical inuries weren't the ones that would need time to heal.

Drew's jaw was steel as he watched the honor guard carry the flag-draped coffins. Next to him, Hannah's mental voice added a reverent layer to the moment.

—restores my soul. He leads me in the paths of righteousness for His name's sake. Yea, though I walk through the valley of the shadow of death, I will fear no evil; for—

She'd arrived on a direct flight into Vilstein; General Dale had arranged it. Whatever she'd been doing with the experiments back at Ganzfield, apparently Matilda was now able to handle it—Hannah's thoughts rarely left the people who needed her help here.

Trevor and I had spent the rest of the day taking turns watching over each other, but we'd been too upset and in pain to get much sleep. Hannah had come to my trailer as soon as she'd arrived. She'd drawn a sharp breath when she'd first seen the injuries. She'd had to remove my stitches—the memory made me wince—before she'd laid her hands on my shoulder and properly repaired the slashes. She'd repeated the process on Trevor's leg, as well. Then she'd touched his face and healed his broken nose. Once she'd finished, her mind flooded with pink embarrassment. *Oh, no! I should've checked how it'd been set! It didn't heal right!* Trevor's nose now had a slight crook in the bridge. Indecision made her freeze, eyes wide. *Should I re-break it and set it again?*

Trevor had shaken his head. "Not today."

Hannah had startled as she'd realized he was reading her thoughts.

I'd held up our linked hands. "Special connection, remember?"

She'd smiled. "You're talking normally again."

I'd choked up at that, since my recovery had been Heather's doing, and now Heather was in a box and being loaded into the plane like cargo, and she'd never—

I shook my head, trying to force the memories to subside. I focused back on the ceremony. Lieutenant Richardson, the same chaplain who'd married us, read the names as they were loaded one-by-one onto the cargo plane, carried with formal military ceremony.

"Captain Jacob Bell." I flashed back to the first meeting we'd had with him, when he'd taken us and what we could do seriously, rather than looking at us as a bunch of stupid kids.

"Lieutenant Daniel Moran."

Cecelia stood slightly apart from the rest of us and her jaw quivered with the sense of lost possibilities.

Don't die.

Her last words to him hadn't been enough, no matter how much charm resonance she'd put into them. Even though Hannah had been able to finish the repairs that Heather had started of her ripped throat and vocal cords, Cecelia still hadn't said a word.

The names continued.

"Lieutenant David Cohen."

"Lieutenant Samantha Hathaway."

"Staff Sergeant Elena Cavallo." A wisp of smoke curled up from Drew's shoulder as his hands clenched into empty fists.

"Staff Sergeant Gregory Meadows."

"Staff Sergeant Jonathan Truman."

"Specialist Cheyenne Carter."

"Doctor Heather McFee." Drew's churning emotions congealed a lump in my throat and his hands fisted again as the final coffin—Heather's had no flag—followed the others. The official story was that a "mechanical accident" in an airplane hangar had taken the lives of the nine people whose bodies now filled the hold of the plane.

And it was Christmas Eve. The timing just made it all seem even worse. My jaw started to quiver again and I squeezed my eyes shut to stop the tears.

My fault.

Heather had been on my team. I'd been responsible for her being here—none of them would've been here if I hadn't told Dale we needed the whole team to come in the first place, back on that night at Ganzfield when everything had gone so well—just before everything had gone to hell. I'd pushed to go after Katya when we'd learned she was in danger. If only we'd stayed back in the hangar while they'd interrogated Tania! When Goran and the other astral had come for her, I would've seen them and Trevor could've grabbed them. The two of them would've ended up in the tank with Tania and we could've gone and rescued Katya a few hours later.

No one would've had to die. My soul deflated as guilt soaked into me.

Maddie, it's not your fault. Trevor's grip tightened around my waist. *We thought Katya was in immediate danger. It made sense to go after her.*

Heather was my responsibility. Catching the astrals was my responsibility. I shouldn't have split up the team. I screwed up and now all these people are dead.

Trevor closed his eyes as he pressed his forehead against mine. *You had no way of knowing that they'd —*

Tania knew they'd come for her.

Tania HOPED they'd come for her.

And she had two little kids. I... I fried somebody's MOM. Those boys don't have a mother anymore because of me.

You saved my life. You saved Drew, and Dmitri, and Katya. They were trying to kill us on the road, and they'd already killed people here. You didn't take innocent lives, Maddie. You didn't do anything wrong.

I sniffed and tried to make that register as more than a nice thing to hear.

You didn't do anything wrong.

Drew was the first of our group to move. He took a shuddering breath and then grabbed Heather's bag along with his own. He moved as though his feet were cast in iron as he trudged up the ramp into the plane. Collapsing in his seat, he stared at a spot a couple of feet in front of him on the floor.

Hannah's thoughts pinged with concern as she watched Cecelia struggle to wheel her bag into the plane. Jagged images pierced her soul as she stared at the coffins secured in the cargo hold.

Trevor lifted his duffel in one hand and the cat cage in the other. I grabbed my own bag, never letting go of Trevor's wrist. Velcro kept up a plaintive monologue as the carrier swung between us.

Dmitri and Katya came last; Dmitri had a plastic shopping bag of things he'd retrieved from his car, but Katya had nothing but the jeans and sweater she wore—the ones she'd borrowed from me—and the jacket one of Dale's people had gotten for her from the PX. The loading door slid up with a hydraulic hiss and sealed with a thunk.

We strapped in against the fuselage and stared at the coffins the whole trip home.

END OF BOOK FIVE

Keep reading for a sneak preview of:

SOULMATE

THE SIXTH GANZFIELD NOVEL BY

KATE KAYNAK

Coming in early 2013 from Spencer Hill Press

Soulmate

CHAPTER 1

Wintry, early morning light fell in pale stripes between the slats of the window shutters of the old church. Sliding into Trevor's bed, I pillowed my head against his chest and closed my eyes. His heartbeat thrummed against my cheek, and each slow breath he took made the top half of my body rise and fall. Smiling, I gave an audible sigh.

Perfect.

Trevor's thoughts shifted into cloudy focus, and his arms tightened around me, first the warm, actual ones, and then the invisible set. He took a sharp breath and stiffened, suddenly much more awake.

You know it's too dangerous for you to keep doing this.

I opened my eyes and propped myself up to meet his gaze. *And "good morning" to you, too. Don't worry; I was awake the whole time, and I can take care of myself.* I flexed my own invisible arms, grasping his golden ones and arching them like wings above us. Wings? Hey, there's a thought. *Did you ever—?*

Trevor shook his head. *We looked into it, but I weigh too much. I can't make enough surface area to get any lift.*

That would've been cool, though.

Yeah. He cupped my cheek in his hand. *So, did you risk your life this morning for any particular reason?*

Just the missing-you-even-when-I'm-in-the-same-room one.

He sighed, but a shiver of delight ran through him at being so cherished. *Maddie, we've been through this. I can't risk hurting you.*

I ran my fingers in a light touch across his face, stroking the crooked little bump on his nose where it hadn't been perfectly re-set. *You won't hurt me. You haven't even hurt the cat, and I was pretty sure she'd end up flying across the room the first night we brought her back.*

Actually, with all the yowling she'd been doing while stuck in her cat carrier, there'd been a point when I'd been considering playing "Go long!" with a furry little football.

As if she'd sensed we were discussing her, Velcro jumped up onto the end of the bed and made her way across the comforter to head-butt Trevor's chin. She'd grown from a trembling little puffball into a sleek, half-grown silver-grey cat in the three months we'd been back at Ganzfield. Invisible fingers scratched behind her ears, and Velcro arched back into them, eyes closed. Little green tendrils of happiness ebbed and flowed with the rhythm of her purr.

So, I played with the lock of hair that fell across Trevor's forehead, *we have more than two hours before we're due at training. Whatever will we do with ourselves?*

The cat jumped off the bed with an affronted squawk as Trevor pulled me closer. His warm brown eyes twinkled as his lips quirked. *Let's see if I properly understand the situation. I'm in bed*

Soulmate

with my beautiful wife... and we don't need to be anywhere else for hours?

My heart stuttered in my chest at the ideas that filled his head. And how cool was it that my amazing guy truly thought I was beautiful when I was wearing an old t-shirt and flannel PJ-pants?

Love of my life.

I nuzzled his neck, thrilling at Trevor's reaction. Red energy danced between us, and the images that flashed in my head may have been my own or Trevor's. Didn't matter—we were totally on the same page. I moved up to kiss him, feeling my insides go all quivery as his lips moved against mine. One of his hands wrapped around the back of my neck, fingers sliding up into my hair, while the other slid lower. I met his gaze as silver energy flared around us. Sitting up, I reached for the hem of my t-shirt, grinning at the sensation of Trevor's IQ dropping as I pulled it over my head.

A ghostly flash of purple burst through the wall and stumbled a few steps before recovering. Her glowing eyes flashed across the room, zeroing in... and I gasped as she headed right for us.

Coming in September 2012...

Dying sucks—and high school senior Ember McWilliams knows first-hand. After a fatal car accident, her gifted little sister brought her back. Now anything Ember touches dies. And that, well, really blows.

Ember operates on a no-touch policy with all living things—including boys. When Hayden Cromwell shows up, quoting Oscar Wilde and claiming her curse is a gift, she thinks he's a crazed cutie. But when he tells her he can help control it, she's more than interested. There's just one catch: Ember has to trust Hayden's adopted father, a man she's sure has sinister reasons for collecting children whose abilities even weird her out. However, she's willing to do anything to hold her sister's hand again. And hell, she'd also like to be able to kiss Hayden. Who wouldn't?

But when Ember learns the accident that turned her into a freak may not've been an accident at all, she's not sure who to trust. Someone wanted her dead, and the closer she gets to the truth, the closer she is to losing not only her heart, but her life.

For real this time.

Cursed

Jennifer L. Armentrout

Author of Half-Blood

978-1-937053-12-3

Angelina's Secret

As a child, Angelina spent years in counseling learning that Josie, her imaginary friend, wasn't real, but it turns out her childhood friend wasn't imaginary after all.

Lisa Rogers

978-0-9831572-8-1

978-0-9831572-0-5

Half-Blood

Jennifer L. Armentrout

The Hematoi descend from the unions of gods and mortals, and the children of two Hematoi—pure-bloods—have godlike powers. Children of Hematoi and mortals—well, not so much. Half-bloods only have two options: become trained Sentinels who hunt and kill daimons or become servants in the homes of the pures.

Seventeen-year-old Alexandria would rather risk her life fighting than waste it scrubbing toilets, but she may end up slumming it anyway. There are several rules that students at the Covenant must follow. Alex has problems with them all, but especially rule #1:

Relationships between pures and halfs are forbidden.

Unfortunately, she's crushing hard on the totally hot pure-blood Aiden. But falling for Aiden isn't her biggest problem--staying alive long enough to graduate the Covenant and become a Sentinel is. If she fails in her duty, she faces a future worse than death or slavery: being turned into a daimon, and being hunted by Aiden. And that would kind of suck.

Coming in June 2012 from Spencer Hill Press:

BETRAYED
A GUARDIAN LEGACY BOOK

Lil isn't just an average teenager. She's one of the Nephilim—the descendants of humans and angels—which gives her some serious psi skills and a mission for redemption. Just when Lil thinks she's found a balance between her normal life with human friends and her training to become a Guardian, she's warned that someone close to her will betray her. When the boy she loves starts acting strangely and one of her human friends acquires a supernatural ability, Lil begins to realize that someone is manipulating the people she loves... and won't stop until she's been lured to the dark side.

EDNAH WALTERS

Coming in May of 2012 from Spencer Hill Press:

Just because Ella can burn someone to the ground with her mind doesn't mean she should…

But she wants to.

elemental

EMILY WHITE

978-1-937053-04-8

Masters of the Veil

Book One of the Veil Trilogy

There's no "I" in SORCERY.

Daniel A. Cohen

March 2012 — 978-1-937053-02-4

Acknowledgements

After five books, writing acknowledgements gets a bit redundant; many of the same people who made the first four books possible came through again for number five. Thanks yet again to my wonderful editor, Deborah Britt-Hay, and to the Spencer Hill folks who worked on this project: Kendra McCormick, Marie Romero (who delighted me when I realized she'd even made corrections to the phonetic Russian), Jessica Porteous, and Rich "The Closer" Storrs. Special thanks to Emily White for her beta reading and help with getting the military stuff more up-to-date and accurate than my memories of life on base from a dozen years ago. Thanks to Sarah Warren, a.k.a. "Floot," for her help with Russian patronymics. A shout-out to Samantha Hathaway, who won the "Kill me, Kate!" competition on the Facebook fan site and therefore got a character in this book named after her… whom I then killed off. I also want to thank Rebecca Mancini for representing my work, and thanks to Liz Pelletier for introducing me to Rebecca.

Ve Osman, çok teşekkür ederim herşey için, canım.

Photo by P. Alton

About Kate Kaynak

I was born and raised in New Jersey, but I managed to escape. My degree from Yale says I was a psych major, but I had *way* too much fun to have paid much attention in class.

After serving a five-year sentence in graduate school, I started teaching psychology around the world for the University of Maryland's Overseas Program.

While in Izmir, Turkey, I started up a conversation with a handsome stranger in an airport. I ended up marrying him. We now live in New Hampshire with our three kids, where I enjoy reading, writing, and fighting crime with my amazing superpowers.

Come find out more about the books of the *Ganzfield* series (*Minder, Adversary, Legacy, Accused, Operative,* and *Soulmate*) at **Ganzfield.com.**

Made in the USA
Charleston, SC
29 March 2012